Creation of Chaos: Volume I

Pete Altieri

October 2017

Published by

Chaos Publishing

PO Box 554

Heyworth, IL 61745

CreationofChaos.com

*For my mother, Adele, and those many rainy days
spent searching at the Paperback Exchange.*

Table of Contents

Long, Dark Hallway   9

Carnival of Atonement   37

Man With Spots   66

Elvis and the Two Dead Hookers   82

The Jesus Tree   99

They Came to Darkness   137

Unfit For Human Occupancy   177

Cross to Bear   193

Bodies In My Pocket   205

Hand of the Dying   228

Blackened Spiral Down   241

Contraption Number 12   267

Killing Machine   304

Thirteen Nuns   320

Chainsaw House Party   351

Sifting Through the Ashes:

Afterward and Acknowledgements   381

CREATION OF CHAOS: VOLUME I

Long, Dark Hallway

1

Staring at the long, dark hallway at 4:00 am, Joe Cowdery felt a sickening feeling in the pit of his stomach. He had only been working at St. Peter's Hospital for two weeks, but cleaning this hallway was his most dreaded task. As a custodian on third shift, he was tasked to sweep and mop the hallways, when traffic in those areas was at a minimum. He didn't mind the hallways on the first or second floors, but the basement of the original hospital was the one that bothered him. It was in a "T" shape; the top section led to the elevator on one end and the stairwell at the other, while the dimly lit long section formed the bottom. The concrete walls were cold and painted battleship grey, and the old 9-inch asbestos floor tile was dark brown with black streaks. The ceiling was also concrete, painted with a cream color, now stained with years of cigarette smoke from a time when hospital employees could light up in the building. Every twenty feet were mounted aged fluorescent light fixtures that hummed when powered on, and barely cast enough light to see. It worried him not only because the hallway was dark, even with the lights on, but it was because of what was at the far end that filled him with dread.

There was a sign mounted next to the metal double doors that read simply, "Morgue". There was something in that word that instilled a sense of fear in Joe, even though the morgue was moved to the new addition that was built last year, and this area was closed for business. Maybe it was the thought that just about every dead person in McLean County, for the past 75 years, had passed through those doors. They would be whisked out of the morgue, up a concrete ramp and into hearses parked in the alley behind the hospital, waiting to take their fares to various funeral homes in the

Bloomington area. Even the indigent would leave the morgue this way for a burial of minimal expense in a glorified cardboard box in a section of Maple Hill Cemetery, funded by private donations. No customer left the morgue coming back through the metal double doors at the end of the long, dark hallway.

2

"Mr. Montgomery will see you now, Mr. Cowdery," said Christine Conder, the secretary that worked in the buildings and grounds office at St. Peter's Hospital. She was in her early 40's but looked like she was pushing 60, with too much makeup and an outdated mullet-style hairdo, prepared for public viewing each day with a full can of Aqua Net. Her voice was gruff, from years of smoking Pall Mall reds. She looked up only for a moment and forced a smile before going back to her crossword puzzle and gum smacking.

Joe nodded to her, making his way into Doug Montgomery's office. Doug was the supervisor of the maintenance crew and custodians. Joe's father-in-law, Ben, had told him about the custodial job that was posted on the bulletin board near the employee time clock. He was less than six months from retiring from the maintenance crew, and he hoped his influence with Doug would help Joe get the job. Joe and his daughter, Betsy, were only married a year and were expecting their first baby in less than two months. Ben wanted something more secure for Joe, who was a hard worker but wasting his time bagging groceries at the IGA. He wanted more for Betsy than a bag boy's income.

"Come on and sit down - uh, Joe, right?" Doug said, forcing a wry smile. Distracted, he barely made eye contact.

"Yes, sir. Joe Cowdery." Joe sat down, looking around Doug's office to see if there were clues that might give him something to talk about with his potential boss. His father had suggested that tactic during a job interview. Doug's office was outdated with cheap wood paneling and random pieces of even cheaper furniture. It was cluttered with piles of maintenance parts catalogs and car magazines, and pictures of his wife and two boys at various ages and events in frames on the walls. Also displayed were some of his training certificates and the licenses he had to carry for his position. There was Green Bay Packer calendar on the wall next to a sign that read, "Ford Parking Only". There was also a poster

that said "kiss my ass" with a smiling donkey on it. Doug had a

penchant for interior decorating by garage sale.

Doug had his work boots up on the desk, leaning back in his

chair, with a smirk on his face. He wore a uniform, like the rest of

the maintenance crew, but his name said "boss" instead of Doug.

His workers all made fun of him about it behind his back. The

rumor was he was henpecked at home, but when he crossed the

threshold at work, he was all about being in charge. At the first sign

of trouble, Doug typically would try and pin the blame on others.

Joe figured he was in his late 40's, but the cheesy mustache make

him look older. The fact that his boots were three years old but

looked like he just bought them spoke volumes. Ben had warned

him about Doug and his poor bedside manner, but he explained that

to work at the hospital as a custodian, Joe had no choice but to deal

with him. Doug was judge, jury, and executioner all rolled into one

hell of a complete jerk.

"You know the only reason you're sitting here is because of

Ben, right?" Doug said, absently gazing at Joe's application and

cleaning his teeth with a toothpick.

Joe didn't know how to respond to that. He found himself staring at the toothpick rooting around in Doug's mouth, and listening to the disgusting slurping sounds he made. It grossed him out when Doug took it out, looked at it closely, then smelled it before putting it back in his mouth.

"When can you start?" Doug asked.

"I could start Monday, sir. I just want to give my boss at IGA a few days' notice. They always have kids coming in asking about jobs. So, they won't have any trouble replacing me."

Disinterested, Doug continued to pick at his teeth. Then he picked up his cell phone and was messing around with it, while Joe sat there, shifting in his chair.

"OK. Monday is fine. Christine can give you all the paperwork we'll need you to fill out. You OK working third shift?" He flipped the toothpick at his garbage can but missed.

"Sure. I can work whatever shifts you have. Thank you!" Joe replied and reached out to shake his hand. Doug ignored it, still staring at his phone.

"OK, kid. Be here at 10:00 pm Monday. I'll have someone run you through the areas you'll be responsible to clean. After a couple nights, you'll be ready to work on your own."

"Thank you, Mr. Montgomery."

Doug nodded, still engrossed at whatever was on his phone.

Just like that, Joe started his employment with St. Peter's Hospital. Betsy would be happy, since it was almost four dollars more an hour than he made at IGA and guaranteed 40-hour weeks. Doug told him that sometimes they could work overtime if something big was going on at the hospital, where he wanted to make the building shine. With the baby coming, they would need the money.

3

It was the three-week anniversary of his start date when Joe clocked in on Monday night. An hour into his shift, the four custodians from second shift were clocking out and leaving Joe by himself to work until 7:00 am, when the first shift employees showed up. He didn't mind working alone at all, because he could listen to music on his phone with ear buds and tune the world out while he swept and mopped his areas. Joe liked to listen to heavy metal, and thanks to the ear buds, he could play it as loud as he liked without disturbing anyone. Lester, the custodian that trained him, told him to start on the second floor and work his way down to the basement. Despite three weeks on the job, the basement hallway bothered him in the small hours when there were so few people around.

It was nearly 4:00 am when Joe filled up his mop bucket with steaming hot water from the slop sink in the basement custodial room and a generous amount of Liquid Sunshine, a chemical they used at the hospital for general purpose cleaning. It had a nice lemon fragrance that left the hallways smelling clean when he was done. Doug loved when he got compliments on how good the building looked and smelled, so he was adamant about his custodians doing things his way. Maintenance didn't seem as important to him, since the work they usually did was behind-the-scenes and the average person had no idea of the importance of changing out a valve in the boiler room or re-glazing a broken window pane. It was all about cosmetic appeal and what scored Doug the most points with the brass.

An hour passed, and Joe returned to the slop sink to dump his mop bucket and fill it again with hot water and Liquid Sunshine to do the last half of the long, dark hallway. He was going through his playlist to pick the right music for the worst part of the shift, when he heard a noise that made him jump. Joe's back was to the old morgue. He gingerly turned around when he heard the noise again. It made his heartbeat race, realizing that the sounds were coming from the other side of the doors. He stood frozen in place, in the middle of the hall, now facing the doors, hoping that the noise would not return. A few pensive minutes passed and in silence. He was breathing heavily in anticipation, and his mouth became incredibly dry.

The notification tone on his phone rang, letting him know he had a text message. It made him jump.

Can you pick up some milk on your way home? It was Betsy. She had trouble sleeping the past two months of her pregnancy, so it was not uncommon for her to send him text messages at random times during his shift. Despite her excitement at Joe's new job, Betsy didn't like being home alone through the night. They lived on the west side of town in a bad neighborhood, and it was not uncommon to hear people out at all hours of the night and even gun shots. There were a string of robberies and break-ins in the area recently, and she was already looking for a new place somewhere quieter, especially with the baby coming and Joe's new job.

OK. Joe replied.

Suddenly, he heard the noise again. This time it sounded like a banging of metal on metal. He had never been inside the former morgue, and he had no desire to find out what might be causing the noise. Nervously, Joe looked around in all directions.

Are you busy? I miss you. Betsy messaged him back.

Yeah, I'm real busy. Gotta go, Bets.

He put the phone back into his pocket and began mopping the last half of the basement hallway. Every so often, Joe would look up and stare at the double doors and then to the sign that read, "Morgue". He hoped that the noise would not persist. Joe moved as quickly as he could, trying to get the mopping done so he could leave this dreary part of the hospital. He wondered why they even had him doing this area of the building, since the plan (as he heard it from Lester during his training) was to demolish the original part of the hospital in two months, once they moved all the offices and patient rooms over to the new addition. When he asked his father-in-law about it, Ben told him to not question it and to just do his job.

"Just put in your eight hours, Joe. That's all anyone can ask of you," Ben had told him on Saturday night when the family went to eat at Lucca Grill. "Don't ask too many questions. Bosses don't like that. Keep to yourself, because people talk and you'll wind up getting in trouble." Ben chomped on his Baldini pizza – a Lucca Grill staple and his favorite thing to eat.

He managed to get the rest of the hallway floor mopped, his bucket dumped and put away without hearing any other noises coming from behind the double doors. When the first shift guys came on at 7:00 am, Joe thought about mentioning what he heard to one of them, but he figured they would just make fun of him about it. He thought that maybe it was something perfectly explainable, and there was no use in making himself out to be a problem child. So, he punched out at 7:30 am sharp, picked up the milk that Betsy wanted, and went home to get some sleep.

4

It was 4:00 am the following day, Tuesday, when Joe found himself back in the basement hallway. Staring at the metal double doors, he began to mop the floor, slowly making his way down the long, dark hallway he dreaded. An hour passed, and he was nearing the halfway point of his mopping when he heard a noise again. It was the same metal on metal sound he heard before. He turned off his music, stopping dead in his tracks. The noise persisted, and Joe could feel the terror course through his body like a raging fire. He turned around, hoping that maybe someone was in the hallway that could vouch for the obvious banging sounds in the former morgue. There was no one else. He turned back around, staring at the doors.

Joe's grip tightened on the mop handle, his knuckles white in anticipation. He grabbed it like it was the only thing he had to defend himself (which it was) from whatever was moving around beyond the doors. The banging rang out again, yet this time it was followed with what sounded like someone walking, feet shuffling across the tile floor. He didn't know what to do. Thoughts raced through his mind. Should he turn and run away? Joe knew that the guys would never let him live that down. Should he call out to whatever was making the noise? Maybe it was an employee moving equipment or furniture? His fear would not allow him to confront it. Instead, like the night before, he decided to work as quickly as he could, the mop water sloshing about in his bucket, the equivalent of whistling in the graveyard.

He found himself glancing at the doors every few minutes, hoping that the noises would not return. In his mind, he wanted to just call it done and hope that no one decided to check his work for the last section of the hallway. As dark as it was, a person would practically need a spotlight to see if the floor was swept and mopped. Since the hallway was no longer used in this part of the basement, Joe wondered why he was even sweeping and mopping it anyway. But, he thought about what his father-in-law told him about not asking questions and that he should just do his job. He could see Ben saying it, a slice of the Baldini pizza in one hand and a beer in the other.

Suddenly, the shuffling of feet could be heard. This time it sounded like it was just on the other side of the doors. Joe was no more than ten feet from the end of the hallway, paralyzed in terror.

Then it sounded like someone on the other side was jiggling the door knob. Joe's eyes got real big, and he stared at the knob shaking in place. Slowly, it began to turn! Joe threw down the mop as he watched the knob turn and the right door creak open. A strong, musty odor swept out from the opening in the door, and only darkness could be seen within. Joe turned and ran. He ran like he was on the track team and never looked back, his footsteps echoing.

He turned the corner to the left, still running with everything he had. He was desperate to make it to the elevator. He hoped that it was already in the basement, so the doors would open quickly. Reaching the elevators, Joe repeatedly pushed the button to go up, but the doors did not open. His breathing was heavy, and he did what he could to slow it down, hoping not to hear any noises behind him. He heard nothing. Against his will, Joe turned around quickly while the doors considered opening, but he saw nothing behind him.

"Come on, damn it!" he said under his breath, as he watched the old elevator finally begin its descent to the basement. He pushed the button again, knowing it did no good.

The display above the elevator showed the car was in the basement, yet the doors still would not open! He pushed the "up" button again, but still no response. He knew the stairs were on the other end of the hallway, and he would have to run past the long, dark hallway to make it to the other side of the "T" where the door was that led to the stairwell. He took a deep breath and ran once again, this time toward the stairs. As he ran by the dreaded hallway, Joe glanced toward the old morgue. He thought he saw movement in the hallway as he ran, but he wasn't sure if it was a figment of his imagination. All Joe could think was to run faster, and if there was something moving in the dark shadows of the hallway, he would make it to the stairway first.

He was only a few feet from the stairwell when he felt something ice-cold grab his right foot. The grip was tight, and the last thing he remembered was falling face-first to the hard tile floor, and then everything went black.

5

"Joe, can you hear me?" said a soft, female voice. It sounded like she was talking through an empty paper towel roll.

Joe's eyes fluttered as he regained consciousness. The first thing he noticed was how sore his face was. He was in a hospital bed, and a nurse was standing next to him, calling his name and taking his blood pressure. She was thin, plain-looking and in her 50's. She wore blue scrubs and was smiling at him.

"Yes, I can," he replied, noticing his voice sounded funny, like he was heavily medicated. "Where am I?" He looked around the room.

"You took one hell of a fall. You're at St. Peter's Hospital. You picked a good place to get hurt, I guess. We don't know how long you were lying in the basement. A security guard found you while making his rounds," she said, writing some things down on his chart. "My name is Sabrina, if you need anything. I brought you some ice water." She gestured to where she set the pitcher and cups down.

There was a pause. "I felt something grab me before I fell." Joe knew it sounded strange, but he was tired of not saying anything.

"Really?" She looked up from his chart and stared at him for a moment.

"There were noises in the old morgue. I've heard them several times this week," he said, looking at the nurse. She wasn't making eye contact. "Something was in there. It was opening the door, so I ran."

She smiled at him and patted his shoulder gently. "I'll go get the doctor to talk to you. Get some rest now. Your face is starting to bruise up good. You are lucky you didn't break anything."

Joe didn't respond. He knew it all sounded crazy. He knew what people would think when he mentioned that he heard noises in the old morgue. That's why he hadn't mentioned it to anyone. There was no mistaking it, though. He felt something grab his foot and pull him down with tremendous strength. He remembered it was ice cold. Joe looked at his right ankle, and it was red and swollen. Joe knew something down there in the old basement grabbed him. He didn't want to even think about having to go back there. Not right now. Not ever.

6

"So, the doctor said you have a concussion. He said you need to be off work for 48 hours," said Doug Montgomery, standing next to Joe's bed at the hospital. He was wearing his uniform, holding a Styrofoam cup of coffee. "Can you believe that shit?"

"Yes, that's correct," Sabrina added, with the doctor's note in her hand. "Did you want a copy, Doug?"

"I already got a copy of it. Thank you." He was obviously annoyed at the situation. Sabrina quietly left the room.

Doug walked to the door and shut it quietly. "You've got to be fucking kidding me, Cowdery," he said under his breath through gritted teeth. "What's this bullshit about hearing noises down there. Something grabbing you? Are you high or something? Drunk?"

Joe knew Doug wouldn't believe him. "None of that. But I have heard noises the last couple nights down there."

"What kind of noises, for Christ's sake?"

"Banging noises. Footsteps. Plain as day."

Doug took a sip of his coffee and slowly shook his head back and forth. "You've been watching too many movies, Cowdery. Been listening to that screaming hippie shit too loud. That's all we need is people here at the hospital talking about our department like we're a bunch of weirdos. They'll think we're all nuts. Me included!"

Joe didn't respond. He knew it didn't matter what he said.

"That basement is about the only place in the hospital that's not on the security cameras. So, whatever you imagined happened down there, we can't know for sure. But, if I was a betting man, I'd say you just were just clumsy and fell. Probably on your damn cell phone." Doug downed the coffee and threw the empty cup toward the garbage can, missing by two feet.

"Yeah, maybe." He knew arguing with Doug wasn't going to help. He just wanted him to leave the room. Joe just wanted to get out of here and go home. He looked at the clock. It was just past 8:30 am.

Doug also looked at the clock. "Shit. I need to get going. Some of us got work to do. See you on Monday. I'll work your shift tonight if I can't find someone to cover it. No more talk about Jason or Freddy chasing you with machetes or anything. Got it?" He turned and left the room and muttered "Christ on a damn Christmas tree!"

Joe glanced down at the redness on his right ankle. He felt a cold, clammy, shivering sensation sweep over him, wondering what the hell had grabbed him in the basement. There was a horrible feeling of dread, wondering if whatever it was in the basement would come looking for him. He wasn't sure if he would be able to go back down there again, but for now, he was thankful of a three-day weekend with Betsy. She would help him forget about it, or at least try.

7

It was Friday at 4:30 am, and Doug Montgomery was finishing up sweeping the basement hallways. Now it was time to mop. He could not find a custodian to cover Joe's shift, and rather than let anyone else know about the incident, he just figured he'd work it himself. He didn't mind getting a jump on the weekend, with plans to go to the dirt track in Farmer City that night to watch the races. It was the first stock car race of the season, and he enjoyed taking the boys, especially now that they were old enough to actually watch the races with him. Doug thought he might even splurge and get pit passes so they could meet the late-model drivers. Hell, he would probably take his wife, Sandy, and make a regular family outing of it. She also enjoyed going, as long as some of her friends were going to be there. The track was supposed to have a local country cover band, Tommy Simms and the Cow-Tippin' Six, play between heats. Doug would have one of his maintenance guys, Stan Arbuckle, cover for him after the overnight shift so he could go home to catch some sleep.

As Doug pushed the mop bucket into place, he stared down the long, dark hallway at the metal double doors. He laughed to himself, thinking about what Joe told the doctor about hearing noises coming from the old morgue. Impossible! Doug supervised moving the old equipment and supplies when it closed and personally walked through the area to be sure it was secure. He had the locks changed and re-keyed to keep everyone out of there. Most of the equipment was too old to do anything with, so it was scrapped at the local recycling center for cash. A few items were given to a funeral museum in Springfield. He knew that nothing should be in there, and certainly no one making the noises that Joe claimed he heard. Doug chalked it up to a wild imagination from a young kid who watched a few too many scary movies. The devil-worshipping heavy metal music he listened to sure didn't help matters. Doug liked listening to old country like Alabama or the Oak Ridge Boys and songs about simpler things in life. He thought everyone should as well.

He had only been mopping for ten minutes when he thought he heard something. It sounded like banging, metal on metal. Doug froze in place and stared at the double doors. The noise did not repeat. Doug figured it was the elevator doors behind him and continued to mop, humming the melody to one of his favorite songs, *Elvira,* by the Oak Ridge Boys. Despite the fact he hadn't done any manual labor in years, he found a certain solace in mopping the tile floor. Dealing with a variety of emergencies throughout the day and catering to the whim of administrators, Doug rather enjoyed the mindless task of mopping.

My heart's on fire, Elvira!

Suddenly, the banging sound rang out again. Doug stopped humming. He was about twenty feet from the double doors, and this time, he knew the sound came from there. Doug didn't want to believe it, but there was no mistaking it. He would never admit that young Joe Cowdery was telling the truth, but again the banging noise persisted. It was loud and prominent in the empty hallway.

Giddy up, oom poppa, oom poppa, mow mow!

Doug hoped humming along with the song would make the noise stop, but it didn't. He thought about calling security and having them send someone down to the basement to check out the

source of the noise. He knew that they would all get a big chuckle

out of that. Doug had his share of arguments with security over the

years, especially with the overnight crew and their supervisor,

Ronnie Wilson. Doug had turned Ronnie in on more than one

occasion for not doing his job and spending his shift shuffling

around with a coffee mug, spending way too much time in the

bathroom and watching movies on his laptop. Ronnie's aunt was the

director of human resources at the hospital, so complaints never

went anywhere but her trash can. It pissed Doug off to no end, yet

he filled out written complaints about Ronnie on a weekly basis.

Heigh-ho silver, away!

The banging noise sounded again. Now Doug was

determined to find the source of it. As creepy as it was in the dim

light of the hallway, at an hour where no signs of life were to be

found in the old basement, Doug thought there had to be an

explanation for the noises. He set the mop down in the bucket of

water and Liquid Sunshine and walked toward the double doors. His

steps were slow and deliberate. Doug thought once more about

calling security, just in case there was an intruder in the former morgue. He thought about Ronnie and the stupid jokes he would

make about the call for help and decided against it once again.

Doug's hand steadied on the old door knob. It was cool and

smooth and should be locked, since those were his instructions when

they cleared out the room two weeks before. Yet Joe claimed

someone on the other side opened the door the day before. He

twisted it to the right, and sure enough, the knob turned easily and

was not locked at all! Could it be possible that Joe's crazy story was

true?

"Well, I'll be damned!" he said, pushing the door open.

Doug looked behind him for a moment, making sure no one else was

around. No one was there.

"Hello? Is anyone in here?" he called out, his voice echoing

inside the shell of the former morgue. He pulled out his small

flashlight, looking for a light switch. A narrow beam of light moved

across rows of the old metal drawers, where the bodies were kept in

cold storage, awaiting autopsy, identification by family, or a ride to

one of the local funeral homes. There was a VA hospital in Marion,

Illinois that was supposed to be purchasing the drawers and having

them moved three hours south in a large truck. The new morgue had a more modern system and didn't need the drawers from the 1940's.

Doug slowly stepped into the morgue and found the light switch on the wall. He flipped it up, but no lights came on. He remembered that the electricians removed the ballasts and bulbs to use them in another part of the old hospital where the outdated fixtures were the same, and getting older parts was becoming increasingly difficult. He would be happy when the old hospital was demolished and he no longer had to try to find parts out of production for over twenty years.

Just then, Doug heard movement to his left. He shined the flashlight beam in that direction but saw nothing. Then it sounded like it came from his right. Pointing the light in that direction yielded nothing either.

"Who's in here? I'm calling the police!" Doug shouted, his voice a bit shaky. He moved his light in every direction, but nothing was there.

Suddenly, one of the drawers slid fully open. Worn metal casters grinding on the stainless-steel tracks shrieked, piercing the stillness. Doug stared directly at it, his flashlight beam capturing the movement, and then it slammed shut abruptly. Then another drawer on the far-right end opened quickly, only to slide shut again, making a loud banging noise. Without realizing it at first, Doug pissed his pants, a darkened stain spread from his groin. There were ten drawers total, and they were opening and closing in rapid succession. The noise was nearly deafening!

"What the hell?" he cried out, the drawers opened and shut in a macabre choir of metallic fury, as if they were alive and wanting to be fed. Doug took a step back, his left hand reaching behind him for the door knob. The other hand held the flashlight, and its beam was now flickering, almost in time with the insane banging of the metal morgue drawers. It was sheer madness.

As Doug finally found the knob, he turned and began to frantically twist it. It would not turn! He tried the other door, but met with the same result. The drawers behind him continued to slide open and then slam shut, a cacophony of metal on metal that was raging in the pitch black.

"Help! Help me!" he screamed, dropping the flashlight to the floor and banging on the metal doors with both fists. His muffled cries went unanswered in the long, dark hallway where only his abandoned mop and bucket were witness to the mayhem.

Then he felt a clammy, cold touch on the right side of his neck, and then on the left! He screamed, but to no avail, as something moving in the blackness had him by the throat. It was pulling him across the floor as Doug's legs kicked and thrashed about, desperately trying to gain footing. The hold was a vice grip of ice.

"Help!" he barely gasped. The hands on his throat were building pressure and now cutting off his air supply. Doug grabbed at whatever had a hold of him, yet it was too strong. It wasn't letting go, and he continued to be pulled across the slick tile floor, helpless to stop it.

Suddenly, above his head, Doug heard one of the drawers open and felt whatever had a hold of him pick his body up and throw him inside like a rag doll. He could feel the coldness of the drawer. His entire body was now lying inside. Terror had a grip on him that refused to let go, and in a moment the drawer slammed shut, trapping Doug inside its stainless-steel confines. He screamed himself hoarse for what felt like hours, but no one could hear him. He banged his fists bloody and kicked his feet until they were numb. There was no one that could hear his tormented cries and frenzied banging in the gloom of the long, dark hallway.

Carnival of Atonement

1

It was the second Friday in December, and the Carnival of Atonement would begin in less than two hours. A growing mass of dark clouds began to make their way across Cochise County and encircled the town like an ominous, churning wreath. The vibrant lights on the fifty-foot Ferris wheel, the intoxicating calliope music of the merry-go-round, the rushing swoosh of the Tilt-A-Whirl, and the tantalizing smells from the funnel cake and pizza stands were set in contrast against the foreboding ceiling of clouds. The scene was disjointed and rang out like a dissonant chord.

Every year when the carnival came to Atonement it brought with it the richest ironies and clashing emotions, mixing the unbridled enjoyment of the citizens with the harshness of its true purpose. To the citizens who counted down the days to the carnival, it brought raw excitement. To those who would have to atone, the carnival brought with it an incredible sense of dread.

Atonement was a small, unincorporated town of 2,900 people (according to the last census) 80 miles southeast of Tucson, Arizona. People traveling on I-10 in southern Arizona would likely miss it. An exit off Route 191 that reads, "Wilcox Dry Lake Annex", is the only paved access to Atonement, and unless a person was really trying to find it, they would continue east to New Mexico or south to Mexico. The citizens of the town preferred it that way. Visitors are not welcome in Atonement because of the harsh standards they place upon themselves. There is no police department. Even the Cochise County police stay away from the unincorporated town. A small family diner, a gas station, hardware store, and an IGA were the only commerce to be found. There was of course the Atonement Church of God on the very north edge of town. That was the source of all that was just in the small town that most never knew existed.

The middle-aged pastor of the church was a purveyor of fire and brimstone who shook the rafters every Sunday when he delivered his sermon. Revered Clayton Henry was the grandson of the original pastor who founded the Atonement Church of God in 1899. Reverend Clayton had a wild mane of red hair that flowed in curling locks to his shoulders. He was married to his childhood sweetheart, Suzanna, and they had twin teenage sons, John and Peter. Both boys were looking to follow in the Henry family tradition and become preachers themselves.

Reverend Clayton usually wore a wide-brimmed black parson hat, black jacket, neatly-pressed white dress shirt, bolo tie, black slacks, and highly-shined black shoes. No matter how hot it got in Atonement, the reverend was in the same dress he wore on Sunday, every other day of the week. His sparkling hazel eyes and measured tone was captivating to the townsfolk. When the reverend spoke, it was as if they were speaking directly to God.

Since the 1800's with his grandfather, Revered Jonathan Henry, the Atonement Church of God had established a council of three men who were respectable members of the town. When a

citizen was found to have done something wrong, they would appear

before the council in the meeting room in the back of the church,

where judgement would be made and their atonement assigned. The

council handled minor infractions that were easily fixed. Last week

Ben Shipley was made to pay $250 and three chickens to his

neighbor, Diego Sanchez, for accidently damaging his fence when

doing some work on his property.

When it came to matters that were beyond minor infractions,

Atonement had a truly democratic style of discipline. The citizens

would gather at the downtown square and cast paper ballots to vote

and decide the fate of the accused. Each person 18 or older was

given a ballot to pick guilty or innocent. If the citizen felt the

accused was guilty, they would vote for which punishment was a

proper atonement. It wasn't often that this was necessary, as the

citizens of Atonement were there because they wanted to be. The

fear of having to face the wrath of your fellow citizens and the fire

and brimstone of Reverend Clayton, was enough to keep most on the

straight and narrow. This obedience was ingrained in them from

birth, now three generations in perpetuity. They might discuss among themselves that the arcane way of things was stifling

progress, but deep down they craved the structure and security that

the rules gave their lives. Frankly, they wouldn't know what to do

without the rules.

Reverend Clayton picked the best men available for the

council every five years. He would also lead the meetings at the

square, with the help of several volunteers, and explain the crime

that was alleged to the citizens. Upon collection of the ballots, the

council would count the votes and pass the verdict to Reverend

Clayton. He would stand behind an ornate podium, while the lights

around the square cast him in a sort of angelic aura. For this reason,

the reverend would have such meetings in the square at night, when

he could maximize the desired effect. The preacher knew what

power the pulpit wielded, and he made no bones about playing it like

a musical instrument.

2

Earl Whitecotton was fidgeting in his seat on the second

Friday in December 1977. He was sitting in the bleachers along the north wall at the Atonement Elementary School to watch his

granddaughter sing in the Christmas program. His wife, Helena, sat

next to him, fanning herself with the programs they handed out upon

arrival.

"It's so hot in here, Earl. Aren't you hot?" Helena asked,

beads of perspiration building across her forehead. She mopped her

brow with a handkerchief.

Earl pretended that he didn't hear his wife. His mind was

somewhere else, thinking back many years ago, on the night of the

Christmas program in 1927. Hearing the chatter of some men sitting

behind him, Earl knew he wasn't the only one thinking those same

thoughts. The entire room was packed full of the people of

Atonement, and they all knew how special this night would be.

Immediately following the program, everyone would walk to the

town square and enjoy the carnival, which would run until Sunday

night, when it would be rolled up tight and put away again until the

following December. Waking up the next day, it was as if the

carnival was never there. Where it went from there no one knew.

No one asked. It was just gone.

"Earl! Earl!" Helena said urgently, her voice raising an

octave. "Did you hear me?"

"Yes, dear. It is hot in here." Earl never looked over at Helena. His eyes were fixated on the double doors that led to the gym.

The large gym with the barrel ceiling and lattice woodwork was unique in design, but did nothing acoustically for the room. The murmur of the crowd was nearly deafening, and the excitement was palpable. Like Earl, most of the adults were glancing to the double doors in anticipation. It was as if they were awaiting the entrance of a king or queen, or the entire Barnum and Bailey circus. The curtains were drawn closed on the stage, but some movement could be seen along with the flashing of lights in some sort of code that likely meant, "get ready", to the students who would be performing.

Harold Carr sat in his seat in the front row, center stage. This was the reserved seat he had every year for the Christmas program. His wife, Mary, had passed away six years ago from lung cancer. Harold wished Mary could have been alive to see this. They had talked about it often, especially when the topic of the Christmas program came up in conversation. Harold's friends and family hated to bring up the subject of the Christmas program when he was around, only because they knew that it would result in getting him upset. But this year was different. For the first time in a very long while, Harold had a smile on his face and a certain twinkle in his eye as he waited in his front row seat, glancing every so often over his shoulder at the double doors that led into the gym.

The gym was completely silent the moment the double doors opened inward. As light from the hallway poured into the darkened confines of the gym, three elderly men slowly entered. With their heads bowed, looking at the floor, they walked to the front of the stage in single file. Within ten seconds the first voice rang out in the hollow silence, to be followed by an onslaught of jeers, insults, and curses. Within moments, it was boiling over with genuine hatred spewing from the mouths of the audience. Teachers, secretaries, factory workers, farmers, nurses, cashiers, and more from each walk of life, spouted a raw, visceral reaction that erupted like a volcano.

"You bastards! You don't deserve to live!" one woman cried out from the seats at stage left.

"Burn in hell, you sinners!" screamed one man, his voice hoarse and raspy.

A shower of paper cups, newspapers, and other items were

being hurled at the three men as they continued their slow walk

toward the stage. Some of the items bounced off them, yet they kept

their heads down in shame and kept walking. The crowd continued

to scream and throw items at them. Several even stood up and spit

into their faces. The three men were stoic.

A custodian was in the aisle with a flashlight to guide them to

the three metal folding chairs that were set up directly in front of the

stage, about ten feet in front of Harold. As if on cue, the gym

became perfectly silent again once the three men were seated. With

saliva dripping down their faces, the three sat motionless and staring

ahead. The curtains on the stage were pulled back to start the

program. The silence was deafening in anticipation.

3

The Christmas program had just concluded in 1927. While

the crowd moved in an orderly fashion out of the school and toward

the carnival set up in the town square, four boys were up to no good.

They had snuck outside during the program to a farm on the edge of

town. One of the four, David Sutter, was the one who suggested they go to his grandpa's barn where no one would see them. David

knew his grandparents were going to be at the program, just like the

rest of the town. Charles Bonfield had stolen two big cigars from his

grandpa. The boys wanted to smoke them before heading to the

carnival. A third boy, Artie Daniels, was lighting one of the cigars,

trying to act older than his 11 years by imitating his father when he

lit up a pipe. Charles bit off the end of his and lit it.

A fourth boy was Kenny Carr, and he didn't want to smoke

cigars with the rest of the boys. He had tried a cigarette one time

and threw up for an hour afterward. Kenny was a little slower than

the rest of the kids at school, and they teased him a lot. But Kenny

had an older sister, Charmaine, that the boys in his class all drooled

over, so they were letting him hang around in hopes to see more of

her. To make things worse, Kenny also had a stutter, so he said as

little as possible. He was just glad to feel like he was a part of the

group, even though he suspected they only wanted to be able to see

his big sister and her bursting 17-year-old boobs. It was all they

talked about.

"Come on, Kenny. Give it a try!" said Artie, coughing out a

cloud of smoke.

Kenny didn't take it. "I don't know guys, I really d-d-don't w-w-want to."

Charles and David laughed out loud. Artie tried to hide it, but followed along and laughed too. Kenny kept his head down.

"Oh, come on. Just take one puff, Kenny. Just one," said Artie.

Kenny reached for the cigar, his hand quivering slightly. He dropped it to the ground. In the darkness, despite it being lit, they couldn't see the cigar.

"Oh, shit. Where the hell did it go? I can smell something burning!" cried David.

The four looked around nervously. The smell of hay burning became evident.

David started to stomp on the hay that was smoldering, but was unable to get it to go out. Then flames started to rise, licking up the side of one of the horse stalls.

"Hurry, grab some buckets. This barn will go up fast if we don't put that fire out!" David yelled out. He was panicking, thinking about what his grandfather would do if he found out they caused the barn to burn down.

"I'm s-s-sorry, David. I didn't m-m-mean to drop it."

The other three boys were trying to get buckets of water on the fire, but it was getting out of control quickly.

"You dumb son-of-a-bitch!" David yelled at Kenny, who was now standing in the middle of the chaos, crying.

"I'm s-s-sorry!" Kenny whimpered, tears streaming down his face.

Artie cried out, "We need to get out of here. This thing is going up!"

David picked up one of the empty metal buckets. It was a heavy, galvanized metal.

"Not without me killing this little bastard!"

He swung the metal bucket and connected with a crunch. Kenny toppled over into a pile of hay. Flames began to shoot up in every direction as the loft above them started to catch fire. The fire spread to the ceiling joists. The smoke was thick. There were two horses in the barn that David had to let loose for fear they would die in the fire. The entire time he could only think about how his grandfather would whip him for being involved with this. That is if his father didn't kill him first.

"He's out cold, David!"

"Yeah, you might have even killed him!"

David stood there, frozen for a moment. Trying his best to think amid the confusion. There were only minutes left before they would all be trapped inside, as the roof started to groan and creek under the strain.

"If we leave him in here, they'll just figure he started the fire. We could sneak into the carnival and just say we were never here," David said to the group.

Flames were crackling in the crisp night air as a thick black smoke poured out of every crevice. David knew someone in town would see the blaze. He didn't have time to think it over any more. He was sure the only answer was to leave Kenny in the barn and get out while they could. No one would have believed they were not at the carnival. The story would work. David convinced himself.

"I don't know, David. I don't think we could keep a secret like that," said Artie, trying to shake Kenny awake. He was breathing shallow, but alive. The main support beam was directly over him and the fire was charring it quickly. It would only be moments before it would fall and kill the boy.

"We're all in this together. We gotta promise never to tell. We're all guilty," said David. Then he turned and ran for the barn door. Charles and Artie followed behind.

There was one thing that David, Charles, and Artie didn't realize. Kenny's younger sister, Elizabeth, had seen the boys leaving the Christmas program, and she was worried her brother would get mixed up in some mischief. She knew how the kids picked on her brother. It took her longer to walk in the dress and fancy shoes she wore to the program, but as she made it to the barn, she saw the fire and the three of them run away. She wondered where Kenny was, but assumed he had run like the rest.

4

As the curtain opened at the Christmas program in 1977, the stage lights came on and set the scene of a typical Christmas program in an elementary school. The classes, from kindergarten through sixth grade, each performed two Christmas-themed songs, much to the enjoyment of the audience and the music teachers who had worked hard with them for the past two months.

The curtain closed once again for a brief intermission before opening ten minutes later. This time the lighting was somber. A replica of the barn at the Sutter Farm was built to fit the stage, and it was set up so the entire audience at the Christmas program could see inside. They used three of the sixth-grade boys at the Atonement Elementary School to play David, Artie, and Charles, and a third-grader to be little Kenny. The attention to detail was incredible with the hay, stables, and the brand of the cigars, Swisher King Albert. They even had the old red-painted horseshoe that Grandpa Sutter had hung over the door.

In the three metal folding chairs, the three older men sat still and stared ahead at the performance. Tears welled up in David's eyes, and Charles' too. Artie was not giving the crowd the satisfaction to show the performance upset him. He was the most bitter of the three of them. It was their atonement to come to the Christmas program every year to watch what they did, over and over again. The rest of the year they lived on the outskirts of town in three run-down farmhouses only a few miles from each other, and they were shunned by the rest of the citizens. They had to stay in Atonement. It was part of the enigma that made the town such a unique place with unique rules. No one ever left, no matter how bad

it got. Even David, Charles, and Artie stayed, despite being treated

like lepers and tormented every year on the second Friday of

December. Now this was the 50th time they had to watch the

Christmas program.

In late December of 1927, at a town meeting in the square,

the three boys were brought before the assembly of citizens. Kenny

had been found dead in the embers of the barn the morning after the

fire. At first, it was a mystery as to what he was doing in the Sutter

barn and why there were remnants of two cigars found near his

body. Then Kenny's sister, Elizabeth, came forward to tell what she

had seen that night, and everything became perfectly clear. The

citizens each cast a vote, and it was a unanimous guilty verdict for

all three. Their atonement was being shunned like they were and

having to come to the Christmas program every year to see what

they did. But that wasn't all. Not for murder.

On the 50th anniversary of the murder, the three were going

to experience one last atonement. David, Charles, and Artie had

dreaded this day for the past 50 years. They would discuss it among

themselves in the confines of their homes. They knew it was

coming, and the fact it took 50 years to get there made fearing it that much worse. That much slower and painful. Everyone in the crowd knew something big was going to happen, even the children in the play. This year, the Carnival of Atonement would be a truly special event. It would be an atonement no one in the town would ever forget.

The rest of the play went on as the audience watched, mesmerized. Most were only able to think about what was coming after the performance, including David, Charles, and Artie. As the children on stage acted out Kenny being struck in the head with the metal bucket, the simulated flames the younger children made with yellow and orange construction paper were used to remind the three what a fiery hell they chose to spark that night in 1927. If the gym building hadn't been a wooden structure, the town probably would have had them light it on fire every year for dramatic effect.

While the boys on stage ran out of the barn, the spotlight was on the smaller boy who was playing Kenny's part. Then the spotlight went out, and the audience was perfectly silent. The stage curtain was drawn shut slowly as the gym overhead lights came on. No one said a word as they silently and in an orderly fashion shuffled out of the gym and into the main hallway which led to the

front entrance of the school. They all knew what was going to

happen next, and most were anxious to get a good spot to watch.

The last people to leave the school were David, Charles, and

Artie. They walked slowly toward the town square behind the mass

of citizens making their way to the same place. The Carnival of

Atonement was waiting for them. The big Ferris wheel was

spinning, and its lights were flashing brightly enough to see it many

blocks away at the school. The carnival workers were making their

last-minute safety inspection of each ride. The games were ready to

go, and the smell of the funnel cakes, pizza, nachos, and tamales

were enticing.

Reverend Clayton was also there waiting and already perched

behind the podium, running through the speech he had written years

before, knowing this day would come and that he would be the one

to enforce the atonement that his grandfather laid out in December of

1927. Oddly, it was a crystal-clear night with a brisk chill in the air

not common in southeastern Arizona, just as it had been in 1927.

The reverend spent extra time primping his flowing red locks and

making sure to adjust the lights so the podium was the focal point and not the carnival that surrounded it. This would be his time to shine, and Atonement would remember him forever because of it.

5

The crowd gathered in the square as the three men were led to chairs to the left of the podium. Reverend Clayton wore a dramatic countenance, held his hat firmly, and stared at the three sitting next to him. The men looked considerably older than their years. Those 50 years of exile had not been kind to them. The crowd was quiet, but it was only a matter of time before their rage would explode, and the ugly underbelly of the town would be revealed. While the citizens liked to think of themselves as pure and living in a utopia where they didn't need police, that was the furthest thing from the truth. Even so, their piousness was beyond compare.

Looking out at the faces before him, Artie knew many of their dark secrets. He kept his opinions within the confines of the private conversations the three men had over the years. They all heard the rumors around town about which married person was sleeping with someone else. Living in the shadows made it easy for the three men to listen to people talking, assuming the three shunned men were like inanimate objects. It was no different than any other place on the face of the Earth. There were shady business deals and people that took advantage of others less fortunate. There were illegal drugs to be found if a person knew the right places to go find them. There was illegal betting, gambling, and an assortment of other vice crimes, including prostitution. In some ways, the fact that the town acted high and mighty, handing out punishments to those unfortunate enough to get caught, made it that much worse.

"I would like to welcome everyone to the 1977 Carnival of Atonement. This has been a tradition in our town since its founding in 1895," boomed Reverend Clayton from the podium. His voice was clear, and his diction was almost perfect. He looked back and forth, scanning the crowd before him. The atmosphere was electric, and he reveled in it.

"Fifty years ago, these men were given an atonement to carry out in this very square. My grandfather, Reverend Jonathan Henry, stood in this spot and read the sentence that was unanimously decided upon."

David thought back to that night in December of 1927. It

seemed like forever ago. Fifty years at least. There were very few nights where he didn't dream about that night. He could see the empty stare of Kenny after he crumpled to the floor of the barn, the smoldering hay surrounding his thin frame. He felt a tremendous amount of guilt over what he had done. David felt bad for the Carr family, and he couldn't look any of them in the eye after that happened. He knew they all hated him. Just as he hated himself. Despite the many years that had gone by, it didn't seem to get any easier. David also was burdened with the guilt that the other two, Charles and Artie, were given the same sentence he was, despite the fact they were only there and gone along with his plan to leave Kenny to die in the fire. David was the leader of the group, and if he decided to do something, Charles and Artie followed.

Charles was also thinking about that night and wondering how his life would have been different if he hadn't gone out to the Sutter farm with the others. He resented David for being the one who organized the meeting in his grandfather's barn and for smashing little Kenny Carr with the bucket. Charles knew that he was the one who had gotten the cigars. He had taken them from his grandfather's private stash. Charles wished he hadn't been there that night, and having to relive it every year with a dramatic performance was a recurring nightmare he wished would go away.

Artie had a bottomless amount of guilt inside him, thinking about letting Kenny die in the fire that night. He had let that guilt fester without an outlet, and it had turned into a jaded bitterness. Artie was sick and tired of waking up angry every morning for the past 50 years. Going through the day hating the world was too much for him now. He looked out at the crowd, the sound of Reverend Clayton's voice fading into the background. Artie could see the expressions on their faces. They hated him. Having to live in exile for another day was too much to bear.

Reverend Clayton was raising his voice even higher, as the audience sat in awe.

"It was Jesus, in Matthew, from the New Testament who said, 'Ye have heard that it hath been said, an eye for an eye, and a tooth for a tooth: But I say unto you, that ye resist not evil: but whosoever shall smite thee on thy right cheek, turn to him the other also,'" his voice resounded throughout the square, and his hands were up high, appealing directly to God to give him the strength to do what was needed. "So, I ask you, citizens of Atonement, do we take an eye for an eye or turn the other cheek?"

The crowd was silent, and then they stood up as Reverend Clay stepped away from the podium and motioned for David, Charles, and Artie to rise as well and follow him. The three did as they were told, moving solemnly in a procession.

As they walked, it was obvious what was different about the carnival this year. In the middle of the square was a life-sized replica of the barn. It was almost identical to the one that Jim Sutter had built in 1910 on his farm. The hay, the stalls, the red horseshoe over the door were all in place. It was like taking a time machine back to that chilly December night in 1927. Each of them had a sickening pit in their stomach, seeing that barn again like a page torn from an old photo album discovered in an attic.

The crowd followed the procession and was gathered around to see the spectacle for themselves. It was the most extreme atonement that had ever been brought down, but since there had never been a murder in town before, and not one since, it seemed appropriate. Suddenly, there was some movement at the rear of the barn. David noticed it at first, and then Charles and Artie did as well.

"My grandfather placed the decision on how the atonement was to be carried out firmly on my shoulders. The crime of murder had never happened here in Atonement, and because of that, the citizens had to make a difficult decision. The punishment was not clear, yet I feel that God himself has spoken to me and told me what to do," said Reverend Clayton, his voice still strong and firm.

While David, Charles, and Artie stood only a few feet from the barn, with the crowd behind them, silently watching on, the reverend moved back and forth, still talking about the decision that he was forced to make. The whole thing was playing out like a dream, and the movement inside the barn was concerning the three men. They didn't know what was going on. Some of the citizens began to whisper to each other, not understanding Reverend Clayton and his apparent confusion to carry out the final phase of the punishment his own grandfather read 50 years before.

From the shadows inside the barn, out walked Harold Carr. He was visibly upset, yet he did not hesitate to stand in the center for all the audience to see. The murmurs of the crowd became louder as the citizens realized there was something different about to happen than what was expected.

Reverend Clayton opened the door of the barn and motioned for the three men to step inside. The crowd inched closer, realizing that things were about to get interesting.

Someone from the reverend's right handed him a lit torch, the flame shooting out at least a foot, dancing in the cool breeze. The crowd instantly focused on the fire. Fifty years of thinking about this night was about to end for those old enough to remember that December in 1927. Those younger would have heard the stories told by their grandparents and parents, passing through the generations like a priceless heirloom. Everyone in Atonement knew about the murder of little Kenny Carr and the three despicable ones who had carried it out. They all wanted their revenge. They all wanted to see this Judgement Day on Earth and to put an end to this travesty for once and for all.

"So, I hand this torch to you, David Sutter," Reverend Clayton began, "so that you may be forced to confront the demons that have haunted you these 50 years."

David took the torch, his hand quivering slightly. He had no idea what was going on. This was not the atonement that had been decided on 50 years ago.

"If we were to carry out the punishment as it was first decided, the three of you would be placed inside this barn and burned to death at the hand of Harold Carr. An eye for an eye. But I think it would be far worse that you light this barn on fire, and the three of you stand outside with the rest of us, while poor Harold Carr burns alive! Just like what you all did to his cousin 50 years ago!" The Reverend's eyes were wild. The crowd was dumbfounded!

Harold stood there, his eyes now closed. He had spent the last 50 years waiting to avenge the death of his cousin, Kenny. He was the one to light the fire and watch those three men burn to death. Now the tables had turned because Reverend Clayton wanted to carry out what he thought was a worse punishment. Harold was struggling with it, but he was raised not to question the reverend, whomever it may be. God Himself was speaking through him.

The reverend continued, "To live the rest of your days, shunned by the town, coming to watch the Christmas program every year, and to have a fresh memory of burning Harold Carr alive, would be a living Hell that you would be forced to endure. Knowing of course that when you die, you will all be condemned to spend eternity in actual Hell. For you three, dying tonight would be far too easy. It would be like letting you off the hook. Not on my watch!"

David stood in the middle between Artie and Charles. He looked at each of them as he held the torch. They offered nothing. The look in their eyes was the same as his own. They were confused and horrified at the thought of living another day like they had for 50 years. What if they lived into their 80's or 90's? Could they endure living the way they had? Leaving town and suicide were not options for anyone in Atonement. They just didn't do that.

The crowd inched even closer and slowly. From the back of the group, a chant began to grow. It was quiet at first, but each time it went on, the volume increased. Within two minutes it was almost deafening.

"Light the fire! Light the fire!" the crowd chanted.

David's hand shook, and the flame from the torch seemed to move in rhythm with the chant.

Harold stared directly at David in defiance. As scared as he was to die like his cousin did, Harold was honored that the reverend decided to make him a martyr. He realized now that it was going to be more painful to the three of them to watch him die and have that on their conscience for the rest of their days. Harold knew he was going to Heaven. He was going to see Kenny again and many other friends and relatives who had passed on. He was now at peace with it. Harold was serving a higher purpose.

"Light the fire! Light the fire!" the crowd continued to chant, each time louder.

"Go on, David. Light the fire. Go on. Do it!" Harold cried out over the crowd noise.

As if in a dream, David leaned forward and allowed the torch to touch the piles of hay. It caught fire in seconds.

"Light the fire! Light the fire!" the crowd continued.

As the flames shot up quickly, the frame was on fire within a few minutes. Harold felt the incredible heat on his legs as he was surrounded in black smoke and flames. His screams were primal and horrifying. It was the stuff of nightmares to watch him burn alive. He made it a point to stare at David, Charles, and Artie as long as he could, his body completely engulfed in fire. His screams faded in the raging inferno.

As the replica of the barn burned to the ground, the crowd began to scream insults at the three men as they had done inside the gym. Sticks, rocks, and other items were hurled at them without mercy. The men were made to stand there and take the abuse, thus

beginning the second part of their atonement, as decided by

Reverend Clayton and the Atonement Church of God.

Man With Spots

1

"You little son-of-a-bitch!" said Richard under his breath as he shut the door to his step son's bedroom. It was 2:10 am.

Jimmy sat on the bed, shaking with fear after having another one of his vivid nightmares. It was a dream that came to him nearly every time he closed his eyes. He could see a leather belt with a heavy brass buckle coming down on him over and over again. He tried to cover himself with the comforter on his bed, as if that would shield him from the blows, but Richard pulled it violently from him and tossed it to the floor. Jimmy knew he wasn't dreaming now, but

Richard scared him more than the leather belt. He knew Richard was capable of worse.

"I have to get up for work tomorrow, you little bastard. You wouldn't know what that means – having to get up for work," Richard said through gritted teeth and clenched jaw, so as not to awaken Jimmy's mother, Kim. He was only an inch from Jimmy's face as he uttered those words. Richard's eyes were wide open and alive with contempt for the smaller-than-average boy before him. In some sick way, Richard despised any attention being taken from him. The way Kim would coddle Jimmy was less affection Richard was getting. Jimmy was quivering in fear at his hateful words. He didn't know what to say that wouldn't put Richard over the edge.

Jimmy had nightmares often. In his dreams he would re-live the horrible times he experienced with his real father, Donald, and how he would beat him with a belt for trivial things. Jimmy remembered having his arm broken one time, shielding himself from his father's punches, only because he didn't turn his television off one night. Donald didn't care much about waking up Kim. Donald really didn't care much about anything except drinking whiskey and sleeping around. It was when he came staggering in the front door, his clothes disheveled and the strong odor of whiskey on his breath, that Jimmy and his mother feared what he might do. Kim experienced the abuse herself. She knew of Donald's womanizing, and when she brought it up, he would lash out at her both verbally and physically. Jimmy could hear him yell at his mother and hated him for it. She tolerated it, because she didn't see a way out. Kim was worried that she wouldn't be able to make it on her own, especially with a 9-year-old son. Her job at Murphy's Irish Pub as a waitress and bartender didn't bring in much money. Even with Donald's meager income as a house painter – they struggled. So how could she possibly do it on her own? Donald worked for cash under the table, so there wasn't going to be any child support, and she knew it. She was all too aware Donald beat Jimmy but found ways to justify it her mind. The prescription pain killers she was eating like candy helped hide the pain and reality of a life gone wrong. Kim was raised in a house where her own father beat her mother, much in the same fashion, over too much drinking and running around with loose women.

Her prayers were answered a year ago when Donald ran into the husband of a woman he had been having an affair with, at one of the bars he frequented. The two got into a heated argument in the bar, and Donald left and went home to get a shotgun. Upon returning to the bar, he found the man in the parking lot talking with some friends. Without a word, Donald shot the man in the chest and killed him instantly in front of at least a dozen witnesses. The police were there in moments, and Donald didn't even put up a struggle. He was convicted of first degree murder and sentenced to 40-years-to-life in state prison. The last time Kim saw him was at his sentencing. As he was taken away, she felt like a tremendous burden was taken off her shoulders, but the fear she had of being alone with Jimmy crept back in soon after.

Only a few short months later, Kim began dating Richard, who drove a truck for a restaurant supply company based in Chicago. He made better money than Donald and didn't drink nearly as much. He also seemed to like Jimmy, as the two appeared to hit it off right from the beginning, and nearly six months to the day of Donald's sentencing hearing – they were married.

Things with Richard were good at first. Kim and Jimmy moved into his house on the east side of town, a much nicer neighborhood than the apartment they had been living in on the west side. Then things changed. At first, Kim began to get the feeling

Richard wasn't being totally honest with her. Money seemed to be

short all the time, but she knew the paychecks that he was bringing

home should have allowed them to be much more comfortable.

They began to argue about money all the time. She suspected he

was spending the money on other women and at the local watering

holes. Kim still thought he was good with Jimmy, but every now

and then she would hear him raising his voice to the boy, but when

asked about it, he would make her think she was imagining things.

Jimmy didn't bring it up to her, so Kim was able to believe things

were fine. She didn't realize he was petrified of Richard, and that's

why he didn't say anything.

Jimmy was having nightmares often, mostly about his father

and the abuse he had dealt. Richard would not allow him to sleep in

their room on nights the dreams petrified the boy. Still, Kim didn't

want to believe he was being harsh to Jimmy. She didn't want to go

through that all over again. It was easier to pretend it wasn't

happening. Her choice in husbands had not improved, despite her

new lease on life the day that Donald was taken away in handcuffs

and a prison-issued jumpsuit.

There was, however, another person who knew what was going on with Richard and Jimmy. It wasn't a concerned neighbor or a friend from school, because Jimmy was too scared to say anything. It was the man with spots. That was the name Jimmy had given him. He knew what was going on, and he didn't like Richard at all. The man with spots didn't like anyone who didn't treat Jimmy well. Right now, he was sitting in a chair by Jimmy's bedroom window, slowly rocking back and forth, and watching Richard throw the comforter on the floor and yell at Jimmy. His beady eyes were seething with anger as he watched the spectacle before him. The man with spots was not an imaginary friend of Jimmy's. He lived inside the television in Jimmy's room, and most nights, he crawled out of it and sat quietly in the closet, or lay underneath the bed – a mere breath away. When there was an altercation and he felt that he needed to be more involved, the man with spots would sit in the chair by the window and watch. No one but Jimmy could see him. If they did see the strange man, they would have run away screaming. His appearance was disturbing to say the least, but Jimmy knew he wouldn't hurt him, so the man with spots didn't scare him at all. The man with spots didn't like Richard one bit, and it was only a matter of time before he would tear him into pieces -

very little tiny pieces. That's what he told Jimmy he would do to his

stepfather if he ever raised a hand to hit him like his father had.

It was after Jimmy's father went to prison that the man with

spots first started showing up. He didn't say much. In some strange

way, he connected with Jimmy and didn't need to communicate in a

normal way. As odd as his appearance was, Jimmy knew he wasn't

going to hurt him, so the man with spots was not feared. When he

made his presence known to Jimmy, there was a certain calmness

that washed over his bedroom, knowing that no one was going to

hurt him again. There would be no more beatings. No more leather

belts with large buckles pummeling him in the night. The man with

spots wasn't going to let that happen ever again.

"You're going to sleep in your own damn room and leave us

alone! Only sissies have nightmares and cry about it!" Richard

kicked his mattress as he turned and shut the door behind him.

Don't worry, Jimmy. Go to sleep now. I'll stay awake until

the sun comes up to make sure you're OK. He won't hurt you.

Jimmy smiled as he picked the comforter up off the floor and

lay back down. He knew the man with spots was rocking in his chair behind him, keeping the bad stuff away. He was fast asleep in ten minutes.

2

Three nights later, Jimmy woke up from another nightmare. He was screaming. It was only 9:45 pm, and the man with spots was still inside the television. He normally didn't come out until midnight or so, and he was back inside before the sun came up.

"Oh my God! What was that?" Kim cried out, groggy and out of a deep sleep in their bedroom at the other end of the hall.

Richard heard it. It was hard not to, as the hairs on the back of his neck were standing at attention from the shrill scream coming from Jimmy's bedroom.

"God damn that kid!"

Kim winced at his words as she felt her husband climb out of bed and reach for his bath robe. She knew he was upset. Richard got up every day at 5:00 am for work, especially during the summer months when he was busy, and the humid temperatures meant they had to get started early to avoid unloading their trucks in the afternoon sun. Working 10-hour days at least six days a week took its toll, and he was very cranky when he didn't get the sleep he needed.

"I'm sorry, Richard. Please don't yell at him. He's had a tough time dealing with Donald going to prison," she said, sitting up in bed now wide awake.

Richard grunted something indistinguishable as he walked out of their room and into the hallway toward Jimmy's room.

Kim was grateful to have such an understanding husband and went back to sleep.

3

The door of Jimmy's bedroom was flung open as Richard stood in the threshold, angry that he was awakened with the high-pitch scream. He had a long day ahead of him at work, and every minute he wasn't sleeping was going to make the day that much more difficult. Jimmy was sitting up in his bed shaking uncontrollably as his stepfather turned on the light and stepped into his room.

"What is your problem, Jimmy? Another nightmare scaring you?" His voice was taunting the frail boy who still quivered in his large shadow. Richard was nearly 6'2", and Jimmy was small for his age. The hand-me-downs from his cousins draped over his little body like yard sale clothes on cheap plastic hangers.

"And what did I tell you about leaving that damn television on? That's probably why you're having nightmares. Christ!" Richard was turning red now, as the rage that was typically simmering was now ready to spill over. He walked over and turned it off.

"I'm sorry R-r-ichard," the boy stammered to get out.

"You're sorry? Sorry? I have to get up an hour early tomorrow, and you're sorry?"

Jimmy began to wonder if the man with spots was already out of the television and in his room somewhere. He didn't see him in the chair. Maybe he was under the bed or hiding in the closet again?

Richard went over and pulled the electrical cord from the television and picked it up over his head.

"Please don't hurt me!" Jimmy was cowering on his bed, looking around for something to defend himself with. He knew that Richard was madder than he had ever seen him get. He knew the man with spots warned him that his temper was even worse than his own father's.

"Oh no, I won't hurt you. Your Mom wouldn't let me live that one down you little bastard!" he said as his voice was escalating to yelling now. "I'll do something worse!" Then he threw the television across the room, and it smashed against the hard plaster wall, shattering the screen! The loud crunch of glass woke Kim up.

"No!" screamed Jimmy, wondering if the man with spots was still inside. He still didn't see him by the window. There was no sign of his large friend. Just then, the bulb in the overhead light in Jimmy's room shattered. The room was dark except for the nightlight near his bedroom door. It also seemed to get about 10 degrees cooler in an instant.

Kim heard all the yelling and the glass breaking, and feared the worst. She knew that Richard's fuse was lit, and she hoped she could get to the bedroom in time before things got out of hand.

Then the bedroom door slammed shut with a resounding crunch. It appeared the heavy wood was on the verge of breaking in two! Jimmy was petrified, as Richard was now coming at him in the dark bedroom with the door shut and no sign of the man with spots!

"Jimmy! Richard! Open this door!" Kim cried out as she began to pull and push on the doorknob to no avail. It didn't move! The door was firmly in place and would not budge. She began to pound on it in desperation but only heard silence on the other side. Had she been too late? Had Richard done something terrible? Kim could feel her eyes well up in terror.

Now Richard stepped over the broken television on the floor, and he was nearly upon Jimmy, who was shielding himself from his enraged stepfather with his frail little arms. He closed his eyes and hoped that the man with spots would show himself. He was supposed to be there to protect him in the hour of his most dire predicament – he needed him now!

Richard felt something grab his leg. He figured his pajama pant leg got hung up and tried to shake it off, but it was something else. Then he felt a very strong grip on his other leg as something in the darkness below had a firm grasp on him. The pressure on his legs became stronger by the second.

"What the hell?" Richard cried out, his voice raising an octave. The pain was intense.

Jimmy cracked his eyes open just a little bit and could see two arms raising up from the broken television. They were large muscular arms covered with spots. The nightlight near his door cast a dim glow, but he knew what was happening.

"Jimmy! Richard! Open this door now!" his mother screamed on the other side of the door, her fists pounding with urgency. The door would not budge. Tears were streaming down her trembling countenance.

Richard began to cry out as the sharp claws dug into his skin, pulling him down to the floor, as the man with spots crawled out of the shattered screen. His body was large, somewhere between muscular and fat, and his skin had a blood-red hue. He was covered in crusted-over black spots of various sizes. They covered every part of him, and his eyes glowed with evil green, surrounding black pupils inside. His head was large and bald, covered with spots like the rest of his body. His teeth were sharp and now gnashing at the flesh of his stepfather, who was screaming and flailing around on the floor like a rag doll in the grasp of the man with spots.

Jimmy found himself almost taken out of the scene, as though the screams of Richard and his mother were coming from a distant place – far away from here. The man with spots was making low growling noises as he tore Richard into pieces, blood splattering all over the walls, floor, and ceiling. Jimmy wasn't afraid. He knew the man with spots was doing just what he promised he would do. He was tearing Richard into little tiny pieces.

4

When the sun came up that next morning, Jimmy pulled the sheet down from his face, afraid at what he was going to see. The act that had taken place at the foot of his bed had been the most violent thing he had ever witnessed. The screaming coupled with the sound of the man with spots eating his tormented stepfather were going to stay with him for a while.

As the sunlight poured into his bedroom window, Jimmy saw the television back in its usual place and unbroken. There was no blood anywhere to be found on the walls, floor, or ceiling like it had been only a few hours before. His bedroom door was open, and there were no signs of the tremendous pounding that his mother was exerting during the struggle. As he climbed out of bed, he couldn't help but wonder if the whole thing had just been a strange dream. Was it another nightmare to add to the long list of scary dreams he had endured?

His heart raced as he walked around to the foot of his bed, where he had dreamed Richard encountered the man with spots. On the floor in a neat pile were tiny pieces of plaid fabric – the same plaid fabric that made up Richard's pajamas! The pieces were dime-sized and neatly piled up on the floor, only a couple feet from the television! There was no blood or anything else, just the tiny swatches of fabric.

"Jimmy. Are you up? I had the strangest dream last night," Kim said as she stood in the doorway, yawning.

Jimmy didn't say anything. He was trying to process what had happened.

"Have you seen Richard? I figured he would be gone for work by now, but his truck is still in the driveway."

That was when Jimmy knew that the man with spots had taken care of Richard just like he promised. He pushed the pieces of fabric under his bed and ran to his mother, hugging her tightly. It would be OK now.

Elvis and the Two Dead Hookers

Elvis had no idea where the two dead hookers came from. He had never seen the two young girls before. He couldn't deny the facts. The car was his. The hookers were dead, and they were in his trunk. It was as simple as that. Right now, as the hot afternoon sun baked everything in sight, Elvis Lee Lewis was hiding in the shade under some random back porch on Clayton Street. He was panting heavily after running from the cops for the past half hour. He was out of shape, and the smoking didn't help. Speaking of smoking, he craved a Marlboro right now, but in his frantic foot race from the police, he lost the pack he kept rolled up in his shirt sleeve.

Less than one hour ago, he had been cruising down Lincoln Street in his hometown of Bloomington, Illinois. He was on his way home from his job as a mechanic for Taylor's Tire and Auto on the west side of town. It was a blistering August day in 1982. It was Friday, and all Elvis (and his pelvis) could think about was getting home, taking a nice cool shower, picking up his girlfriend Cindy, and going out to Dawson Lake for her birthday. This had become an annual tradition for them and their close friends. Elvis and Cindy had been an item since their junior year at Bloomington High School. He had grown up a lot in the last few years and hoped they would get married soon.

Elvis installed a modern stereo in the blood red 1950 Ford Mercury his grandfather left him when he died three years ago. He had restored the car as his first real project after high school and spent a lot of time searching for as many original parts as he could find. His dad let him use the garage at work when he needed it, since it had a hydraulic lift, and got him any parts he came across at the junkyard. It was decked out with rear fender skirts and a chopped top, just like the 50's bad ass gear heads would have done it. The stereo needed to be modern so he could play his massive collection of 1950's music that he had. Elvis knew that people made fun of him and his family, but he didn't care much at all. Some days he wished it was the 1950's all over again - a much simpler time.

With a name like Elvis Lee Lewis, it was no surprise that he loved the 1950's. Well, his parents were mostly to blame for that. His father, Odell, went by "Buddy" due to his obsession with Buddy Holly. He had an impressive 1950's record collection, but his Buddy Holly memorabilia was considered one of the most extensive in the country. Every year, on February 3rd, Odell spent the day listening to only Buddy Holly, Ritchie Valens and the Big Bopper, in tribute to the fallen three on the anniversary of the plane crash that ended their lives far too soon. If he could, he would even take the day off work. His mother Daphne was also a huge fan of the era and loved to travel the Midwest with her husband to attend the cruise nights and stock car races during the summer season. She would shamelessly jump up and scream "go Big Daddy" when he rounded each turn. When Elvis was born, Odell wanted to name him Buddy, but Daphne won out by naming him after her two favorite 50's crooners – Elvis Aaron Presley and Jerry Lee Lewis.

Their house on Bunn Street was small and modest, adorned with not only 1950's collectibles of their musical icons, but also old TV shows like Perry Mason and Maverick, St. Louis Cardinal stuff, vintage car models, and much more. They had a vintage jukebox in the living room that played nothing but 50's music. Odell sported a duck-tail hair style and worked at the junk yard on Bunn Street, across the street from their house, where he tinkered with cars all day. His hands were permanently oil-stained. He didn't make much money, but had full access to parts he needed for his own stock car that he raced on dirt tracks in nearby Fairbury, Farmer City, Canton, and Peoria throughout the spring and summer. He was also always in the middle of restoring at least two or three cars in their two-car garage. His mother had a poodle cut hairdo and wore vibrant colored dresses straight out of the 50's. So, it's no wonder that little Elvis liked the 1950's as much as he did. It was in his blood.

He glanced down at his dashboard and was surprised his gas tank was nearly empty. Elvis decided to stop at the Freedom gas station near his parents' house. He lived in a small apartment above their garage. He paid rent and helped around the house, so they didn't mind at all having their only child around in his 20's. All six of the pumps were busy, but as Elvis pulled in, one of the cars drove

away – giving him access to a spot to fuel up. He got out of the car,

his lanky 6-foot frame clad in jeans and a white t-shirt. He changed

out of his uniform at work. He put the gas nozzle into the Mercury,

showing off his tattooed fingers that said "ROCK" on the right hand

and "ROLL" on the left. His short sleeves were rolled up and

displayed the ace of spades tattoo on his left forearm and the pair of

dice on his right. He also loved to wear his hair in a duck tail, but

when he was at work, they required him to wear a ball cap to avoid

getting his hair caught in a moving part of one of the cars he was

working on. Most would look at Elvis with a bewildered amusement,

but the Lewis family had been in Bloomington for a very long time,

so they didn't give it much thought. He had his share of run-ins with

the police as a teenager, but most of it was petty stuff that only made

them bring him to his parents in a squad car. The kids in the

neighborhood enjoyed watching the spectacle and hearing Odell give

him the belt good when that happened.

After fueling up, Elvis went inside the Freedom gas station to

pay and also to use the restroom. The colas he loved to drink by the

bucket-full were catching up to him, and he wondered if he would make it home without taking a piss while there. There was a long line at the counter, so he decided to use the bathroom first. It was a small one-man-show with a toilet that looked like it hadn't been cleaned for a year and a urinal that was perpetually running water into the disgusting pool of scum at the bottom. The smell of sour piss was strong, and Elvis did the best he could to do his business and run water across his hands to make it feel like he washed them before shutting off the light and closing the door behind him.

As Elvis emerged from the restroom, he could not believe his eyes. It was as if he was in a dream, and he actually shook his head a couple times back and forth. What he saw before him was a completely different gas station than he saw less than two minutes before. There was none of the same merchandise displayed as was there before. They were replaced by old-fashioned coolers with only Pepsi, Coca-Cola, 7-Up and Hires Root Beer. A small display of candy lined the small space under the counter. Two aisles of grocery items were there too and the store was immaculately clean. There was a black and white checkered ceramic tile floor and a large display of motor oil in old-style containers like he had seen in his grandfather's garage growing up. Even the man behind the counter was different than the scruffy 30-year-old cashier he saw moments before. He was much older, with a military-style haircut and some thick horn-rimmed glasses, similar to the ones that Buddy Holly used to wear. He was smoking a cigarette and staring at Elvis – like he had seen him before.

Elvis wanted to say something to the man, but he thought maybe someone was playing a joke on him, so he didn't want to look any more stupid than he already felt. Now there was no one else in line, like there had been a few minutes before. He took out his wallet and put a $20 down to pay for his gas. He was fixated on a calendar behind the counter that showed it was 1957! It definitely had the look of a gas station from the 50's, but how was that possible?

"You already paid the gas jockey son," the man said, pushing the bill back toward him.

"I did?" Elvis was surprised, since he knew he didn't pay anyone. He also wondered *what the hell is a gas jockey?*

The man nervously smiled back at him. Then he looked down like he was trying to find something. Elvis stepped out of the gas station and into the bright summer afternoon sun.

As Elvis walked toward his car, he saw what he assumed was the mythical gas jockey the old man referred to, washing someone's windshield as the gas pump filled up their thank. Elvis had only seen that in movies. Even the gas pumps, now only two instead of the six that were there when he arrived, were the old style that he had only seen pictures of. The sign out front said the gas was only 44 cents a gallon! *What the hell is going on?* He stared at his car, which looked like someone had put a fresh coat of paint and wax on it while he was inside! The blood red paint job was glistening in the bright sunlight. It looked amazing!

Opening the door of his car, he marveled at what he saw. The interior leather was pristine, like it had been in 1950. As he sat down behind the wheel, he immediately noticed the cool chrome skull on the floor shifter, wired to the headlights to glow when they came on! This was definitely not in his car before he went inside, and it looked so cool, he couldn't believe it. That's when he noticed the radio. It was not the modern stereo he installed, but the original radio that came with the Mercury. He turned it on, and thankfully on came the music he loved - *Jailhouse Rock* by Elvis Presley. Still, Elvis could not understand what was going on.

He began to look around and noticed that all the cars at the gas station and driving the streets were classics like his. He saw old Chevy, Pontiac, and Ford cars and trucks like he was at a cruise night somewhere. The houses in the neighborhood on Lincoln Street were also different. The kids that ran the streets wore clothes from the 1950's. Their hairstyles were from the 1950's. Elvis was shocked and wondered again if he had been dreaming. Could it be possible that he was somehow transported back to the 1950's? It had always been his dream, but now that it was his reality – it was disconcerting.

"What the hell?" he said out loud. He fired up a smoke and drove off, leaving the time capsule of Freedom Oil behind. The massive big block engine of his tricked-out Mercury roared.

Now Elvis wondered what he would find when he got home. His parents should still be there. His dad had a race tonight in Fairbury, but they would probably not be leaving for another hour or so. Maybe they could explain what was going on to him? Maybe he would awaken from the dream before he got home?

He barely drove two blocks before a police car sped up quickly behind him and then suddenly the lights and siren turned on. Elvis pulled over and put the car in park.

"Son-of-a-bitch!" he exclaimed, slamming his hand against the dashboard, not wanting to be late to pick up Cindy. *She's going to be pissed off,* he thought.

His bony fingers nervously tapped the steering wheel as he saw not one but two cops exit the squad car. Both had .38 revolvers drawn! Elvis could feel his pulse quicken, not knowing why the cops would be approaching a simple speeding violation like this. He assumed that's what they were stopping him for.

Only a few feet from the car, one of the cops stopped and crouched, with his gun pointed at Elvis. The other cop stood on the passenger side of the car, his gun also drawn.

"Get out of the car with your hands up!"

Elvis couldn't understand what was going on. He knew they must think he was someone else. He didn't think he did anything wrong at all. Not even speeding! Then he wondered if the old man at the Freedom called the cops, saying he didn't pay for his gas. He knew he didn't pay, despite what the man behind the counter said.

As Elvis got out of the car, the cop closest to him grabbed him forcibly and shoved him up against the car. *Careful of the paint job you fucker,* he thought.

"Grab the keys Tommy, and let's open the trunk. I don't see anything in the back seat from where I'm standing."

"What's going on man? I haven't done anything!" Elvis pleaded. Despite the fact it was Friday afternoon at a time when the roads were typically busy, it was eerily quiet. The cicadas were the only noise Elvis could hear right now. They were loud in the trees above.

"Just be quiet son," said the cop who had him up against the car. His grip was incredibly strong.

The other cop took the keys out of the ignition and opened the trunk. Elvis watched him as the massive trunk popped open.

"Oh Christ! Oh fuck! Sarge, come look!" His mouth was agape. He took a step back, putting a handkerchief up to his nose.

The Sergeant who had a hold on Elvis pulled him toward the rear of the car with the trunk wide open. Inside the trunk were two young women. They were definitely dead, entangled limbs and hollow eyes in distant stares stuffed in the large trunk. One was blonde and wore way too much make-up. She was wearing a red bustier with a short skirt. Both of her shoes were gone. The other was older, brown hair, and glasses. She also had on a short skirt and was only missing one of her high heels. Their skin was a sickly gray color, like they had been dead a while. Elvis didn't know what to think. The world was spinning around him.

"Son-of-a-bitch!" said the Sergeant. "Get on the radio. Tell them we found the two hookers from the 76 truck stop from last night and the sick bastard who killed them."

Now he threw Elvis face first into the pavement, forcing his arms behind his back to prepare to handcuff him. His knee was planted firmly in his back. Elvis could hear the rattle of his handcuffs, and he prepared to put them on him.

"What's your name you sick son-of-a-bitch?" He reached for one wrist to put the cuffs on.

Elvis was trying to hold his face up off the hot pavement. Tiny pebbles were stuck to his sweating face. He spit out some dirt that got in his mouth.

"Elvis. Elvis Lee Lewis."

The Sergeant laughed. "Yeah, right. You're Elvis, and I'm the fucking Easter bunny. You think this is funny? Do you?"

"I didn't do anything wrong!"

In the distance, Elvis could hear the other cop on the radio. He was talking about two hookers that were killed out at the truck stop on the west side of town, only a few blocks from Taylor's Tire and Auto. He knew they thought he killed the girls, but he had never seen them before in his life.

"You got the wrong guy! I didn't kill anyone!" he cried out, wiggling to get free so he could explain that he just got off work and was going camping for the weekend.

As Elvis wiggled, the Sergeant that was on top of him lost his balance and fell toward the squad car, hitting his head hard on the bumper. It knocked him out. Elvis acted on impulse and jumped up while the Sergeant was down on the pavement next to him, and the other was on the radio inside the squad car. It wouldn't be long before he realized Elvis was free. So Elvis ran. He ran as fast as he could, hoping that they would soon realize they had the wrong guy. *But how the hell did those two hookers end up in my trunk?* Some neighborhood kids who were playing catch with a baseball now stopped to watch the spectacle taking place on the side of the road. One cop was down, the other was a rookie who was stumbling out of the car with his gun and starting to run after the tall skinny guy with the tattoos. They hadn't seen this much excitement all summer, so they watched for as long as they could until the skinny guy ran down Evans Street and into the backyards of the houses that lined the east side of the street.

Elvis darted from yard to yard, hiding behind whatever he could find. Garbage cans, swing sets, barbeques, bushes, flowers and hedges. He was cut up, scraped up, and gasping for air. He hadn't run like that since gym class in high school. Even then he was in terrible shape. His two-pack-a-day habit was definitely catching up to him. The fast food and colas were also not helping matters. Covered in sweat and soaked to the skin, Elvis was now under the porch where this strange story started, wondering what his next move would be. He figured it was close to 6pm. He debated whether he should wait until dark and then try and get away.

Nearly two hours had passed. Elvis was still under the porch. Dusk began to settle in. He thought he would make his move once it was dark. He was lucky that the porch he decided to hide under was at a house where no one was outside in the back yard, or had a dog that would know someone was hiding there. His mind was racing the entire time, not knowing how all this happened. He ran through the events of the day over and over while he hid, waiting for darkness. There was nothing that happened that made any sense. All he did was go into the bathroom at the Freedom and when he came out – BAM! It was 1957. As much as he loved the 50's, Elvis didn't know what would happen to everyone he knew. Would they be the same age like he was? Or would they not exist?

It was just after 8pm, and Elvis decided it was dark enough to crawl out from under the porch. His plan was to make it back to the Freedom gas station and go back into the bathroom. Maybe it would transport him back to 2015? It sounded crazy, but then so did the entire course of events leading up to this moment. He was stiff from being under the porch all that time, and he brushed the dirt off his bare arms and jeans as he stood up and made his way back toward the Freedom.

After moving as stealthily as possible, Elvis made it to a house next door to the Freedom, hiding in the hedges in front of the home. He decided the best thing to do was to just walk into the gas station and not hesitate. The sooner he could get into the bathroom, the better. He just hoped that the old man wouldn't prevent him from going into the bathroom in some way. Would the cops be there waiting?

As Elvis walked up to the Freedom, he noticed that the lights inside were off, and the gas attendant was no longer outside in his uniform. It appeared the gas station was closed! He pulled on the doors and confirmed the Freedom was closed. The posted hours showed they closed on Fridays at 8pm. He knocked on the door, hoping maybe someone was still inside that would let him in. He didn't know what he would say, but it was worth a try. He had no other ideas.

Just then, he heard a car from behind him, then a second and a third. The lot was awash in bright headlights and police car lights!

"Freeze!" a loud authoritative voice cried out. "Get down on the ground, or I'll shoot!"

Elvis slowly turned around, hoping no one got trigger-happy. He made sure his hands were up high.

Just then, a shot rang out as he jerked back against the doors. A rookie cop thought he saw Elvis reach for a gun in the dim light. He was hit in the left shoulder. The pain was intense. Then another shot – and another. Elvis was now down on the asphalt in front of the Freedom; blood pouring from his wounds. Lying on his back, all

the noise around him began to muffle as a feeling of peace swept

over him. Elvis couldn't help but smile while his vision slowly

dimmed, as one of the police squad cars was playing *Hound Dog* on

the radio.

Across town at the Bloomington drive-in, his parents Odell

and Daphne were on their fifth date and having sex in the back seat

of Odell's Pontiac Chiefton. Little Elvis was being conceived as 24-

year-old Elvis was bleeding out in the parking lot of the Freedom Oil

gas station, a cool summer evening breeze soothing him as he passed

on to the other side.

The Jesus Tree

1

I don't think I will live to see another day. From the sound of it, they've got my house surrounded. If you could hear the creaking of the sturdy wood frame of this 60-year-old home, you just might understand my predicament. I don't expect anyone to grasp the extreme peril that I am currently in. The candlelight I'm using is flickering now, and as the boards moan and groan under the tremendous pressure, I know time is short. I've taken to writing

down the events that have led to this moment. There is a neat stack
of papers I've got in the side table drawer next to my makeshift bed.
I'm going to try and stay awake all night to finish what has taken me
nearly a month to compile; however, at my advanced age and
condition, that has become increasingly difficult. My breathing is
shallow, and I can feel the beating of my heart weaken with every
stroke of the pen.

They say that there are no atheists in fox holes. I believe that
now more than ever. I never was much of a religious person (much
to the distress of my mother), but after what started in July of 1925, I
changed my mind. It didn't take long for me to seek out the help of
the clergy when things started to go wrong. With all their good
intentions, even the men of the cloth weren't able to do much more
than prolong the agony a little.

I need to tell my story, as difficult as it may be, so that people
know what happened to Franklin Phillip Manville. I believe that
once they are done with me, there will be nothing left. Earth to
earth, ashes to ashes, and dust to dust will be the literal end for this
miserable thing I've endured called life. I can't blame anyone but
myself for all of this. When I'm done writing this down, I can only

hope that in some way, I can prevent such a cursed thing from ever happening again.

The wind is howling outside. Despite the fact they have the house surrounded and in their firm grasp, I can hear it nipping at the asbestos cement roof shingles, and shaking the storm shutters. I can also hear the wood continue to creak, like it might snap at any minute and bring the entire house down upon my wretched self. I can also hear the faint sound of fireworks in the distance. That means that it's the Fourth of July.

Where my house sits, I can hear the annual fireworks from both Danbury on the Connecticut side to my east and the Brewster New York side to my west. For most people, the 4th of July is a time of fun in the sun, and a celebration of our nation's independence. Yet for me, it's an annual date with the reason why I'm hiding in my attic, eating canned goods, and praying each night that I live to see another day. Every Fourth of July she comes to pay me a visit. She slithers into my house, and no matter where I manage to hide, she finds me. I can smell the rot and decay before she shows herself. I can hear that high pitched laugh of hers from a distance, before she comes to call. She reminds me of what I did to cause the horrible curse that has descended upon the once great Manville family farm and estate. I see that grotesque face in my dreams each night. She never lets me forget. I know that just before midnight she will be here to taunt me. She will remind me once again what I did, and why my life has been one long, tormented curse. Today marks 50 years since that humid night in July of 1925 when this all began, and I shudder at the thought of what she has in store for our annual get together. I boarded up the attic access hatch, but I know it's no use.

For now, all I can do is write as quickly as my gnarled, arthritic fingers will allow. My body is falling apart slowly, and my mind has trouble focusing like it did in my youth. Yet I must continue, as the wind shakes the house to the foundation, and the cracking sounds of wood breaking begin to escalate with the ticking of my clock. It's almost midnight. She will be here soon. I think I can hear that godforsaken laughing coming from downstairs. God help me.

2

I was born in 1887 in New York City to Christopher and Anna Manville. My father was born into the Manville family fortune that revolutionized the building industry with the wonder product of the early 20th century – asbestos. My grandfather, CB Manville, merged with HW Johns to form Johns Manville, and they made roof shingles as well as a variety of other materials with asbestos. These products were used in just about every building built in the early 1900's and well into the 1970's. The fortune was immense. My father was one of four boys and two girls, and all of them were born into privilege. Not all made good choices with their riches, but my father was definitely one who did. He decided to leave the hustle and bustle of New York City and moved as a young man to Putnam County, New York, very close to the Connecticut state line. In the sleepy town of Brewster, New York, my father built a beautiful estate on a 250-acre patch of ground where he started a very profitable farm. The farm was one of the largest employers in the area at the time, and he built rows of cottages where his best workers were allowed to live and raise their own families. My father was a genius when it came to business, which was a Manville trait of course, and before long, he had the largest apple orchard in western New York, and an extremely viable livestock business where he raised and sold cows, hogs, and even stud horses for wealthy men who enjoyed racing them.

My father also invested in highly profitable real estate in neighboring Westchester County, where many of the more affluent who worked in New York City, but who wanted to get away from the city lifestyle, would build houses. My mother didn't have to work, but kept herself busy with a variety of social functions. She often entertained at the estate, and had a knack for bringing in new money to the area. She enjoyed her time gardening and competing in the apple pie contest each June at the Putnam County Fair. I was their firstborn in 1887, followed by my brother Ernest, sister Cicely, and the baby of the family – little Raymond. We all did chores at the farm, because despite our tremendous wealth, my father always instilled a hard work ethic in us. He made sure we all knew what it meant to work hard for little money, so that we would all aspire to greater things.

Little Raymond grew up to be the biggest of the brothers and moved to upstate New York after college to start a general contracting business. My sister Cicely was the brains of us all. She finished college and went into teaching at a prestigious boys' school in Wooster, Massachusetts, then married a young heart surgeon from Boston. My brother Ernest joined the Army at the end of World War I, and got out after his enlistment to work for our grandfather, running one of the mills on the lake shore of Chicago. He died young in a freak accident at the mill involving a falling load from a crane.

I was the only one who decided to stay and run the family farm. The rest of my siblings seemed very eager to leave the nest and move away. I, however, felt an attachment to the estate and didn't mind taking the business side over in 1910. I graduated from the University of Connecticut the same month our father had a massive stroke. It nearly killed him, yet despite surviving the ordeal, he was not able to return to work. It was hard to see our father, who was always sharp and willing to work 16-hour days, reduced to sitting in his chair all day and listlessly looking out the window of his bedroom. My mother was still very active, and faithfully stayed through the worst of it, and helped us with his care, until he died in

1919. She died six months later from lung cancer. Years of

smoking had finally caught up to her.

The farm was running great and business was good, as I

became the sole family member at the estate. I moved my second-

floor bedroom to the first floor, in the rear of the house, with a

picturesque view of the valley and mountains that comprised most of

Putnam County. No matter the time of year, the view always takes

my breath away when the sun comes up in the morning. I met a

wonderful young girl, Amanda, from our local Holy Family Catholic

Church. She was from nearby Pawling, and had recently moved to

the area. I mentioned earlier I was not a very religious person, but I

had always been taught it was proper to go to church every Sunday,

and while my mother was alive, there was no getting away with

missing mass. Our English ancestors had been devout Catholics.

Amanda and I married after dating for a year, in the fall of 1919, and

she began to put her touches on the house to show off her flair for

interior decorating. She blessed me with twin boys in March of

1920. Elijah and Christopher were born very healthy and were the

apple of my eye from the start. I enjoyed nothing more than

spending time with them, as an escape from the responsibility of running the business. Thankfully, Amanda also enjoyed playing with the babies, and together with our housekeeper, they were well maintained but highly spoiled.

In August of 1923, our housekeeper, Beatrice, asked if she could bring her niece along to help on days where she had a lot of heavy lifting or long shifts. She wasn't getting any younger, and we agreed that it was a good idea to take some of the strain off her. Her niece was a beautiful 16-year-old girl from Carmel, named Rosemarie. Rosemarie had long dark brown hair, bright blue eyes, and an angelic face with a surprisingly developed figure for a girl her age. The staff kept her busy, but I always made it a point to look for her each day to say hello. She was a bit backward, and blushed like a red rose in June, whenever I paid her a compliment.

It was at our annual Christmas party in early December that year, when I saw her in a nice dress that flattered her curvaceous figure. I found myself keeping an eye out for Amanda, so she wouldn't catch me talking to Rosemarie, even though our conversations were innocent enough. After seeing her in that blue dress and black silk stockings, I found it hard to look at her the same way again. The weeks that followed, when she was in her work uniform, things seemed different. I found that Rosemarie would seek me out during her shift, instead of me looking for her. She seemed a bit more flirtatious with me, which as a man in his mid-30's, I found flattering. I still loved Amanda, but with the boys now age five, she was real tired at the end of the day, and so our bedroom life wasn't much at all. Having a pretty girl fawn over you, despite her young age, can really boost a man's ego. That's exactly what it did to me.

I began to dream about her. There was one instance when I woke up nearly soaked in sweat, with Amanda lying next to me, after a very inappropriate dream involving Rosemarie. I think it was at this time, very early in 1924, that our relationship crossed the line into something forbidden. I would find ways to meet up with the beautiful Rosemarie during lunch at a hunting cabin we had on the very south edge of our property, near Oak Grove Pond. During times of the year where the cabin wasn't being used, it was the perfect place to get away. She would meet me there as often as we could, and after losing her virginity to me on an old rickety bed at the cabin, she became a teenage girl in heat over me. Once again, my hubris got the best of me, and just thinking about being with her got my pulse racing. Those blue eyes had blinded me to how incredibly stupid it was for me to be involved with the young girl on a variety of levels. At that time in New York, 16 was the legal age to have sex, and even get married without parental consent. It was wrong for me to be having an affair with anyone, but with a subordinate employee even worse. I prayed that our long-time housekeeper, Beatrice, would never find out.

It was the morning of July 4th, and Rosemarie insisted we meet at our usual spot. I was busy preparing for a family cookout we usually had at the estate. Since we were in the livestock business, family and friends would come to enjoy the best steaks around. Not to mention, the many other wonderful dishes that Amanda put together along with other wives who spent days preparing. Rosemarie was persistent, so I relented. I figured if we met at 7am, we would have some fun for an hour, then I would still have enough time to get things ready. She would also be at the cookout along with Beatrice. I knew I would be so busy trying to entertain everyone all day, that my only time to really enjoy myself was during the fireworks. From our estate, we could clearly see the fireworks in Brewster and Danbury. It was the perfect spot to enjoy both displays.

When I arrived at the cabin, Rosemarie was already there. She was sitting on the bed in her stocking feet and sobbing uncontrollably. I knew something was wrong, but what she told me nearly knocked me down to the hard wood planks of the cabin. Her pretty face shook with heavy sobs and tears streamed down as she told me she was pregnant. That alone would have been enough of a revelation, but she continued, telling me we should run away and get married. Of course, she knew I was married, but that didn't matter to her. She was of an age where romantic notions were plentiful and rarely grounded in reality. It was when I sternly told her that we would do no such thing, and that she should not continue with the pregnancy, that things took a turn for the worst. Despite being Catholic, I knew the pregnancy could not continue.

She began to scream and throw things about the cabin. I tried to subdue her, and explain that it just could not be. I told her that my stature in the community, and my responsibilities of running the family business were too great, and appearances were important. Having a child out of wedlock was bad enough, but with a 16-year-old girl who was hired help, was simply not possible. It would be an

abomination to the world. Rosemarie would have no part of that

logic. She continued to scream and threaten to tell my wife about

the affair if I didn't at least let her have the baby. My mind was

racing, and fully cluttered with every possible angle of the tangled

web that was woven. As she continued to yell and scream, my

temper began to burn out of control. Every venomous word she spat

was like a searing hot dagger in my back. I knew that I had to do

something to keep her quiet, but no good thoughts came to mind.

That was when I lost all control. I could see the face of my

father and my grandfather, in total disgust at what I had done. I

could also see the countenance of my humiliated wife, hurtful and

crying over the illicit affair with the young and beautiful Rosemarie.

Even though our boys were far too young to understand, I knew that

eventually they would, and how it would hurt them to know their

father did such a dreadful thing. It was all of these things at one time

that pushed me to the breaking point.

It seemed like everything I did after that was in slow motion.

There were no sounds. There was only her horrified face as my

hands reached up and grabbed her by the throat, and threw her down to the bed with ferocity. Her face turned bright red as my hands clenched tighter. The once smooth and luxurious skin of her face and neck was now oxygen-starved and turning blue – veins protruding from her neck in a desperate cry. Her arms flailed as she tried to fight back, but to no avail. She even tried to kick me, but it was no use. Within a few minutes she succumbed, and took her final breath.

I stood up, gasping for breath myself at the outburst of rage. She looked as if she were sleeping peacefully in the bed. The same bed we had used as our playground for the sordid affair. I knew I did the right thing, but I felt horrible about it. I took a few deep breaths so I could formulate a plan to get rid of the body. Thankfully, in the shed behind the cabin, was a variety of supplies that would come in handy. I came back into the cabin with some rope, a black vinyl tarp, and an old rusty boat anchor. I laid the tarp on the floor and put Rosemarie in the center, rolling her tiny body into it, and then using the rope to wrap her up, I attached the anchor. I hoisted her up over my shoulder and walked down to the pond. There was still not a sound as my gaze scoured the horizon, making sure no one else was in sight. Thankfully, I saw no one.

I set her down at the shore, while I stripped off my own clothes, so I could wade out as far as possible before tossing her body into the water. I made sure to go into an area of the pond that was thick with vegetation, which no one typically used for fishing or swimming, and tossed her as far as I could. The tarp must have had too much trapped air, because it took a good minute to sink, even with the weight of the old anchor. That was when I thought I saw the tarp move, as if Rosemarie was breathing inside! I knew she was dead, or at least I thought she was. As the tarp slowly went under, I saw what I thought were a few bubbles rise to the surface. The idea that she was still alive inside the bundle gave me the chills, but I knew there was nothing I could do about it. It was unfortunate, but I was not willing to surrender my family fortune, my marriage, and my standing in the community over this young girl. Yes I had grown to love her, but it was not enough. I realized then that I had done something horrible, and there was no turning back from it.

The bubbles eventually stopped, and I made it to the shore, where I got dressed before anyone would miss me back at the farm. Beatrice spent the entire day asking everyone if they had seen Rosemarie, since she had not shown up at the cookout. I did my best to avoid her, because the image of the bubbles rising to the surface of the pond was all I could think about when the subject came up.

3

The next two months were difficult as the search for Rosemarie went on, with the police coming out to the farm to talk with me, my wife, and our employees. Her family was nearly hysterical with worry, but there was nothing that turned up at the farm, and thankfully no one said anything that would have tipped the police off about our affair. I spent many sleepless nights those first two months, worrying that someone might have noticed the two of us had become closer than we should, or that an employee might have caught a glimpse of us coming out of the hunting cabin. No one did.

Beatrice became ill, likely from worrying about her niece, and from her advancing age. At Christmas of 1924, she put in her two weeks' notice and decided to retire. I was relieved, actually, since seeing her every day made it nearly impossible to not think about Rosemarie. We gave her a handsome bonus and set her up with a nice apartment in Danbury, where she lived close to the rest of her family. I figured it was the least I could do after what had happened. My wife always liked her, so she didn't seem suspicious at the gesture.

The following 4th of July is when things began to change. We had just cleaned up after our annual cookout, and the last of the guests had gone home. Amanda had gone to bed early, as a busy day in the hot July sun had gotten the best of her. The boys were also asleep, and I was drinking a beer on the back porch, enjoying the solitude, when I heard a distant sound that put the hairs on my neck standing at attention. It was an eerie high-pitched laugh that came from the direction of the old hunting cabin. I noticed that it was almost midnight, so I knew it was unlikely that any of the guests could still be around. As I sat there holding my beer, the laughing continued. It sounded like it was getting closer! My eyes were fixated on the blackness of the woods that surrounded the back yard, but I couldn't see a thing. I noted that the usual choir of crickets and typical night sounds were strangely silent. Then I noticed a horrible odor that almost made me gag. It smelled like rotting meat, or a dead animal of some sort, wafting my way. It was faint at first, but then it got increasingly stronger. Now I stood up, not knowing what

direction the smell was coming from. It seemed to almost surround

me from every direction!

Suddenly there was a hand on my shoulder, forcing me back

down in my chair! It was ice cold and wet. The rot smell was never

stronger as my body froze in fear at what was behind me. I closed

my eyes tight, hoping that this was all a dream and that I would

awaken and be in the comfort of my own bed, with Amanda sleeping

next to me. When I did open my eyes, the horror show that unfolded

before me made me cry out. It was a terrible sight to behold! It was

Rosemarie. She was dead, but I knew it was her. She was standing

before me, dripping wet, her rotting flesh gone in places, leaving

bone visible. Her face was eaten away from being underwater all

this time, and her body was as lithe and lean as I remembered. The

black tarp that I covered her in was mostly gone, and some of the

rope I tied her up with remained. The dress she had been wearing

was falling off her in places, exposing a sickly, molded grey flesh

that was stretched tightly to her frame. Her eyes bore gaping holes

into me, as I could not take my glance away from them. Those once

gorgeous blue eyes were now black pools of hate. She let out another one of her high-pitched laughs, exposing a mouth full of rotten teeth and black tongue, and a whiff of that rancid breath brought tears to my eyes.

She told me that I was cursed for what I had done. Her voice was different than I remembered it. It was inhuman. It was rough with a gravelly texture, as if she had been gargling with broken glass for the past year. As she stood before me, uttering her hate-filled words about what I had done, she told me that my life would now be plagued with horrible cursed events. I tried to respond, but I was frozen. I found myself unable to retort, and it was probably best, because the sooner she would go back to her watery grave, the better. The image of her rotten face and cackling laugh haunted my dreams every night since that one-year anniversary of her murder. From that night forward, as soon as I closed my eyes, I would see her. I could not escape her clutches to me in the dream world. Some nights I would wake up screaming, covered in sweat and praying for the sun to come up.

4

It was almost a month after Rosemarie's return in 1925 when the curse began to show itself. A strange parasite attacked the apple orchard at the farm, and we lost an entire crop of apples. This was strange, since that had never happened since my father started the orchard part of our business. Since this was approximately 15% of our business income, it did hurt us financially and did cause me to have to let go eight employees who I hired to pick apples and tend to the trees. Then in September, we experienced a series of strange occurrences at the farm. We had a majority of our cows, hogs, and chickens die from some inexplicable disease that no one was able to diagnose. I knew what it was, though. I knew it was Rosemarie and the curse she told me about on the 4th of July. With all of these uncanny events happening, the farm was in real danger unless things improved in the spring. I could only hope that the curse would not continue, but I could not have been more wrong.

As if the bad things we had experienced were not enough, then we had several bad accidents that resulted in deaths of our staff.

One of our long-term employees, Sammy Ray, who ran the hog farm, died from a fall when repairing one of the hog confinement roofs. Another employee who worked in the dairy was killed by lightning just before Thanksgiving, and one of our housekeepers was found hanging in the back yard for no apparent reason. A series of strange things happened around the house too – such as electricity going on and off, water pipes bursting for no reason, and doors that would lock on their own. Amanda was convinced the house was haunted. I knew she wasn't far off with that assessment.

In January 1926, the curse ratcheted up even more. Amanda had been feeling tired all the time and finally decided to go to the doctor. Our local family doctor set her up with some tests in New York City, where they had the best technology available. She was diagnosed with pancreatic cancer. She got bad quickly and was bedridden in less than three months. Elijah and Christopher took it hard, not understanding why their mother was not able to play with them, read to them, or do much of anything as the cancer took hold and refused to let go. Her constant crying and moaning in pain was maddening, and I did my best to keep my composure, despite the overwhelming guilt, knowing that it was because of my terrible sin that she was looking death in the face. Amanda died in May of that year in a fit of incredible agony, that caused her to scream out for pain medicine that couldn't come fast enough. To watch her die slowly was my penance, and I knew it. To see the pain in the boys' faces was almost enough to push me over the edge with guilt.

Just when I thought the curse couldn't get much worse, the apple trees began to wither and die. As spring came, one by one the trees died. I hired the best arborists on the east coast to come to the farm and try and save them, but it was no use. Each one that came out said they had never seen anything like it. I had the same problem with my livestock. I brought in veterinarians with the highest pedigree to try and save the animals, but, like the tree experts, they were equally baffled. I lost 90% of my animals before the 4th of July. Due to the dire circumstances at the farm, and my wife's recent passing, it was the first year we decided to not have our annual cookout. I also found it difficult to imagine enjoying myself at the cookout, knowing that the anniversary of that dreadful day would bring with it a visit from Rosemarie. I knew she would come to see me again, gloating with the knowledge she had brought such pain in my life.

It was close to midnight on the 4th of July, and this time instead of waiting on the back porch, I locked myself in my bedroom on the first floor. I did my best to stay awake, but with the lack of sleep I had been getting, I began to doze off sitting in my rocking chair. I kept a loaded shotgun at my side, as if that would help me against the undead lover from my past. I was partially in a dream state when a pungent odor woke me up. It was the familiar putrefaction that I experienced a year ago when Rosemarie first made herself known. As my eyes began to adjust to the darkness, her horrific face was only an inch from my own. Her mouth was agape, black and rotten teeth bared, and a hideous, cackling laugh reverberating. I was unable to move, terrified at the sight of her once again. She told me that she knew of my pain, and all the misery that had descended upon my family, and there would be much more to come. She also told me that this visit on the anniversary of her death would be a regular thing between us. I was so fearful of her presence that I forgot all about the shotgun at my side, although I knew it was useless to me against the apparition. Within moments she was gone, and only the lingering odor of her rotting corpse would allow me to reminisce on our encounter.

5

It was two weeks after our last meeting that I decided to confide in a priest. I was concerned about anyone local knowing about the situation at my farm, but already the rumor mill was going around. Almost all my employees were gone, with only a bare-bones crew left that helped me keep the house in shape and to watch the boys while I did what I could to save the business. Thankfully, I had other sources of income from rental properties, and the trust fund my father had established, providing a monthly stipend that now was vital to keep the bills paid and to meet payroll. To avoid further rumors going around the county, I decided to talk to a priest in the small town of Bethel, Connecticut, which bordered Danbury.

Through an old family friend, I learned of Father Dominic Caruso, a retired priest, who might be the right person for me to explain the curse. Of course, I could not tell him about the murder, for fear that he might break the seal of the confessional, if I were to bare my soul about every detail. I knew I couldn't take that chance.

I met with Father Dominic in a small apartment in the rectory at St. Mary's Church. He was very old and somewhat hard of hearing, but he was willing to listen to my story. I told him about a young girl who had died at my farm, that I believed was haunting the grounds. I detailed all the bad things that had happened with my wife, employees, crops, and livestock, and that in my dreams, the girl said it was due to a curse. The old priest listened intently and told me that he knew of something he thought might help. He told me that when he first entered the priesthood, he went to a seminary at a secluded institute, St. Bede Academy, in Peru, Illinois. He said that there was a very devout sect of monks there that grew crops to feed the staff and students, and that he remembered a terrible plague that wiped out their crops for two seasons. He remembered that they were able to ward off the plague with a special holy tree that was called the Jesus Tree. He said the tree was blessed and watered only with holy water until it was strong enough to grow on its own. Father Dominic believed that the monks at St. Bede could grow me a Jesus Tree and have it shipped to my estate in New York. He performed prayers for me with a rosary and promised he would contact them on my behalf. It sounded a bit far-fetched to me, but in my desperate state, I was willing to try anything. I gave the priest a sizeable sum of money to have this tree shipped to my estate and asked him to keep me informed.

Several months later, in April of 1927, I received a call from Father Dominic, who explained that the Jesus Tree was on its way to me. He said that the monks were also sending six experienced arborists along with the tree and that they would also be planting an additional twelve oak trees that were to be situated next to the Jesus Tree, to serve as a symbol of the twelve apostles. The priest assured me that this was suggested by the monks of St. Bede, as an extra precaution to help ward off the terrible curse that had fallen upon me. Once again, I was so overwhelmed with grief from my situation, that I was all too eager to let the monks plant the trees.

A week later, the trees were planted. The largest of the oaks was the Jesus Tree, which they said would bear an uncanny resemblance to what Jesus Christ looked like when crucified, as the tree grew to full height. They planted it to the side of the main gate that was accessible from Federal Hill Road. The other twelve trees were a bit smaller, and were arranged six on one side of the Jesus Tree and six on the other, along the property line to serve as a sort of talisman against the curse. The monks told me that it would take at least twenty years for the trees to grow to their maximum height, but that spiritual powers were already in effect and should ward off the curse immediately. They stayed on the property in the former employee cottages for a month to ensure the trees would take, and then left to return to St. Bede in central Illinois.

The spring and early summer of 1927 were uneventful. Some of the crops returned and I was able to hire some of the staff that I had to let go when the curse started. It seemed that the Jesus Tree had been doing exactly what Father Dominic and the monks of St. Bede had promised. Even the terrible nightmares that had deprived me of sleep had lessened. I decided to have the annual cookout on the 4th of July, hopeful that better times were ahead. Elijah and Christopher were both seven now and growing faster than I could believe, and despite the fact they lost their mother at such an early age, were surprisingly well-adjusted. They were both the picture of health and doing things that most boys their age were doing in sports, in school, and socially.

The boys had a great time at the cookout, inviting several friends from school to the estate. They spent most of the day swimming in the Oak Grove Pond. At first I was mortified to think of them swimming in that water, polluted with the remains of

Rosemarie, but when I thought about the Jesus Tree and the apparent

magic it had been making against her curse, I felt that such things

were in the past. I didn't think any more about it. Instead, I decided

to have a good time eating and drinking with friends and enjoying

the beautiful summer day.

After the fireworks, I waited until the last of my guests left

and the boys were sleeping, and took out a fine Cuban cigar. I made

a stiff drink to sip in the night air. I felt like a new man with the

curse behind me. It was just before midnight when I decided to turn

in for the night. I heard a noise inside the house as I got ready for

bed, and realized it was Elijah and Christopher, both standing

outside my bedroom door, clearly in distress. When I asked them

what was wrong, they both complained of having a fever, headache,

and that their muscles were sore. I assured them that a day out

swimming in the heat could certainly do that to a person. I noticed

both were warm to the touch when I put them to bed, and it appeared

they both had a rash on their neck and face. I didn't think much of it

and went to bed.

It was almost exactly midnight when I heard the hideous laughing. It cut the humid night air like a buzz saw. I sat straight up in bed, and all the fears and nightmares of the last few years came rushing back to me. Rosemarie made her annual visit, like she had the last three years, and told me that the curse was far from over. She told me that planting those trees wasn't going to stop a thing, and the worst was yet to come. The flesh rotting off her face was just as horrible as ever. I cried myself to sleep after she left; not knowing what could possibly be worse than losing my wife and all the rest of the terrible events that had occurred. I had no idea how right she was.

A week later, the boys were still sick. The rash had gotten worse, with visible skin lesions covering their bodies. The muscle soreness had escalated to the point that neither of them could get out of bed. I was very concerned to say the least, so I called our family doctor and asked him to come to the house. After Dr. Edwards looked the boys over, I could tell that it was more serious than he was letting on in front of them. He asked me to step outside the bedroom to talk about it. Nothing would have prepared me for what he was about to tell me. Dr. Edwards was a very serious older man, and his bedside manner was typically not the best. He looked me straight in the face and told me that he believed it was malignant small pox. He advised me to keep the boys in the bedroom for the time being, and to not allow anyone near them, since it was highly contagious.

I buried both boys on the property just before Labor Day. It was by far the worst of what the curse had thrown at me since it started. I thought losing Amanda was difficult, but a parent losing their children was pain beyond compare. The nightmares got worse. I was seeing Elijah and Christopher in my dreams as little undead monsters, following Rosemarie, like a growing army of my worst fears. It was terrible.

I stayed up for days on end, wishing that the curse would take me too, but it did not. I was hardly eating and shuffling through life, barely able to keep the business going. As 1927 came to a close, I was down to only five employees, since most had either been let go due to decreasing business, and the rest fled for fear the curse would strike them too. I honestly couldn't blame them. Strange things kept on happening around the property, and rumors were going around throughout the county. My life continued as if I were in some strange dream-like state. The years rolled by, and slowly,

everyone I knew died. Before I realized it, I was all alone. I cursed

the day I had ever met the beautiful Rosemarie, and wondered what

my life may have been like had I not set eyes on that face.

6

The year was 1945 when I first noticed the Jesus Tree and the

others had moved. I know it sounds insane, but they were getting

closer to the house. It was a very slow process, but looking out my

second story bedroom window, I could see them moving a little

more each day. As the monks had said, the Jesus Tree did resemble

Christ on the cross, if you looked at it the right way. It now towered

at almost 30 feet high. The priest and monks had been wrong about

the power of the Jesus Tree, because it did not ward off the curse. If

anything, it seemed to make it worse, bringing small pox to my two

sons. I wondered if them swimming in that polluted water of Oak

Grove Pond was the reason for the disease, and couldn't rule out that

maybe Rosemarie took offense to them swimming where her body

had been so callously thrown away like garbage. No matter the reason, they were gone, and now with all my staff gone, I was all alone in the large home. I moved my bedroom to the second floor when I realized the trees were moving closer, for fear they were coming for me. Rosemarie didn't miss a 4th of July to come to me. Her midnight visit was the one thing I could count on in the miserable existence I was enduring. No matter how many times I begged for her to kill me – she would only laugh. It was that high-pitched maddening cackle that always preceded her visit.

By 1955, the trees were now within twenty feet of the house. They made a perfect rectangular shape around my home. No one else ever came to the estate to visit, so there would not have been anyone else to show. Not that they would have believed me anyway. I know it sounds like the rambling of a crazy man, battling dementia into his old age, but it's the truth. All 13 trees now towered over the three-story house, and I moved my bedroom up to the third floor, in hopes of escaping their eventual destruction of whatever I had left. As I entered the 68th year of my life, I wondered how many more years I would have to endure. With no health problems that I could detect, it seemed like Rosemarie would have me live on forever.

The mere thought of that challenged whatever remained of my sanity.

As 1965 approached, the house was beginning to deteriorate. The once great Manville estate, built solidly of brick and mortar, was now starting to crumble. Year after year of harsh east coast winters and blistering hot summers had begun to take their toll. Time's dark captains would continue to march upon the three-story structure and humble it into ruin. Most people say that the years fly by as you get older, but nearing 80 years of age, I can say that they were creeping by at a glacier's pace. Day after day of sitting by my window and watching those cursed trees, planted so many years before by the monks of St. Bede Academy, inching ever closer to me. By now, the branches were starting to touch the house on all four sides. During the spring and summer months, I could barely see the sun through their dense foliage, as the trees were growing at an alarming pace. Still, Rosemarie would come for her yearly visit, taking great joy in my eternal misery. Every night in my dreams, I could see those bubbles in the pond, as the black tarp sunk ever so slowly into the water. I could see her rotting flesh sway back and forth as she stood before me and laughed at my predicament. I would see Amanda,

Elijah, and Christopher, wandering around the house like ghosts of

my past that refused to let me forget it was me that caused them to

depart the living so early. Yet there I sat, day after miserable day,

waiting for death to come and take me far away from the cursed

ground I called home.

7

So now we find ourselves on July 4, 1975 – exactly 50 years

since the murder of Rosemarie. At the beginning of my tale, I was

hiding up in the attic, hearing the frame of my house cracking under

the tremendous pressure of the Jesus Tree and the 12 disciples of

terror. Their branches were intertwined around the house, pulling it

into their grasp. From outside the home, you could barely see

anything but the branches. The roots had dug down deep and were

choking the house at the foundation, the branches squeezing the life

out of the old estate from every side and now even the roof. I was

slowly being buried alive inside my own house.

As I stated before, I had nailed down the attic access hatch in

a futile attempt to keep Rosemarie away. With my arthritic hands, that was no easy task. The last few years started to wear on me, as I felt like my body was slowly giving out. I could only pray for death to put me out of my misery. I knew midnight was coming. I was concerned that on this 50th anniversary of her death, that she just might have something extra horrible in store for me. The cracking of the boards became more pronounced as the nails crumbled under the intense strength of the trees. The wind howling became louder as I strained to listen for that insane laugh that would warn me that she was coming to visit. I could hear it ever so faintly, amongst the wind and the snapping and cracking as the house began to crumble, sending me hurling down into the blackness. I was plunged head first into nothingness. I knew Rosemarie would be waiting for me in the end.

8

When I awoke from my fall, I wasn't sure if I was alive or dead. I wasn't sure if it was reality or a dream, since the past 50 years my life seemed like one long, never ending nightmare. Everything around me was completely black. I couldn't see sun, stars, or anything resembling light whatsoever. My eyes attempted to adjust themselves, but still I could see nothing. I had no idea where I could have been, but I hoped that I was dead.

That's when I heard the laugh that I had learned to dread a little more each time I heard it. With the laughing came that miasma of rot that always told me that Rosemarie, the undead nightmare, was coming to call. This time, I could not see her rotting flesh, but I could feel her ice-cold hands grabbing me by the arm pits and dragging me away. Where she was dragging me to, or from, I had no idea. I still couldn't see a thing. Maybe the fall had made me blind? Maybe this is what death is like? I called out to her, but she only laughed and kept dragging me along. It felt like I was being taken through grass, brush, and a variety of surfaces as she kept pulling me further and further away.

It was then that I felt wetness. She was pulling me into water of some sort. I still couldn't see anything, which made the sensation of being dragged into the water that much more horrifying. It was then, as I floated on the surface, partially submerged, that I realized where I was. The smells and the sounds were eerily familiar. We were out at the old hunting cabin in Oak Grove Pond. She was taking me out in the water just like I had done to her 50 miserable years before.

As I was falling slowly into the water, I was no longer able to breathe. My lungs were burning. For some reason, I was now able to see. I could see sunlight above the water, but looking through the murkiness, I couldn't see it clearly. I could see Rosemarie, just as she looked 50 years before, with her beautiful angelic face and sparkling blue eyes. She was smiling at me as my body fell deeper and deeper into the pond. Bubbles rising from my mouth were percolating at the surface of the water in the hot 4th of July sun.

9

It's hard to believe ten years have passed since that day Rosemarie dragged me into the pond. I now find myself emerging from the water, the smell of my own rotting corpse, sickening even to me. I walk the grounds, devoid of purpose. The Jesus Tree and the twelve other trees completely engulfed the old house. To look at the plot of land where it once stood, you would never know a house ever existed. There is not even a splinter of wood left behind. I wonder what happened to the pages of my tale, that I spent all that time compiling, but I'm sure it was destroyed and digested with the rest. Unfortunately, no one will ever know what happened on this cursed ground.

The Jesus Tree and the twelve other oak trees are back to where they were the day the monks from St. Bede Academy planted them. Of course, no one will ever believe that they moved hundreds of feet to destroy my home. There is no trace of their movement. Only I know what happened here. I am as lonely in death as I was in life. The beautiful Rosemarie has moved on, while I am sentenced to an eternity wandering the grounds in rural Putnam County, in the shadow of the Jesus Tree.

They Came to Darkness

1

They came to Darkness on a dreary Thursday afternoon in September. Heading south on route 119 in rural eastern Kentucky, the Robbins family was lost. They left at 9:00 am that morning from Indianapolis and found themselves on a detour that forced them to exit I-64 just east of Lexington. Jeremy Robbins had taken a promotion with the accounting firm he worked for, Bell and Johnson, at a new branch in Tampa. Jeremy, his wife Amy, and twin

9-year-old girls Annette and Alexandra were very excited about the move, despite having to leave their friends behind. Knowing they would be living 90 minutes from Disney World gave the girls plenty of incentive to leave Indianapolis. Like most girls their age, they dreamed of visiting the magical kingdom, filled with princesses and everything Disney. Amy didn't want to leave her family and friends, but she was supportive of her husband, and the that fact the girls were excited about the move made it OK. She started substitute teaching at the girls' grade school last year, hoping to be full time next year. However, Amy was confident she would find a teaching position in Florida. Researching the subject, it sounded like the Tampa area was a very good place to be looking for a job as a teacher. It didn't hurt to know that it was 80 degrees today in Tampa, in stark contrast to a chilly 35 degrees on the winding route 119, lost somewhere in Pike County. Each family member gazed out the windows of their SUV, thinking about the promise of a new start in the land of fun and sun.

"This can't be right, honey," Amy said, looking at the map in the atlas they kept in the pouch behind the passenger's seat. Their State Farm agent gave it to them two years ago, but with the GPS feature on their cell phones, Amy and Jeremy had little use for an atlas. Now, lost in the mountainous terrain of eastern Kentucky, somewhere past Pikeville, neither of them had a signal on their smart phones. They were grateful for the atlas, and their phones didn't feel very smart or useful now.

"I don't think so either. I haven't seen a sign for several miles. Should we turn around?" Jeremy asked, "You guys getting hungry?" He looked at the girls in the rear view mirror. They were arguing about what Minnie Mouse would be wearing when they got to Disney World. Jeremy promised that they would spend the coming weekend there, before the tedious task of getting the new house ready. Bell and Johnson sprang for the moving expenses, so they only had enough clothes and necessities (a grey area living with three women) for a week. The movers would arrive Monday with the rest.

They both replied with a hearty, "Yes!"

Amy laughed. "Me too."

"Well, I suppose we can stop somewhere," he said, as route 119 twisted and turned into several curves, with mountains on each side of the road. Some of the drop offs were steep, and Jeremy tried not to look down, for fear he would drive off into the dense green abyss below.

"It's beautiful here, but I don't see any towns or places to stop. I wish my phone had a signal," Amy said, looking intently at the atlas to try and figure out where exactly they were. According to the map, there wasn't much to see on route 119 unless you were looking for places to hunt, fish, or hike in the mountains. Neither of the Robbins' were much into the outdoors. The had both grown up in a suburb of Indianapolis all their lives. Since Amy met Jeremy at the University of Indiana, the two knew they were destined to be wed, and they were the perfect couple ever since – even down to the two kids and white picket fence surrounding their house in the suburbs. She didn't know it at the time, but Amy was two weeks pregnant with what would be their third daughter.

"It is really nice. Not flat like Indiana. If we don't see anything soon, we'll just turn around. That town we passed, Pikeville, looked like it was a decent size. I'm sure we can find something there." He looked at the girls again in the mirror, and now both were arguing over what ride they would go on first at Disney World. Jeremy shook his head, laughed, and put his attention back on the road as it winded to the east.

Several miles later, Jeremy thought he saw a green road sign up ahead.

"Amy, see if you can read that sign." He pointed toward it. "See it?"

Amy took her reading glasses off.

"It says 'Darkness 4 miles'."

"Darkness? Is that the name of a town?"

Amy put the readers back on and was looking at the atlas. "If it is a town, it's not on here. That is a weird name for a town, but we've seen a lot of funny ones today." She kept the girls' interest reading aloud the odd names of towns. The one that had them all laughing was Raccoon, Kentucky. A close second was Hi Hat, Kentucky.

"Interesting. Well, kids – looks like we're going to Darkness!" he exclaimed, as the girls both cheered from the back seat of the Dodge Durango. They forgot about their Disney World arguments for the time being.

2

Jeremy could see a small town up ahead and an old weather-beaten painted wood sign that read, "Welcome to Darkness – Nestled Away From the Rest of the World". He could make out a tall water tower with Darkness painted on the side, rising above the trees ahead. The beautiful fall foliage was enticing. As they passed the sign, the Durango shuddered slightly, and the check engine light came on.

"Are you kidding me?" he said, helplessly looking at the dashboard, the engine light blinking.

"What's going on?" Amy asked, setting the atlas down. She felt the vehicle shudder.

Jeremy pulled the SUV to the gravel shoulder of the narrow two-lane road that led to the small town. As they came to a stop, the Durango shook again, then stalled out. Within moments, the smell of burned plastic or rubber permeated the cabin of the truck. A thin wisp of grey smoke began to rise from under the hood.

"Well, that doesn't look good," Jeremy said, trying not to alarm Amy or the girls. He knew that he was useless when it came to working on cars, aside from pumping gas into it and running it through the car wash. Usually the automatic one.

"Ew, what's that smell?" Alexandra asked, holding her nose.

"Let's get out of the truck, I don't like that smell, either," Amy said. "I don't trust it. Come on girls."

Standing on the side of the road, Jeremy felt small staring up at the steep mountains and dense terrain. Neither had a signal on their cell phones. The town was about a half mile from where they were. It was cold out as a biting wind bore down from the mountain to the west. He tried to think about being in the welcoming sun of Tampa instead of freezing on the side of the road in such a remote place as this.

"What are we gonna do, Dad?" asked Annette, shivering. She held on to Amy.

"I don't know. I think I'll walk to town and get some help. Mom can stay with you guys." He ran his hand through his hair and exhaled loudly, thinking of his limited options.

Amy hugged on both girls. "You're not leaving us here. We can all walk to town. It's not that far." She forced a smile. "It will do us some good after being trapped in the car all day."

Just then, they heard the rumble of a truck coming toward them from the north. It slowed down as it got closer, and appeared to be a tow truck. Jeremy thought it must be a sign, someone was telling them things would be fine.

"Well, I'll be damned!" Jeremy said.

The truck pulled up alongside of them. It was white and a bit rusty, but in their predicament, it was a welcome sight. Painted on the side doors was Earl Lee's Towing.

The driver leaned over to roll down the passenger's window. He was in his 40's, a bit scruffy, wearing a flannel shirt, a down vest, and a Syngenta Seeds baseball cap. He smiled at them with one of his front teeth missing.

"You folks need some help?" He smiled again, tipping his cap slightly.

Jeremy gingerly walked closer to the truck. "Yes, we do. Thanks for stopping."

"No problem. I can hook you up in a jiffy. Take you into town if you want to ride with me. I got plenty of room. I just gotta clear stuff off. I'm not used to company." He laughed, then reached behind the seat, moving some things out of the way.

"Thank you, that would be wonderful," said Amy, smiling back at him. Deep down inside, she wondered if this was going to be like a hundred horror movies she had seen, where people break down in some godforsaken town. She thought he seemed nice, but was still on guard for the girls. She was in Mom mode.

The driver pulled in front of the Durango and began to lower the wrecker to hook it up. He shook Jeremy's hand. "The name is Earl Lee. You all from Indiana, I see?" He pointed at their license plate.

"Yes, we're moving to Florida. We got lost on a detour, and now our SUV broke down," Jeremy said. "It shuddered a bit, then the check engine light came on, and it stalled." He helped the girls into the extended cab rear seats, as Amy climbed in after them. The inside of the truck smelled like dirty gym socks, greasy food, and stale cigarette smoke.

"It stinks in here, Dad," said Annette in a whisper. Jeremy smiled and shook his head slightly.

"Just get in. We'll be fine."

The tow truck hydraulics kicked in and began to whine as the front of the Durango raised up from the gravel shoulder.

"Well, you lucked out. Darkness isn't much, but my uncle Ray has a car repair shop a couple miles up the road. Across the street from a motel and restaurant." Earl checked to be sure everything was hooked up correctly. "My cousin Shirley runs both. Best biscuits and gravy in Pike County."

"Sounds good," Jeremy replied. He knew Amy was a stickler about staying in shape and eating right. He didn't think she'd like the biscuits and gravy much. He would have eaten one of Earl's dirty socks at this point, he was so hungry.

"Ok, then. You folks ready?" Earl Lee opened the driver's door.

Jeremy smiled, getting in the passenger's seat. "Looks like we're all present and accounted for." He looked back at Amy, who was doing her best to remain positive, but the grimace on her face spoke volumes.

3

Helen Rogers was looking out her living room window with a pair of binoculars. She was watching her 3-year-old grandson,

Stevie, who was playing in the guest room with some blocks. She saw the Durango coming from the north, and then watched it break down, smoke pouring out from under the hood. She used the CB radio in her living room to call Earl Lee. He was only a mile away at the time. She saw his tow truck pull over to talk to the family in the broken-down Durango. Then Helen saw the tow truck raise the front tires of the SUV and watched the family pile in.

"Grammy, what are those for?" Stevie was standing only a few feet away and startled Helen.

"I just keep an eye on things. Nothing for you to fret over. Go on and play."

Helen put the binoculars down and went back to watching an episode of The Waltons on her TV. Her job was done.

4

The downtown of Darkness wasn't much. The houses that lined Main Street were old single-story structures and run down, built in the 1920's and 30's. The exterior paint was flaking off on most and the yards were not kept up with. The shops that were visible looked abandoned for the most part, with two taverns and a

gun store that were obviously open for business. Alexandra and

Annette stared out the dirty windows of the tow truck, as Earl Lee

drove slow, with old country music playing on the stereo while he

hummed along.

"Like I said, not much here. But Uncle Ray's place is up

ahead. He'll fix you up."

Moments later, Earl Lee pulled into Ray's Repair and Bait

Shop. It was an ugly site to behold on the edge of Darkness. There

was a huge collection of junked cars and trucks fenced in behind the

shop, which consisted of two garage bays attached to a small office

with a desk and two chairs. The place was a mess with stacks of old

car trader magazines everywhere. An old tabby cat walked amongst

the mess, looking for mice. The tow truck tires crunched on the

gravel in front of the shop.

"Hi, Uncle Ray. Got one for you. These folks broke down

north of town." Earl Lee stepped out of the truck. "They're from

Indiana."

A slight man came out of one of the garage bays, where an

old Ford Ranger was up on the lift. He was probably in his 60's, wearing a blue mechanic's uniform, a military-style buzz cut that had gone solid grey, hands and forearms soiled in motor oil and calloused from years of hard manual labor. He walked toward them, wiping his hands on a rag. His name tag said "Ray".

"That's fine. I'm swamped today, though. Gonna be tomorrow 'til I can even take a look." Ray smiled at the Robbins family in the tow truck. He had all his teeth, but they were a cornucopia of colors, featuring shades of yellow, brown, and grey. He took a cigarette from his front pocket and lit up.

Jeremy heard him through the gap in the passenger's window. He stepped out of the truck, looking briefly at Amy, who was still repulsed in the back seat. None of them had gotten used to the awful smell of Earl Lee's truck. Alexandra was holding her nose, but knew enough not to say anything out loud after the look Jeremy gave them earlier. Annette had the top of her shirt up over her nose and mouth.

"We appreciate it, Ray." Jeremy reached out to shake his hand. He smiled warmly.

Ray nodded. "Not a problem. I'll get you going. You don't wanna shake my hand, son. Hard telling what the hell is on these bastards," he said with a laugh.

"You all can go across the street and eat something. I'll let Shirley know you all want a room for the night. She'll fix you up," said Earl Lee.

"What do I owe you for the tow?" asked Jeremy, taking out his wallet.

"Not a thing. Consider it my good deed for the day," Earl Lee replied, tipping his cap again.

Jeremy was surprised. "Well, thank you!"

"We like to be neighborly 'round here. Hope you enjoy your stay." He got back in the tow truck.

"I'm sure we will. Some food sounds good right now," Jeremy added, and he waved as Earl Lee drove away.

The Robbins family made their way across the street to the Griddle and Grub Family Restaurant. Jeremy knew Amy was going to complain about the place, just from the looks of it on the outside and the ridiculous name. Some grub sounded good about now.

5

Hours later, the Robbins family was making the best of things in room 3 at the Darkness Motel. The room was sparse and dated back to the 1950's with yellowed wallpaper, popcorn ceilings, carpet in obnoxious colors that was faded and piling, and two double beds with spreads that matched the hideous carpet pattern. A two-drawer dresser with cigarette burn marks held the small 19-inch television that got only three channels. The lime green rotary phone on the nightstand between the two beds was the icing on the proverbial cake. The Robbins kept up appearances, but behind closed doors were repulsed with their evening digs.

Annette and Alexandra both took showers and got ready for bed. It had been a long day, and miraculously Amy found a Hollywood award show on the TV, and they watched it quietly. Amy was doing a little reading in bed after she took her shower. It had been cut short when the hot water turned to ice. She wasn't too happy about it, but she knew making a big deal about it was not going to help matters, and the last thing she wanted was to scare the girls.

Jeremy was sitting on the edge of the bed, unable to consider sleeping. He was concerned about the Durango and what could possibly be wrong with it. He also wanted to be in Florida by tomorrow morning – on Friday. That would give them three days at Disney World before they would need to start unpacking at the new house. So many things were on his mind. He also considered the new office opening in Tampa, and the uncertainty of working for a new branch manager. Jeremy got along very well at the Indianapolis home office. He hoped it would be the same in Tampa. He also wouldn't admit it out loud, but he was also stressing about Amy and her obvious disdain at this small town they had no choice but to live in until their SUV was fixed. Jeremy was worried that Amy wouldn't be able to keep it under wraps, making things more difficult dealing with these hearty small-town folks.

He got up from the bed, Amy watched him walk to the window. He slid the curtain back slightly, preventing the bright outside light from coming in and waking the girls, who were now sleeping. Jeremy noticed a flashing Budweiser sign in the front window of the Griddle and Grub. They ate there earlier, and the food wasn't bad at all. He didn't realize they sold beer too. A beer sounded good now after a long, stressful day.

"Why don't you go over to the restaurant and have a beer or two? Probably do you some good," said Amy, who was suddenly standing next to him in the window.

"You wouldn't mind?" He was surprised.

"No. Go ahead. I'm getting ready to go to sleep myself." She figured letting him have a few beers after the day they had wasn't such a bad idea.

Jeremy grabbed his jacket and put his shoes back on, and with a smile, he opened the door from room 3 and walked toward the Griddle and Grub. A cold beer sounded like a good idea.

6

Jeremy opened the door of the restaurant. The air inside was warm and smelled like fresh baked bread. Something was different about it as compared to what he saw when the family ate dinner only a few hours before. Jeremy couldn't put his finger on what was different, but he quickly dismissed it as probably the lighting inside at night, compared to daytime conditions earlier. He felt an odd sensation that he had been in this place before – years ago. It was familiar.

There were only two tables occupied in the restaurant. The one closest to the door was a family of four – mother, father, and two young children. The father smiled and nodded his head at Jeremy.

"Welcome! It's always nice to see visitors in Darkness," the wife said pleasantly.

"Thank you, everyone has been very nice to us since we got here." He continued past them, as he noticed a bar in the back of the room, that he didn't see earlier.

At the other table was an elderly couple, who also smiled at him as he walked to the bar.

A waitress came out of the kitchen with a tray, and said, "Go on back there, and William will take care of you, sir."

"Thanks," Jeremy replied, still feeling the sensation that he had been to this place before today.

There was an elderly man sitting at the bar nursing a drink, talking with a middle-aged male bartender, who Jeremy assumed was William. They stopped conversing as he approached.

"Good evening, sir. What can I get you?"

"You must be William."

"That would be me, sir." He smiled as he washed some glasses behind the bar. He was in his mid-30's and wore a white dress shirt and a black tie. His hair was slicked back, and he moved with the skill that only a seasoned bartender displayed. He wore wire-framed round glasses.

"I'll take a Budweiser, William. As cold as you got it. It's been one hell of a day," Jeremy said, sitting on the middle stool, two down from the elderly man who was keeping to himself. Jeremy set a ten-dollar bill down.

William poured a draft of Budweiser into a frosty mug and set it down on the bar. He looked at the ten and pushed it back toward Jeremy.

"Your money is no good here, sir," William said, smiling.

"Well, thank you. I don't think I've ever been to a town that was as nice and friendly as this. I can't accept it, though, I don't want you to get in trouble, William." The ice-cold mug felt really good in his hand.

"John here said he would take care of it for you. He always enjoys having someone here at the bar to drink with," he said, and

John nodded at the end of the bar, a wry smile across his weathered face. "We've both heard each other's stories a dozen times or more."

The elderly man was partially in the dark where he was sitting.

"My only request is that you move closer, son. My hearing isn't what it used to be. I'll be 90 next year," John said. He looked to be American Indian with his complexion, facial features, and the long braided grey hair that hung down nearly to his waist in the back. The creases in his face were deep but symbolic of an inner wisdom that he appeared to possess, stoically sitting there.

"Well, of course." Jeremy moved to the stool next to his, and William dried off his hands and walked away.

"John Whitecotton," he said, reaching a hand out to shake.

Jeremy shook his hand, "Jeremy Robbins."

"You must part of the family that broke down outside of town earlier," John said, sipping at his drink.

"Yes, we got lost on a detour just after Lexington. We ended up on 119, and just as we saw the welcome sign for Darkness, the truck stalled out, and the check engine light came on." Jeremy took a good sip of his beer, and it tasted wonderful. He couldn't

remember the last time he had a beer.

"Ray will fix you up. He's a whiz when it comes to anything

with an engine."

"That's what I hear. I hope it's nothing too major. We're on

our way to Florida, and my girls are anxious to see Disney World."

"Well, while you're here in Darkness, you'll be well taken

care of. We don't see visitors often, which is why most of the

townsfolk bend over backwards when we see someone new," John

added, sipping at his drink.

"Speaking of Darkness, that is an odd name for a town."

Jeremy took another drink of his beer as William came back behind

the bar.

"William, get me another and one for our guest here," John

said as he set his empty glass down. "You don't have to be

anywhere anytime soon, do you?" he continued, considering

Jeremy's eyes. John's eyes were a rich brown and warm, like a fire

on a cold winter night.

Jeremy looked at the clock behind the bar. It was almost

11pm. William set another frosty mug in front of him.

"No, I don't. Not at all."

John took a sip of the new drink William gave him and closed his eyes for a moment. Jeremy could only see the left side of his face, as he blended into the dark shadows at the end of the bar.

"It's really not an odd name for our town, if you know the history of this area. My people, the Cherokee Indians, occupied much of Pike county back in the 1700 and 1800's," he said as Jeremy became fixated on the rhythmic nature of the old man's voice. Everything else around him at the Griddle and Grub dissipated into the background as the story of Darkness began to unravel like a ball of string with many dark surprises deep inside.

.

7

A small Cherokee village occupied the valley that is now known as Darkness, at the base of the Pike Mountains, that span nearly 100 miles in Eastern Kentucky and into West Virginia. While the Cherokee were a powerful tribe, and their village was filled with able-bodied warriors, they were subject to periodic attacks. These fellow Indian attackers wished to occupy the valley, as it was rich with fertile soil for planting a variety of crops, and had a river and

two lakes that were filled with trout, bass, and salmon, there were

plenty of deer, rabbit, squirrel, and birds to eat and clothe them. In

addition, the steep Pike Mountains provided excellent cover during

attacks, and the surrounding dense woods with unforgiving terrain

made it difficult for outsiders to approach without being noticed.

A secret that the Cherokee had and kept very close to the vest

was the fact there was a mysterious dark figure that roamed the Pike

Mountains. Legend has it that the entity is a shape-shifting creature

that blends into the shadows, but is powerful beyond compare. He is

said to live in a cave among the steep, rocky inclines near the

summit of one of the mountains. In the late 1800's, a Cherokee

claimed to have found piles of human and animal bones in one of

these caves, but found no sign of the shape-shifter. At night, the

Cherokee say you can sometimes hear the horrified screams of a

deer or other game being captured and consumed. Their terror-filled

cries served as a reminder that the entity was ever-present. For some

reason, the thing never attacked the Cherokee villagers, but rather

protected them from foe, bad weather, and brought general good

luck to the entire valley below its dominion

The elders of the tribe told fantastic stories about the shape-shifter. Some claimed it looked like a giant wolf or bobcat, with tremendous fangs that could snap a man in half without regard. Others compared it to a bear, two or three times the size of the largest seen in the Pike Mountains. Some even said it bore a resemblance to a man, but with features of several wild predators. Whatever the description, hearing stories of the shape-shifting entity would scare the Cherokee, even though they knew the thing had been protecting them for generations. They gave it the name Ulasigavi. Translated to English, his name was Darkness.

Darkness seemed an appropriate name for the nocturnal creature who kept the entire valley safe for more than one hundred years. Storms that ravaged neighboring areas were somehow averted. Other tribes suffered terrible loss to crops due to disease or insect infestation, but they did not affect the Cherokee under the watchful eye of Darkness. It was because of this tremendous bounty and good fortune that they decided to name the town after him in 1837. They did not mind paying homage to the shape-shifter who protected them so vigilantly for so long.

Even as the white man moved into the area twenty years

later, and as many of the Cherokee moved to the rougher terrain to the east, the unincorporated town remained known as Darkness. Some of the Cherokee stayed behind and assimilated into the white culture. Darkness remained a unique blend of these very different cultures for another 100 years, all the while protected by Darkness, who remained a fixture in the Pike Mountains. Stories continued to be passed down, and the occasional citizen of Darkness or nearby hunters who had the bad luck of being confronted by the shape-shifting being spun wild tales of their harrowing escapes. Some even had horrific wounds from sharp claws or teeth that served as a constant reminder that Darkness was there and he was still relevant.

It was September of 1966 when things changed in Darkness forever. Those who remembered how the valley flourished before then, would tell those who were too young (or born later) to remember just how great it once was. It was Friday, September 23rd, when a school bus full of high school football players and cheerleaders from Lexington East High School were traveling through Darkness on their way to a tournament in Richmond, Virginia. It was their first time in the tournament, so all the players, coaches and cheerleaders were very excited about their weekend trip.

The bus driver decided to take the shortcut on route 119, despite the twists and turns it made through a very rural part of the state, just as dusk was beginning to settle in. The kids and adults were having a great time singing songs and talking about what a great weekend it would be. The driver was a custodian at the school who volunteered to drive the bus for the trip and was a big supporter of the school's football team.

As the bus was going south on 119, coming toward them on the other side of the road was Darren Childers, son of the Darkness mayor, Harold Childers. Darren was with two other high school boys, and they had spent the day fishing and drinking beer. They were now headed north to Pikeland to meet up with some girls they had met the weekend before at a party. Darren was drunk, as were the other two, and he didn't realize that he was driving too fast for the winding road, especially at dusk. In his impaired state, Darren began to weave his blue Ford Mustang along route 119 as the three listened to Led Zeppelin on the state-of-the-art 8-track player his father had installed.

The driver of the school bus jerked the wheel as the Mustang swerved abruptly into his lane. Instinctively, the bus driver swerved to the left to avoid the collision and barely missed the oncoming car.

The bus careened sharply, nearly tipping over and unable to stop

before hitting the guardrail. With the tremendous weight of the bus,

occupants, luggage, and equipment, it was sent hurtling down the

sharp embankment on its side before flipping over twice. The

occupants of the bus were thrown from one side to the other,

thrashing in a human blender and screaming in terror as the bus

continued its death spiral to the bottom of the rocky hillside. The

driver was thrown from his open side window about halfway down,

before the bus flipped, and watched in horror as the bus began to

catch fire, with 51 trapped souls burning alive inside. Horrific

screams filled the valley. The driver's efforts were valiant, despite

his broken bones and concussion from his ejection from the bus. He

broke out the back window and attempted to save some of them, but

the fire was too intense. The black smoke that poured out of the bus

was overwhelming, and the driver passed out behind a nearby tree,

which saved him from the tremendous explosion that could be seen

and heard a few miles away in Darkness.

Everyone in Pike County (and beyond) was devastated by the

accident. It made national news. Of course, Darren and his friends quietly drove back to town and never admitted to being there when it happened. The driver of the bus took weeks to recover at a burn unit in a Lexington hospital, and he gave his account of what happened, describing the blue Mustang that ran him off the road. The mayor of Darkness knew that it was his son who was involved in the accident, but he made sure that no one had seen him, or his friends, in their intoxicated state. When anyone mentioned that the car sounded like the same one that Darren drove, he provided an alibi that the boys were at his house that night, helping him move some furniture and watching a movie. The mayor even went so far as to pay the hospital bills (with tax dollars) that the bus driver incurred, and he made sure he had a job with the town where he didn't have to do much for the rest of his working life. The mayor had him doing small projects for him, and he made sure the driver kept the job even after he left public office. No one said anything in public, but many knew that it was the mayor's way of trying to right such a terrible wrong. Strangely, Darren died a year later when he was driving to Tennessee to attend college. He was in a head-on collision with a large box truck on route 119. He bled out slowly and died hours later at a nearby hospital. He was sober, swearing off alcohol after the incident with the bus. His guilt from that accident was overwhelming, and it haunted him until the moment of his death. Darkness had ways of settling a score.

There was a plaque installed at the site of the crash, listing the names of the 51 victims and the date that will forever exist in infamy throughout Pike County – September 23, 1966. The town of Darkness would never be the same again. A series of very unfortunate events plagued the tiny town, and their shape-shifting namesake appeared to have cursed the community it once protected. Crops were infected with some unknown bacteria that killed off anything they tried to grow for several years after the bus crash, and when things did improve, their yield was 25% of what it was previously. The fish and wild game seemed to thin out and not flourish like they had before, as high levels of mercury in the water wreaked havoc for a long time. The following summer, the valley saw terrible storms that flooded homes and businesses and tore the roofs off many more.

Some of the families in Darkness tried to leave the town. Those that did met with terrible ends. Darkness didn't want anyone to leave. Sometimes they would die in their vehicle, driving away from Darkness, just like Darren Childers on his way to college.

Others got very ill after leaving town and died weeks later. Some

were found hanging from a beam or with a bullet hole in their

temple. There were lots of rumors going around about the curse, that

no one was allowed to leave, but no one really knew for sure. They

still heard the horrible screams of animals being devoured in the

night.

On the anniversary of the accident, September 23rd, Darkness

was not content eating the wild game that roamed the Pike

Mountains. He demanded human flesh as a punishment for what

they had done, allowing the atrocity to go unpunished. Darkness

would come down into the small town and take as many children as

he desired, either eating them on site or dragging them away

screaming to his mountain domain. They were never heard from

again, and no search parties dared to venture to the top of Pike

Mountain to confront the beast.

There was only one way for the people of Darkness to avoid

these annual raids. They would have to supply a human sacrifice to

him. The Cherokee that still lived in the area spoke of these

sacrifices often, to appease their gods. But in this case, it was the mysterious Darkness, and since no one could leave the town, getting someone to be the sacrifice became increasingly difficult in the remote area. Children were the preferred sacrifice, as adults provided no guarantee the monster would not feast upon their young as well. No one really knew what Darkness was thinking, so their terror would build to a blackened crescendo until the dreaded date would arrive each year.

Schools were closed on September 23rd, as were most businesses. Everyone stayed home, protecting their families – especially the children. When night came, that was when he would descend from the mountain, sometimes seen by those brave enough to be outside, or peer from a window. Just like the legend, the descriptions varied greatly, with no one sounding more believable than the rest.

The secrets remain within the boundaries of Darkness. They dare not say anything to anyone else, because the stain of what happened on route 119 that day in September of 1966 was their own burden to bear. It was a filth that covered the town and made them remember the day and what they did to cover up the atrocity. It was a day that they would have to relive every year until eternity, as

Darkness prowled about, delivering justice in his own evil way.

8

"That is one hell of a crazy story, John," said Jeremy,

finishing the last of his fourth beer.

John didn't say anything. He stared down at his own drink, a

feeling of sadness sweeping over him, telling that tale to his guest.

The old man finished the last of his drink. He wasn't sure how many

he had sitting there. When he was telling the story, he seemed to

drink more than usual. He noticed Jeremy looking at his left hand.

It was scarred badly.

"It's not a story. That's the truth about why the town is

called Darkness. You wanted to know," John said, slowly turning

his body to the left, to face Jeremy directly.

Jeremy's head was swimming, buzzed by the four frosty

mugs of beer. He also turned to his right to face the old Indian. In

the dim light of the bar, it was still visible. Before, Jeremy couldn't

see it, because the man sat in the shadows on the last stool. Yet now

it came to life, and Jeremy could feel his heart thundering inside of his chest, ready to burst open. The entire right side of John's face was a mass of scar tissue. It was a tangled web of skin grafts, done in a second-rate hospital at a time when such surgery was in the dinosaur ages compared to what they could do now. His right eye was milky and dead, swimming in a white sea on his face. He looked like something from a fright night feature on TV, with half of his face with the normal wrinkles of a 90-year-old man and the other in mid-stream of melting flesh from his face.

"What the hell?" Jeremy cried out, staggering a few steps before gaining control. The room began to spin. He looked over at William, who was back to washing glasses again and smiling. He said nothing. William had seen that face before, many times.

John began to laugh as he got off the bar stool, standing at nearly 6-feet-tall but slightly hunched over. His thin frame still had plenty of gas in the tank.

"Maybe you ought to get back to your room, Jeremy. You should make sure your family is safe and sound," John said, still chuckling in deep tones.

Jeremy felt his heart pounding louder, the horrible face of the Indian appeared to be moving, melting all over again. He glanced at

William, and over his head there was a digital calendar and clock. He saw the date and immediately began to panic. It was now past midnight, and it was September 23rd! Was the old man telling him the truth about this shadowy monster who comes down into town every year to avenge the ones who died in the bus accident? Seeing John's face contorting before his eyes, he also came to the realization that John was the driver. He was the one who risked his life and suffered horrible burns over his body. Jeremy saw his hand clutching the glass at the bar. It was covered in scar tissue too, uneven tissue stitched together to mask its grotesqueness.

"So, get going, my friend. Get back to your family," John said, walking slowly toward him.

Jeremy turned and ran from the Griddle and Grub. There was no one in the dining room as he staggered through, knocking over two chairs and banging into the door before getting outside. The chilly September air was nipping at his exposed skin as he ran to the motel. He looked at the sign that read, Darkness Motel, and the fear of what might be waiting for him in room number 3 was maddening.

9

Helen Rogers was sitting at her kitchen table, and it was just past midnight. There were two small windows in the kitchen that faced west toward the Pike Mountains. She remembered sitting there most nights with her husband Sam before he passed away five years ago. Throat cancer got him after chewing Levi Garrett for almost 50 years. They used to enjoy sitting at the kitchen table after supper, watching the sun set and the beautiful view of the mountain. Sam had seen Darkness one time while hunting pheasant. He had nightmares about that thing. Helen remembered him waking up many nights screaming and dripping with sweat, carrying on about something chasing him and how it was growling and snorting.

On this night, she made it a point to watch out the kitchen windows at midnight, just so she could see if Darkness was coming to pay her a visit. She assumed the role of the lookout after Sam died. She promised him she would, and he told her that Darkness would spare her and anyone inside their house. Helen didn't know if she could believe that, so she kept a loaded shotgun on the table in front of her, just in case. She wondered if even a shotgun would stop the shape-shifter, and decided against thinking about that too much.

She was worried about Stevie, sleeping soundly in the guest room. Her daughter was working overnights, and rather than wake him up at strange hours, Helen insisted she let him stay with her for the week.

Suddenly, Helen thought she saw movement at the tree line where the powerful lights that Sam installed had reached their limit. Then she saw it again and was sure something was out there. Then the table shook slightly as a low, demonic growl resonated throughout her small single-story home. Her pulse quickened. Darkness had come to call!

"Grammy, what was that noise?"

10

Jeremy fumbled with his key in the lock of room 3. He heard nothing inside and hoped that meant Amy and the girls were sleeping. He prayed the old man was just the town drunk and off his meds, making a spectacle by scaring tourists late at night. The TV was off, and the room was pitch black. He didn't want to wake Amy or the girls up by turning on a light, so instead, he quietly shut the door behind him and used his phone to light his way to their bed. At least it was good for something after all.

11

Stevie was back in bed, tossing and turning. Helen was fixated on the kitchen windows as Darkness slowly crept through her immense back yard, lit up like a Friday night high school football game. The shotgun was now in her lap, with her right hand close to the trigger. After all the years of living in Darkness and hearing people tell their stories about seeing the beast, especially her own husband, she had a visual in her mind of what he looked like. Most people did.

But what she saw now was not what her imagination had drawn up. This was an abomination and like nothing she had ever seen before. It moved smoothly, almost like liquid, but in the form of a shadow or dark, soupy mist. Inside the swirling haze, Helen could see various faces and body parts. At one moment, she saw the face of a bear, and a second later the roaring face of a mountain lion.

It slithered like a snake across the tall grass, snarling and growling in low tones, causing the glass of the two windows to shudder in place. Helen was frozen, staring at the shape-shifter known as Darkness. It was the perfect name. It was blacker than black, and despite the bright lights, looking at the mass was like peering inside of a thunderstorm, with the same ferocity and power.

Darkness paused only ten feet from the kitchen windows. Helen had her finger on the trigger now and the barrel of the gun resting on the table, facing the monster. It snorted, steam rising from the abyss. Deep inside the miasma were two yellow eyes, about the size of dinner plates, and they were intoxicating. She looked away. The demon snorted again, and then moved on, toward town.

Helen breathed a sigh of relief and set the shotgun down. She could hear Stevie snoring softly in the guest room. Sam had been right after all.

12

Jeremy sat down on the edge of the bed, his head still swimming from the beers. He reached over to steady himself and noticed that Amy was not in the bed at all! He reached for his phone but couldn't find it on the end table in the dark. He turned the lamp on, and spinning around, he saw horror like he never had before. The motel room walls were painted in bright red blood, with bits and pieces of Anette and Alexandra on their bed, the floor, the ceiling, and the back of the motel room door. The room was trashed, huge claw marks dug into the wood paneling, and parts of the old carpet were shredded down to the concrete pad. The mirror in the room was shattered. He let out a primal scream from deep down inside. He knew what had happened here. His girls were offered up as a sacrifice to the shape-shifter. Where was Amy?

Just then, the door of the motel room shattered into hundreds of tiny pieces as Jeremy was thrown back into the dresser, knocking the TV down to the floor with a dull crunch. Outside the room, a storm was swirling, sending pieces of houses off into the night sky. Cars were upended, and security alarms were beeping. He turned to face the door just as he could hear someone calling his name.

"Jeremy! Help me!" a female voice screamed. With all the chaos, he strained to hear it, but he knew it was Amy. It sounded like she was far away, and then the screaming started. He could hear her blood-curdling cries until they faded away, as did the violent storm outside. As quickly as it came, it went away, a low rumble in its wake.

Jeremy stood in the threshold of room number 3, inconsolable. Behind him the remnants of his two girls, and before him, the unanswered cries of his wife. He was broken. He was paying for the sins of Darkness, and he didn't understand why. Why had the beast spared him? How could he live without Amy and the girls?

Jeremy suddenly came to the realization that he, too, was going to be trapped in this living hell, because he would not be able to leave the town, just like the others. He was also shrouded in the curse, sentenced to live the remainder of his days in fear at what was roaming the summit of Pike Mountain and wondering if the town had a viable sacrifice to offer every September 23rd.

Unfit For Human Occupancy

1

Dan Taylor approached the condemned house at 1312 E. Cypress Street with caution. It was easy to distinguish from the rest with boarded-up windows, an overgrown front yard, and the sign nailed to the peeling front door, which read, "unfit for human occupancy". In the stifling heat of a mid-July day, the gnats were attacking his sweaty face while he contemplated what would be the easiest way to gain access inside.

Dan didn't have a very good feeling about this. It was something he had to do for his new job with Banner McBride, an engineering company based in Decatur, Illinois. They had other offices throughout the Midwest. He was hired to do an engineering study of the structure before demolition. The City of Decatur hired his company to do this type of inspection all over town. He wasn't an engineer but with training, he was able to do the necessary field work that one of the engineers back at the office could sign off on. The real engineers sat back in the air-conditioned office while the field grunts got to wade through the filth of it all.

Dan had been laid off for two years after the Firestone plant shut down. He was almost 50, and options were dwindling in this new fast-paced world. His wife got tired of him not working and loafing around the house depressed. She sued him for divorce and left town with some truck driver she had been seeing. Thankfully, they didn't have any kids. His unemployment was about to run out, and the bills were piling up like sandbags bracing for a flood. A neighbor stuck her neck out to get Dan this job, and he was determined to hang in no matter how bad things got. Standing in front of this junk heap that was once called home at 1312 E. Cypress Street, he wondered what could possibly be worse than this.

There were dozens of houses in the Near North Development of Decatur that the City was razing. They had been doing it for years through a federal grant. The City was suffering from the economic downturn that drove several factories out of business. Thousands of workers were fighting for the same minimum wage jobs, and some just gave up and turned to drugs and alcohol. The homeless problem had quadrupled in the past ten years because of it, and these abandoned houses that the City now owned, were a breeding ground for a variety of nefarious activity. Gangs and local degenerates were taking over the neighborhoods.

Dan walked down the driveway to the back of the house. This was the first survey he was doing on his own, and he could feel a lump in his throat. He also couldn't fight off the strange feeling that someone was watching him. He looked nervously over his shoulder but saw no one. Dan clenched his mag light and continued. He carried a small backpack filled with some of the things he needed to do his job, but going into these houses, what Dan really wished he had was a big gun. A really big gun. Maybe a flamethrower!

As he approached the back of the house, the smell of rotting garbage and mold was overwhelming. In the heat, the odor was powerful. A miasma of putrid foulness seemed to be making its way from the back entrance, where the door was completely gone. He learned the hard way to check the back door before spending lots of time trying to break down the front door. Many of them were open already – like this one. He had to duck down to get his large frame through the opening.

Sweat continued to pour down his face. Dan could feel his polo shirt soaked to his skin. Being overweight didn't help matters. He fought back the gag reflex to vomit as he entered the kitchen. Years of dirty dishes were piled high in a crusted tower, half empty cans of indistinguishable food were scattered on the counters and floor, and rodent droppings were like foul chocolate sprinkles on every possible horizontal surface he could see with the aid of his light. A mix of rot and growing mold got stronger as he made his way inside.

Dan continued into what was the dining room, through a makeshift path that had been cleared between the piles of garbage and various discarded clothes, furniture and more. He could hear water dripping somewhere in the house. To his right, Dan could hear something scurrying in the trash. His senses were at the point of exploding. He figured it was a mouse or a rat, but he did his best to not think about it. He knew enough to use rubber bands to cinch his pants at his ankles, to avoid something crawling up his legs. Dan heard more noises like this as he waded through the filth – scratching, moving, and gnawing. Despite the urge for him to take the notebook from his backpack to record the condition of the structure, Dan knew he needed to walk through the entire house to be sure no one else was there. During his training, he was taught to do a quick sweep to verify no other humans were present. As his light illuminated the blackness, Dan couldn't imagine anyone wanting to be inside such a terrible place.

As he entered what appeared to be a living room, Dan could see some daylight from above. There was a hole in the roof, causing the wood floor to be a little spongy beneath his feet. This was likely the source of the dripping sound. He shined his light to the floor to see what condition it was in when suddenly there was a dull creak, then the splintering of wood, and he began to fall through the floor into the dank basement below. Instinctively, he closed his eyes, and the last thing he remembered was how embarrassed he would be to have to call his boss to tell him what happened.

2

Across the street at 1313 E. Cypress Street, Duane Lanham watched the large man with the flashlight walk down the driveway to the back yard of the house. Duane had been staying at 1313 for the past three months, making himself a bed from an old mattress and some clothes he got from a local shelter. He managed to keep himself fed by standing in line every Tuesday and Thursday at the food pantry, taking whatever canned goods he could scrounge up. He had been homeless for the last five years since he lost his job at the glass factory. His drinking had spiraled out of control – putting him out on the street. Now he resorted to hand-outs to eat and a rat-infested old house that no one wanted for a place to sleep. Things couldn't get much lower. He avoided looking in mirrors these days, because seeing his graying hair, scraggly beard and gaunt face made him look 20 years older than he was.

From his second-floor window, he wondered if the big man would make it out of 1312 alive. He knew all too well that something evil lived there, something in the blackness of the crawlspace.

3

Dan wasn't sure if he was dreaming. He remembered hearing the creaking and the splintering sounds, but now he found himself in complete darkness in a damp environment. He must have hit the back of his head hard when he fell, because there was a huge bump there. He carefully felt around for his flashlight or backpack, but neither was there. The cell phone he kept in his back pocket was smashed. He tried to turn it on, but nothing happened. It felt like the screen was shattered. Dan deliberately slowed down his breathing to try and not panic. He had enough emergency action training at Firestone over the years to teach him that freaking out was not the answer in an emergency. He did wonder how long he had been at the house, since it was company policy for field people to call in every hour for safety reasons. Maybe someone would be along to see if he was okay?

He tried to sit up and assess if he had broken any bones in the fall. Aside from a sharp pain in his lower back, Dan didn't think he broke anything. Looking above, he could see a large opening in the floor above, which must have been how he ended up where he was now. He must be in the basement.

Just then, he heard a loud noise coming from the space in front of him. His eyes were slowly adjusting to the darkness, but he still couldn't make out anything. Whatever it was, it was not a mouse or rat. It sounded much larger. Maybe it was a raccoon or opossum? Then it sounded again, and it was definitely bigger than that. His heart began to thump in his chest and despite his measured breathing, he felt panic begin to set in. Whatever this thing in the darkness was, it was moving toward him slowly, as if sizing him up. Dan could hear a low growl that was barely audible but seemed to surround him from all sides! The house felt like it shook slightly.

Then he heard rustling and movement from every direction - scraping sounds on the concrete floor and rustling in the garbage. He thought he heard heavy breathing! Before he could do anything, frozen in fear, Dan felt cold and clammy hands grabbing him from all sides. He flailed and kicked, but it was no use. The hands were getting a hold of him and dragging him across the floor toward the large mass before him. He didn't realize it, but he was being pulled toward the crawlspace that was beneath the original section of the house. Inside that dirt floor space was a dark shadow with eyes that glowed. It had an insatiable appetite, and now it was salivating at its next meal, which was squirming on the floor before it like a helpless mouse in a trap.

Dan was screaming. He was screaming himself hoarse as the hands that were pulling him kept dragging him closer to the crawlspace and closer to whatever was inside there that wanted him. They were like humble servants to the evil entity that now had Dan by the feet. He kept on screaming and thrashing about, but it was no use, as the thing sank its razor-sharp teeth into his legs, slowly feasting on the offering.

4

Susan Price got out of her car outside 1312 E. Cypress Street, noting that Dan's truck was still there. She was getting ready to leave the office for lunch when her boss asked if she would check on him. Dan had not called in for two hours, and they were worried. With the heat and Dan's weight, there was concern that maybe he was suffering from a heat injury or needed some medical assistance.

Susan felt responsible for the company hiring Dan, despite the skepticism from her boss that he was too old and not in the best physical shape to be doing this type of work. She felt sorry for him after losing his job, then his wife. Susan and her husband, Scott, had been their neighbors for several years and felt like she needed to do something to help.

Just as Dan did two hours before, Susan felt like someone was watching her. She couldn't shake the eerie feeling as she made her way down the driveway toward the back of the house. She assumed that Dan must have entered from the back, since the front door was intact and the plywood was still screwed tightly over all the windows. The City did that and was adamant that if they had to take any plywood down, they secure it back to keep people out as much as they could. The smell coming from the house was sickening, and she took a handkerchief from her pocket to shield her nose with little avail. One of the engineers gave her a small but powerful flashlight to use, and she had it firmly in her grasp. The humidity was stifling. She was worried about Dan.

As she entered the kitchen, she could see a light coming from further inside the house. It looked like it was coming from the floor.

She was worried that maybe Dan had fallen. Her boss had told her to not enter the house and to call when she got there. But she thought it would be best to check to see if Dan was in trouble or not and didn't want to wait to call in to the office.

Susan tried to focus on anything but the filth surrounding her. She had been in a few houses like this during her tenure at Banner McBride, but it was only during a time when they were cross-training employees. Her boss wanted the office staff to know what it was like to be in the field. Susan knew enough to change out of her dress pants and nice shoes into jeans and a pair of work boots she kept in her trunk.

She could see Dan's flashlight on the floor, pointed in her direction, which kept the gaping hole in the wood floor obscured in shadows. As she bent down to pick up the flashlight, Susan didn't hear anything as she suddenly fell into the hole, straight into the blackness below.

5

Duane was eating some cold pork n' beans from a can that he opened with his trusty P-38. It was one of the only good things he learned from his days as a grunt in the Army. He only served two years before he was medically discharged with a bad shoulder. He watched the pretty blonde woman slowly creep down the driveway like the big guy did earlier. Duane figured it was his wife or someone maybe checking on him. But Duane knew why he hadn't come out of 1312. No one ever did.

He knew about that thing in the crawlspace. One day a month or so ago, he wandered down into that basement and he saw that evil thing slithering around in the crawlspace. He about pissed his pants over the encounter. He begged and pleaded with the thing to let him go. He promised he would watch out and do what he could to get more people like him, the homeless from the neighborhood, to go down into the basement. Duane promised that he would feed him as much as he could. He did just that. With the gift of gab, Duane could talk several other homeless guys into going to the basement. He told them there was beer down there or some stored canned goods. He even led dogs and cats down there with a little tease of something to eat. Duane made up all kinds of stories, just so that horrible thing would stay in that crawlspace and not come out. He didn't want the monster looking for him.

So, he stayed nearby and watched. He waited for anyone wandering down East Cypress Street. These two today were a bonus. Duane hoped that the thing in the crawlspace would live up to his end of the bargain and leave him alone. He ate his cold beans and watched as the woman walked to the back of the house.

Duane thought he could hear her screaming and a distant rumble. It was really faint, but he was sure he heard it. They all screamed like that. It was a terrible sound. Better them and not him. He clanged on the can of beans with his spoon, his own version of whistling in the graveyard.

6

Two weeks passed since Duane had watched the big man and that blonde woman go into 1312 East Cypress Street and not come out again. He saw a police cruiser come by. Two cops got out and looked inside the house. But they came out just fine. Duane was surprised. He had never seen anyone go into that house and come out alive. During the past two weeks, no one had been walking around that Duane was able to lure in the house. He started to worry. The last few nights he found it hard to sleep, wondering if that evil thing in the crawlspace would come looking for him. He barricaded the front door with a heavy dresser he found, and a couch. He even put some old tires he found in the alley along the staircase that led to his bedroom; anything to slow down something that wanted to get him. None of those things made him feel much better when he lay down at night. He could barely sleep.

On this night, he noticed that even the rats were quiet. Usually he would hear the vermin scratching in the walls or attic. Tonight, he heard nothing. Maybe they sensed something wasn't right. Duane wasn't sure. He just knew if he couldn't find someone to feed to that shadowy monster, then that thing would come looking for him. He would want to feed. He thought about leaving the house and running away. But he was sure the creature would know where he was.

It was almost midnight, and the night air was humid. Duane was wide awake on his mattress, afraid to fall asleep. That was when he heard the noise. In the stillness, he heard a rumble. It was a deep menacing growl that shook the house. Duane knew that the thing was coming to get him. He began to panic, trying desperately to open the bedroom window so he could escape out to the porch roof. But the window was frozen in place. Several coats of old paint and humidity made it impossible to open. He looked around the bedroom for something to defend himself with as the growling noise got louder. Duane heard what sounded like wood creaking as something came up the stairway toward him. In a frenzied dash, he took his mattress and shoved it up against the bedroom door. But he knew that it was no use.

It only took a few minutes before the bedroom door shattered into sawdust as the thing closed in on its next meal. Duane was crying in the corner of the bedroom, with only his P-38 to defend himself with. He screamed as the shadows closed in, and the sharp teeth clamped down on his legs, pulling him into a bottomless pit that he could not escape. The fetid breath felt like a hot oven door had opened, enveloping him in a rotting stench of a mouth. In the end, Duane screamed like the rest. He tried to satisfy the creature

from the crawlspace, but despite his efforts, darkness had come to

call.

Cross To Bear

1

Watching his wife die slowly was not easy, but it was Carson Dillon's cross to bear. He knew everyone had something - that one thing in their life they had to deal with. No matter how well off or happy a person appeared to be, Carson knew there was always something lurking in the shadows. There were always skeletons in the closet, and somehow Carson was able to pinpoint what those dark secrets were, despite not knowing the person. It was his gift.

His neighbor across the street in their quiet upper middle class subdivision, who drove the nice sports car and the wife easily ten years his junior, had his own cross to bear. His teenage son was addicted to pain killers and had been through rehab four different times, nearly bankrupting the family. The young intern at his office who bragged about all the cute college girls he was having sex with every weekend – he too had an albatross swinging from his neck. His father had a thing for young girls and was doing a 20-year-bit in state prison. The shame it brought upon the family was devastating. No matter who it was, they all had their cross, and for Carson, it was his dying wife.

Miriam had been dying a little bit at a time now for the past year, and he was helpless to do more than watch and hope it would be over soon. He didn't know what was worse: the incessant coughing, the moaning, or the wheezing while she slept. Those were the sounds of cancer as it slowly crept through her body, devouring everything good in its path. She didn't sleep much anymore, and neither did he. Miriam slept in short naps for a half hour at a time, so she was sleep deprived and cranky much of the time.

Carson loved to read, and despite having more free time as her medical condition kept them homebound, it was nearly impossible for him to concentrate with all the noise. The coughing and wheezing was almost maddening, not to mention the endless hum of the oxygen concentrator she was connected to with an air hose. There was no escaping the noise, no matter where he went in their 3,000 square foot home. His only solace was going to work, but as his retirement loomed large in the next year or so, Carson couldn't imagine what it would be like to watch her die around the clock. As a busy architect, he didn't really have any hobbies. They never had children, as they both devoted their lives to their careers. Miriam was a college English professor before she got sick. Now that was a faded memory, since her home office was untouched for the past year at least.

A year ago they got the diagnosis from her oncologist. It was lung cancer – stage four and inoperable. Thirty plus years of smoking had finally come home to roost. The cancer had metastasized, and there were dozens of tumors throughout her now frail body – four in the brain alone. She was given the choice of an extremely aggressive chemo regimen and radiation, but that would only buy her a few more months. Miriam didn't want that. She wanted to enjoy the final few months of her life at home with her husband, and not be stuck in a cancer center with an IV drip, her hair falling out in clumps, and puking into a bucket. She didn't even want to quit smoking. Carson told her it was her decision to make, and he would stand by her no matter what. Yet that was before he saw her in the current state she was in – a gaunt agonized face, coughing day and night - slipping away with the urgency of a glacier moving uphill and an ashtray heaping over with cigarette butts.

Now he stood over her while she slept. He had a large pillow in his hands and knew that it was time to put Miriam out of her misery – and his. The wheezing and heavy congestion in her lungs was like grating nails across a chalkboard to Carson. He wanted to end this. His vows for better or worse certainly didn't pertain to this torture of watching the woman he loved die a little bit at a time. He shoved the pillow into her face, and in her emaciated state, she barely put up a fight. There was a little resistance, yet he pushed harder. Tears were streaming down his face, and despite his resilience in putting her down, he turned his head to the side, so as not to watch her final death throes - bony arms swinging back and forth to no avail. It was over in less than two minutes.

Carson shut off the oxygen concentrator and marveled at the quiet. No hacking or wheezing and no purring of the concentrator. He then went back to his recliner and watched her for a few minutes, making sure she wasn't coming back to life. She looked peaceful – like she was sleeping - and Carson felt like a weight had been lifted off his chest. Miriam could finally rest, and he finally had quiet. He looked at the bookcase next to his chair in the living room and picked out a book to read, basking in the silence.

The following day Carson realized that he had to do something with Miriam. He covered her with a blanket but knew before long she would start to smell, and he had to act quickly. He was afraid to call the police. Carson had seen enough of the police shows on TV where the husband was always the first one they assumed killed the wife. That's when he realized he really hadn't given it enough thought. Smothering his wife with a pillow was probably not the smartest thing. The police would know she didn't die naturally. They would likely think he had a girlfriend on the side or was trying to get rid of his wife for insurance money. It was true that he had a policy for her, as well as one on himself, through his job at Whelan and Whelan. He knew of course there was no girlfriend. Carson was nearing retirement age and didn't need another woman in his life. The thought of it made his head spin. He also knew that the insurance policy was the furthest thing on his mind right now, but the police would think that way. It was their job to think of that sort of thing. There was no way he could call the police. There would be too many questions.

He also realized that today was Saturday and the cleaning woman would be by on Thursday to do her weekly top to bottom treatment of the house. When Miriam got sick, Carson hired a cleaning lady to come by and clean to take that burden off Miriam and because he did like a clean house. She also fixed some simple meals that Carson could freeze and re-heat later for himself. He hired Jessa Carthage, an attractive 25-year-old college student, on a referral from a friend of theirs. He just enjoyed the company of a vibrant young woman so full of life that provided him a convenient distraction from reality. The fact she really did a great job cleaning the house top to bottom was a bonus. Even the beautiful Jessa had her own cross to bear, though to look at her you would never know.

She had grown up with an alcoholic mother who ran out on her and her two younger brothers, leaving them with a father who struggled to make ends meet.

Carson knew he had to do something with Miriam. He decided that getting rid of her was risky business, so Carson decided the best thing to do was to hide her somewhere in the house. He decided on the perfect place. Carson figured stashing her somewhere obvious was probably the least likely place anyone would decide to look.

2

Almost two weeks had passed since Miriam died. Carson survived his weekly visit from Jessa without her noticing anything was different about the house. Carson told her that Miriam was feeling better and went to visit some family for a couple weeks. Jessa didn't seem to think that was strange, and so she went about her usual cleaning and cooking before leaving. Carson felt cocky about things – like he had come up with the perfect murder and was going to get away with it. Miriam had family all over the US and he figured that would buy him quite a bit of time before he needed to

worry about what to tell people that asked about his wife.

The following day he started to hear strange noises. The

noises were faint at first, but as the days went by, they got louder. It

was difficult for him to pinpoint what the noises were, but to him it

sounded almost like white noise. It was as if someone had a radio on

very low volume, and it wasn't tuned to a station that came in. As

he sat in his recliner reading, the white noise continued. It went on

day and night, and it got to the point that he was unable to sleep at

all. As he lay in bed, the sound was coming from all directions. It

was in the ceiling. It was in the walls and coming up from the

floors. He ran about the house with a flashlight in the small hours,

desperately trying to figure out what the noise was. He used a small

hammer to tap on the walls to see if maybe he could find a mouse or

some sort of animal that was making the noise, but it droned on.

After almost a week of the noise, it changed from a soft

white noise to the sound of a slurping or sucking sound. He couldn't

place the sound, and it was driving him mad. It didn't make any

sense. Carson even went to the main electrical panel in the house

and turned everything off, and still he heard the white noise and the strange slurping sounds. No matter what he did, he was not able to find the source of the noises that kept him from reading or sleeping. Something had to be done!

Carson decided the best thing to do was to go next door to talk to his neighbor who was a maintenance man at the high school in town. Surely, he would be able to figure it out. Carson patiently waited until 4pm, when the neighbor said he would stop by after work and see if he could find the source of the noise.

3

Almost a year had passed and now Carson Dillon found himself in very different surroundings. He was quietly sitting by a window reading a book. He seemed very content to look at him absent his new living arrangement. Two doctors were standing on the other side of the room, talking amongst themselves about his status. They were both psychiatrists at the Benton Harbor Hospital for the Criminally Insane. The wing of the hospital they were in was very secure, despite the heavily medicated patients walking around in pajamas and playing checkers, reading books, or watching TV in the day room. There were bars on the windows and locked doors to not allow them to leave, but inside this special wing, you would really have no idea of the various disturbing reasons why these patients were now calling this home.

For Carson, it was a rather sad story. He was suffering from dementia. He had been for the last eight years. His wife Miriam had passed away nearly 20 years before after a battle with lung cancer, and he had a very hard time dealing with life on his own. There were dozens of pictures of her on the walls. When the dementia set in, family members got him housed at a special nursing home where he could live in an apartment, with staff checking on him often. As the dementia got worse, the staff would check on him daily until eventually he would be placed in the medical wing of the home and be under constant care.

A year before, Carson was found pounding on the door of the elderly couple next door to his apartment, raving about something in his walls making a strange noise. The couple was concerned and alerted the security staff who promptly showed up to try and alleviate the situation. Upon arrival at his apartment, the security guards were taken aback by an overwhelming odor and the fact the apartment was in complete disarray. There were dishes piled high in the sink, furniture tipped over and various other things strewn about the small one-bedroom unit. Carson was raving about a noise he had been experiencing, but the security guards could not hear it. When they tried to subdue Carson, he resisted – punching one of the guards in the face and then reaching for a knife on the kitchen counter before being thrown down and handcuffed.

Police were called and took Carson into custody. The medical staff at the home medicated him and allowed the police to take him to jail for the assault. The smell in the apartment was overpowering and upon further investigation, the police found the source of the odor coming from inside the wall behind the recliner that Carson enjoyed sitting in. They promptly cut into the drywall and pulled it out as a putrid smell poured from the gaping hole in the wall, causing one of the officers to run into the bathroom to throw up.

What they found in the wall was the decomposing body of Jessa Carthage, a nurse at the home that had recently gone missing. Jessa was making daily visits to Carson and many residents at the home, and her husband filed a missing person report when she didn't come home after work. Her body was wedged between two studs in the wall and covered in maggots that, when the room was silent, could be heard eating at her flesh – it was a slurping and sucking noise. Upon closer examination, the drywall had been cut away, her body set inside the wall and the drywall put back. With all the clutter in his apartment and the recliner wedged up to the wall, it was difficult to see in low lighting.

Now Carson's cross to bear was not his wife, but a life sentence at the Benton Harbor Hospital for the Criminally Insane. In an odd way, he didn't seem to mind much at all. His advanced dementia allowed him to forget killing the young nurse and stuffing her in the wall. He also forgot about his wife and her painful battle with cancer 20 years ago. He kept a picture of Miriam next to his bed and gave her a kiss every night. He wondered why she never came by to visit him. He did have his books and plenty of time to read in the stifling silence of the hospital.

Bodies In My Pocket

1

Sergeant Carlos Rivas was squirming in the hard plastic chair in Mrs. Whitney's waiting room. Despite being the Army for 11 years now, he still was annoyed that Uncle Sam wouldn't provide more comfortable seating, especially for someone coming back after his second deployment to Iraq. The big clock on the wall ticked louder than it should have, which made the fact that Mrs. Whitney was fifteen minutes behind schedule that much more obvious. The décor in the old World War II-style barracks, renovated to office

space, was dated almost to the point it found itself back in style.

      Suddenly the door began to open as Peggy Whitney

said goodbye to a patient. Her smile was always warm, and her

demeanor was not intimidating, like many of the psychologists

Carlos had met in the past year. She was a civilian working in the

mental health center on the base. When given the choice of who to

talk to as part of his ongoing treatment for PTSD, Carlos asked to

see Peggy. He felt at ease talking to her, and the way she did things,

it made it seem like they were just friends talking. It didn't feel

clinical like most of the others, clad in white lab coats and using

clipboards to make notes as he spoke. They nodded a lot and did

their best to seem interested in what he was saying, but he always

felt like they were just filling in their government forms and didn't

care in the least about what he had to say. In that sterile

environment, Carlos felt nervous and didn't say much.

      "Good to see you, Carlos," she said, making her way to the

tan plaid couch in her office. It was weird hearing someone call him

by his first name when he was on base. Peggy did that to make him

feel more comfortable. She had her hot tea steeping on the coffee table that separated her couch from the matching love seat. Behind her was a huge bookcase that spanned the entire east wall, with a variety of psychology books as well as the fiction novels she devoured in her free time. There was also an old globe in a pedestal stand. It was a gift from her grandfather, who gave it to her after she graduated from the University of Connecticut with a degree in psychology. Carlos felt like he was home.

"Same here, ma'am," he said, sitting down on the love seat. Carlos could smell the lemon escaping her hot tea and knew he was in a safe place.

Peggy took a deep breath, looking at Carlos behind a soothing smile. Her mouse-brown hair was up in a ponytail like always. She was in her early 50's, but Carlos thought she was a very attractive woman, despite being 20 years her junior. Running two miles a day and eating well had done her right, with a dancer's figure that radiated good health.

"Why don't you tell me what happened the other night?"

"I don't know if I'm ready to talk about it, ma'am." His left eye twitched for a second.

"Carlos," she said as she took a sip of her tea, "I told you that inside this room I'm Peggy."

He forced a smile. "OK, ma'am. I mean . . . Peggy."

They both laughed, and then it was quiet again.

"Why don't you start with what made you go out at that hour?"

He fidgeted on the love seat. Carlos didn't notice, but Peggy did. She had to notice those little things in her line of work. She loved her job. Helping soldiers was the best job she could have. She lost her own father to suicide after he came back from two tours in Vietnam. He wasn't home a month before her mother found him in the bathtub, with half his head on the shower surround and a shotgun in his lap.

"Well, I needed to go to Walmart to get some stuff for the trailer."

"At two o'clock in the morning?" Peggy held the mug with two hands in her lap.

Carlos looked down. "Yeah, I can't go during the day – there are too many people."

She nodded. "I understand. That's a normal reaction from someone who's been through what you've been through."

Carlos continued, "I started to feel really anxious, like I needed to do something."

She smiled again, taking another sip of her lemon tea. "So, what did you do about it?"

"I took out the bodies in my pocket."

"Just like we discussed. That's good."

Carlos looked at her, tears beginning to well in his eyes.

"Did you stall on the first one again, Carlos?"

"Yeah. It was Davenport. He's always the first one. The first body in my pocket."

Peggy leaned back on the couch, engrossed in what Carlos was telling her. "Tell me all about the bodies in your pocket."

2

Carlos was sitting on the couch in the living room of his rented mobile home. He was wide awake at 2 o'clock in the morning. This was an every night occurrence since he got back from

Iraq two months ago. The nightmares were there every time he closed his eyes. They played through like the trailer of a scary movie. Over and over again, it would repeat in his head until he couldn't take it any longer and forced himself awake. Even awake, Carlos had the dreams, only they weren't quite as vivid as in slumber.

When he got home this time, he found a note on the kitchen table. It was from Kayla. He could tell it was her handwriting as soon as he opened the door. The trailer was quiet, so he knew that she and the baby weren't there. The television was off. Even at night, when they were in bed, she kept the television on in the living room. She used to say she needed to hear the noise. After his first tour in Iraq, he agreed and didn't mind having it on all the time. Carlos didn't like the absolute silence, either. It made his mind keep going, and there were too many things rattling around in there which he would rather not think about.

The note was your standard "Dear John" letter that soldiers got all the time out in the field, or on deployment. Now they came in the form of email or even text messages, but he was getting one old school. Kayla told him she loved him, but wasn't in love with him. She said she had met someone about six months into this last deployment, and she didn't mean for anything to happen, but it did. She told him she paid the lot rent for three months with the money he'd been setting aside, and she left him $100, but she was taking the rest to get a new place for her and Carlos Junior, or CJ as they called him. It was like ten daggers in his back, sitting there in the kitchen, his duffel bag still in his hand, reading this note from Kayla. Part of him wanted to go grab one of his guns from the bedroom and kill the guy. Then he thought about CJ and how the last thing he would want is for him to think of his Dad as a murderer. He also didn't like the idea of seeing his son on visitation day at Leavenworth prison. In the silence of the trailer, Carlos sat dazed and didn't really know what to do next.

As time passed, Carlos began to get things on track. He was getting into the routine of his stateside duty assignment at Fort Knox as an instructor at the Armor school on base. He kept himself busy after work fixing things at the trailer, keeping his lawn looking good, and trying not to think about what had happened in Iraq that had caused him to come home three months earlier than the rest of his unit.

Now, as he sat on the couch at 2 o'clock in the morning,

Carlos knew what he needed to do to help get through this anxiety

attack. He could feel himself breathe heavier, and he became jittery

just sitting there. Usually, he would get up and do something, like

the dishes, or polish his boots. Anything was better than sitting idle

when one of his attacks came on. Taking one of the Xanax pills that

Dr. Harrington prescribed helped, but when he was in the middle of

an anxiety attack, they didn't do much. Sometimes the cloudy mind

that they would induce would bring on his vivid imagination and

things he would rather keep locked up tight.

Peggy had been working with Carlos for the last month. He

went to see her every Tuesday after he got off work for the day, and

it had been helping him deal with his thoughts. She showed him a

sort of card game, as she called it, bodies in your pocket. She would

take pieces of heavy paper, the size of playing cards, and write on

them the things you were having trouble with. She would write

down a person's name, if you had lost someone in your life. Or she

would write down a place, or what she would call a trigger word,

that might be a way to remember a tragic event. Peggy would take

the cards and laminate them. She would tell you to keep them in your pocket, and when anxiety began to rise to the surface, take out

the bodies in your pocket and begin to think about them in a positive

way. It was an interesting technique she developed, and it was of

interest to some at the Department of the Army. Many of them had

been after Peggy for years to go back to school and get her MD, but

she didn't want any part of that. She loved working with her

soldiers, and now with the Middle East conflicts going on like they

had since 9/11, Peggy felt a duty to the men coming home more than

ever before.

Carlos took out the bodies. The first one was Charles

Davenport. Charles was always the first one. No matter if Carlos

shuffled the six cards she made for him, Charles was always first.

There were other traumatic events he saw in Iraq. One of his friends

lost both his legs only ten feet in front of him, on a dismounted

patrol during his first tour in 2003. He was the gunner of a Bradley,

a lightweight reconnaissance tank used by the modern cavalry

soldiers, when a nearby apartment building exploded and collapsed

on top of them. The sergeant that was with him in the turret was

crushed to death by the falling debris. Carlos sat there for 30

minutes, staring at the dead face of the sergeant, while he waited for help to come and dig them out of the bricks, mortar, and concrete.

He spent a year on night duty, putting the dead into body bags, and

taking prisoners along with them, to the Iraqi police checkpoints.

Carlos had seen more death than he cared to think about. But no

matter what the event, it was always Charles that bothered him the

most.

There it was on the coffee table in front of him. The name

was Charles Davenport, in neat handwriting, done by Peggy herself

with a medium black Sharpie. He thought about the good things.

They had been in basic training and AIT (advanced individual

training) together. There's something about going through that with

a person that makes you close. The fact he was back at Fort Knox

made him think about it even more, since that's where they did their

training. Carlos remembered how excited they both were to be

going to Fort Hood, Texas together after graduation, and then two

years later both winding up in the First Cavalry Division, in the 1/7

Cavalry regiment.

Charles had met a young woman off post, and they had twin

girls before his first deployment. Coming home from the first trip to

Iraq was when Carlos met Kayla. They would double date often and had some good times out as a foursome. Kayla got pregnant and had CJ only a month before they left for the second deployment – this one scheduled for 15 months. Carlos married her the day before he left for Iraq, and together they had big plans of buying a house and having more children when he returned.

Charles and Carlos both struggled leaving behind their women and children. The patrols they were going on were increasingly more dangerous. Luckily, the army had been putting armor on the Humvees that they used, but it was still common for the crews to suffer major injuries and casualties. In Baghdad, the terrorists were getting more sophisticated in how they gathered intelligence, and many of the patrols had been met strong resistance. Charles and Carlos were both in B troop, and they were sending out 12-hour patrols every day and night, where the crews got 24 hours off at the end of their shift. They would send them out in patrols with eight Humvees, two Bradleys, and a squad of dismounted soldiers. They were talking to the locals to gather as much intelligence as they could. Amazingly, many of the civilians spoke decent English. The patrols always had a medic with them and at least one interpreter.

Carlos remembered when things went to hell. It was June 8th in 2004 when he and Charles ended up in the same Humvee. They had a lot of guys on sick call the last week with some bad water giving many of the troop dysentery and causing the ones afflicted to stay back on base where toilets were close by. For 48 hours, almost half the enlisted men were sick with it.

The lead Humvee, with Captain Sharkey, was down two men, so Charles came over to help out. The Humvee had two privates in the rear that would provide dismount support as needed, the captain in the front passenger's seat where he could access the computers and GPS system, a 50-caliber machine gunner in the turret, and a driver. Carlos knew that the most dangerous place to be in the vehicle was the gunner: the upper part of his body was exposed outside the Humvee. Since he was manning a big machine gun, he would be a likely target. Carlos volunteered to man the 50-caliber so Charles would drive. They were going home in three months, and neither of them wanted to end up in a body bag in the back of a truck, heading to the morgue.

Charles argued, wanting to go in the turret himself. They were both sergeants with a rank of E-5, both on the list for staff sergeant once the deployment was over. Carlos won, and as the patrol rode out at 0500 (5:00 am) that morning, he was already squinting at the merciless Iraqi sun rising on the horizon. The captain was sipping his strong black army coffee, the two privates were putting in the first dip of the day into their bottom lips, Charles thought about his daughters and wondered what they were doing, and they rode down the already-crowded streets of Baghdad.

3

Peggy looked at Carlos, wondering if he was going to break down. She heard so much misery in the stories that came back from Iraq. It hurt her to see soldiers in such distress. She took solace in the fact that she could help most of the soldiers. Of course, some didn't make it back from the dark side. Suicides were all too common, and she felt each one like a railroad spike in her chest, wondering if she could have done something to save them from themselves.

She handed him a bottle of water. "Are you OK, Carlos?"

"Yeah," he said after taking a drink, "but no matter what I do when I see that card, I can't help but go to that day in the Humvee." His voiced cracked slightly at the end. He appeared to be sweating a little. He fidgeted on the love seat.

"I know. That's what the bodies are supposed to do, really. In telling your story or experiencing it, we hope that you can begin to make sense of what happened, and know that you couldn't have controlled it." Her eyes stayed on his.

"I just wished we could have traded places. I would do anything to have been in his boots that day in Baghdad," Carlos said, his eyes burning. His throat felt tight.

Peggy leaned forward and struck a match, lighting one of her many Yankee candles. The smell of that burning match took Carlos back to Baghdad.

4

As their Humvee stopped on the side of the road, Carlos kept a sharp eye out from the turret. It was well over 110 degrees outside, and despite this being his second tour in Iraq, it was still unbearably hot. He took a drink from his canteen and was just about ready to ask the captain if it was OK for them to take a quick break to eat lunch before moving ahead. They had a half case of MREs (meals ready to eat) and plenty of cold water in the back of the vehicle.

Out of the corner of his eye, Carlos saw something move in one of the first-floor windows of the four-story apartment building to his right. The movement was quick, but everything slowed down to a crawl after that. He heard a loud pop, almost like the sound of a model rocket – like the ones he played with as a kid growing up outside of Boulder, Colorado. This was louder and more powerful, followed by a whooshing sound as a shoulder-mounted RPG (rocket-propelled grenade) made its way toward them. Carlos let out a sharp yell, and he thought one of the privates did as well, but the rocket was upon the Humvee in a matter of moments. Just before it impacted, Carlos noted the intense heat it gave off and the strong odor of sulfur. The armor piercing round went through the captain's side door like butter, leaving a gaping three-inch hole.

What followed was sheer chaos. The rocket sizzled through the Humvee, striking Captain Sharkey in the right forearm, then the left hand, severing the limbs from him in a split second. He screamed out, blood pouring from the wounds and onto the

dashboard, door and floor of the Humvee. The rocket hit the metal

frame and bounced toward Charles, hitting him square in the side of

the head. His lifeless body slumped toward the steering wheel as the

rocket exited the Humvee, a pink mist in its wake. Carlos felt an

intense burning in his legs, as shrapnel from the rocket tore into his

flesh. One of the privates in the rear of the vehicle pulled him down

from the turret as they began to take small arms fire up close. The

entire exchange took less than one minute, as the soldier behind

Charles got out of the Humvee and returned fire with his M-16.

It was a bloodbath inside the Humvee. Carlos kept shaking

Charles by his right shoulder, hoping to get a sign of life. There was

nothing. Carlos kept screaming out his name, but it was no use.

5

Carlos was driving to Walmart in nearby Elizabethtown just

after 2 o'clock in the morning. He had just gone through the bodies

in his pocket, and knew he needed to go out for a drive. He did need

some things at Walmart anyway, and the middle of the night was the best time for him to go. He couldn't be around crowds. Even a few strangers bothered him, especially in a public place. Carlos still perspired just thinking about walking the aisles and wondering if someone was going to jump out at him around the corner, or plant an explosive device amongst the produce.

As he drove the winding back roads toward E-town, Carlos noticed flashing lights ahead. As his truck approached, it appeared to be a young woman with two young children in a mid-sized car with their four-way hazard lights on, parked in the narrow shoulder of the road. Fortunately, it was an open stretch of road, and at this time of night, there was no sign of other traffic. Tension began to take hold as Carlos began to feel an anxiety attack come on. He knew that in Iraq, terrorists often used civilians for cover to hide bombs and other explosives to trick Americans. Despite those feelings rushing over him, Carlos slowed down to see if he could be of help. He reminded himself he was in Kentucky and not Baghdad. As he approached the car, he noticed a large bag of trash in the tall grass in the ditch. He swerved away from it and decided to park in front of her. Seeing trash on the road made him think about Iraq again and how terrorists would conceal their roadside bombs in trash. It was incredible how many things would trigger him to think about that shithole of a place – halfway around the world.

"Oh my God, thank you for stopping!" the young woman said, nearly hysterical. "I tried to call my husband, but my phone's battery is dead. It looks like a flat tire." Her eyes were red like she had been crying. "I just got off work and picked my boys up at the babysitter's."

"No problem, ma'am, I can change it for you if you want." He still felt apprehensive about the bag of trash, but tried to put it out of his mind so he could help this young mother who was obviously in major distress. He thought about Kayla and CJ and hoped someone would do the same for them. Still, Carlos felt like his heart was going to tear through his chest. He did his best to conceal those fears.

As he started loosening the lug nuts, he noticed a strong burnt tire smell. She must have driven on the flat tire more than she should have. The odor of burning tires was a trigger. It was something he woke up to every day during both of his tours to Iraq. Over there it was akin to coffee and bacon in the morning. As Carlos continued to loosen the lug nuts, he could hear the sound of small arms fire in his head. He could strongly smell burning tires

and trash he could hear, and a group of people chanting and yelling

in Arabic. He closed his eyes and shook his head to try and come

back to reality, but Carlos was back in the Humvee with Charles

slumped over the wheel. Once he was struck with the rocket, the

vehicle veered off the road and was sideways in a ditch. The intense

pain that Carlos was feeling in his legs from the shrapnel was

incredible, but he knew that the captain was in major trouble with his

injuries, and one of the privates had taken a significant amount of

shrapnel to his chest and face. He was also in shock, like the

captain, and covered in blood.

"Kids, you need to sit down and let this nice man change the

tire," the young woman said, as Carlos snapped out of his vivid

memory of the incident.

The kids were probably seven or eight, and both of them

were making funny faces out the side window to get the attention of

Carlos. They began to bang on the glass and once again, it was a

familiar noise that took him to Baghdad.

With the Humvee flipped over in the ditch, Carlos was doing

his best to get out of the vehicle and call for help. With the bright sun of an early afternoon in June, it was scorching hot outside, and now some of the locals gathered around. In his jumbled state of mind, Carlos was doing his best to assess the situation. All the training and experience of dealing with crisis situations was coming to him, but knowing his best friend was dead only a few feet from him was beginning to cloud his judgement. He was feeling around for his M-16, but it was nowhere to be found. He could reach for Captain Sharkey's sidearm, a 9mm pistol, and held it firmly in his grasp, in case the crowd rushed toward him. As the Iraqis began to circle the wreck, they began to taunt him even more. Some of the younger children were hurling rocks at the Humvee, while Carlos tried to raise someone on the radio to come help. The chanting of "death to America" made his blood boil, and Carlos hoped help would come his way sooner than later, as more locals joined the fray – their chants and cries almost deafening in the blinding afternoon sun.

6

Sergeant Charles Davenport woke up after his third surgery in two days at the Landstuhl Regional Medical Center only a few miles from the Rammstein Air Base in Germany. His mind was still cluttered and groggy, as the events of June 8th continued to play out in his head. He couldn't believe Carlos was gone. He didn't envy Colonel Edwards having to write another one of those letters to the next of kin, in this case it would have been Kayla. Charles thought about her getting that dreaded personal visit from the unit chaplain, telling her that Carlos was killed in action, and it was too much for him to bear. He knew that little CJ would never get to know his father and how much he loved him. They told Charles that after he recovered from this last surgery, he would be sent stateside to the Brooke Army Medical Center in San Antonio, Texas. It was likely he would be getting out with a medical discharge due to the extensive nerve damage to his legs, caused by the shrapnel wounds when their Humvee was hit with an RPG. Doctors expected him to be able to walk eventually with plenty of physical therapy and patience.

The door of his room opened, and a middle-aged woman sat down next to him and held his hand. "Good morning, Sergeant. It's good to see you wide awake."

Charles thought her smile was warm, unlike the coldness of the hospital room he was in.

"I know you've been through a lot, Sergeant. My name is Peggy Whitney. I'm one of the psychologists here. I'm sorry to hear about the loss of Sergeant Rivas. I heard you two were close," she said, trying her best to smile.

"Yeah, we were." His eyes began to well up with tears, and he was unable to look her in the face. "I feel guilty that it wasn't me."

"That's a normal reaction. We call it survivor's guilt. I read through the after action report, and Private Gardner, who was the only soldier uninjured in the attack, said that you both argued about who was going to be in the turret on that patrol. It says here that you insisted on it, and Sergeant Rivas finally relented and drove the Humvee."

It's amazing how the mind works. They say that when you die, your life flashes before your eyes. In the case of Sergeant Rivas, who was the driver of the Humvee that day in June, he saw that rocket only for a split second before it hit his head – killing him instantly. In that fraction of a second, he thought about what it would be like to go home and feel the guilt of his good friend, Sergeant Davenport, dying instead of him. His mind took him through going home and losing his own wife and son, going to therapy to deal with the loss and his own injuries, and even the incident changing the tire that caused a flashback. His mind even conjured up an interesting therapy of imagining all the negative things in his head as bodies in his pocket. The irony of it all was that one of those bodies in his pocket was his own.

Hand of the Dying

Staring death in the face was not something that Roland
Wilson was ready to do that day. He had a typical, relaxing Sunday
afternoon planned: watching the Cardinals on television with his
neighbor and grilling steaks when it cooled down. Things changed
with a phone call. Roland was dozing off on the couch when it rang.

"Roland, can you come over to my Dad's right away?"

It was the neighbor's daughter, April, who lived across the
street. Roland was wide awake now at the urgency in her voice. He
knew something was really wrong.

She was hyperventilating. "Please hurry. It's Dad. I think he's had a heart attack!"

Roland was already up and heading for the door when April starting crying on the phone.

"I'll be there in less than a minute."

In his mid-50's, Roland's mind was racing as he ran across the yard. The August afternoon sun was intense. He was squinting due to the harsh adjustment from his dimly-lit finished basement to the bright glare of the day. He knew that Big John's heart was living on borrowed time after a long life filled with eating whatever he wanted, to excess, and washing it down with plenty of ice-cold beer. Sometimes after a stressful day, John would enjoy bourbon with one ice cube after dinner. There were very few people who could go drink-for-drink with him, without ending up passed out or slobbering drunk. Big John appeared unaffected by alcohol, and his many great stories only improved when the drinks flowed. His bigger-than-life persona was without compare.

Big John was a hulk of a man, and even in his early 70's, the gentle giant was an imposing figure. Back in his college days, at the University of Missouri, Big John was a star left tackle on the football team and held down a 4.0 grade point average in the classroom. He

stunned many of his friends and family when he turned down an

offer to play professional football, for the fledgling San Diego

Chargers of the American Football League. Big John loved football

but he wanted to teach even more, and at the time, professional

football players didn't make very much money. Especially offensive

lineman! He stayed in school to get his master's degree in education

and moved back to his home state of Illinois, to begin a storied

career in education. His tremendous abilities would impact an

untold number of lives as he rose through the ranks as a teacher and

then into administration.

Roland reached the front door and entered the house. He

could see April pacing back and forth in the living room and Big

John unresponsive, lying on the couch. He was still in his bathrobe

and a pair of sweat pants. He could see that Big John was breathing,

but it appeared very shallow. His body was sweaty, and his face was

flushed.

"Thank God you're here, Roland!" April was crying, her

eyes swollen and bloodshot.

"Did you call 911?"

April seemed stunned, like she hadn't been able to process what he just asked her.

"What was that?"

Roland turned April slightly so he could look her in the face.

"Have you called the ambulance yet?" he asked, holding her shoulders square.

"My God, no I haven't. Can you call them, please? I think I'm going to lose it."

Roland pulled out his cell phone and dialed 911. He knelt next to Big John, holding his hand, while he stared at his chest, watching it rise and fall, waiting for the operator to pick up. He noticed it was 2:10 pm.

"Hang on big man. Hang on for a minute," he said to Big John, his throat tightening at the thought of losing someone so close to him. He loved the man like a father. He gripped John's hand tight, and it seemed as if John's hand squeezed back just a little bit. There wasn't much time.

It seemed like an eternity, even though it was only five seconds, before the operator answered the call.

"911, what is your emergency?" she asked, her voice sounding almost robotic to Roland, who was doing his best to hold it together. April was now sitting down with her head in her hands, sobbing uncontrollably. He realized he was on his own with Big John until the ambulance arrived. Death always scared him, and now that he was watching John slip slowly away, the idea sent chills up his spine. Going to visitations or funerals always upset Roland, and at his age, he had only been to a few. Seeing a dead body really bothered him, more now than ever, as some of his classmates had passed on, along with older family members. There was something about the unknown that terrified him.

Roland suddenly realized his mouth was so dry he could barely speak. "It's my neighbor, John Sampson. He's not responding. I think it's a heart attack. He takes medicine for it and had a mild heart attack a few years ago."

"When was the patient last responsive sir?" the operator asked.

Roland looked over at April to ask her, but he knew she wasn't going to be of any help in the state she was in. "I don't know. His daughter found him, but she's almost hysterical."

Roland almost felt like he was detached from what was going on. He could hear himself on the phone and could hear April crying, but the noises sounded like they were coming through a transistor radio speaker. The operator's voice was mechanical.

Hearing her voice made him think of a great day he spent with Big John, shortly after his wife Agnes died. Big John seemed depressed, adjusting to living alone after more than 40 years of marriage. Roland had divorced his wife two years before, after the last of their kids moved out. He could relate to what it was like to live alone, after years of marriage. Roland took him out on Lake Shelbyville, where they loved to go, especially after getting the new boat. Fishing and hunting were second only to eating and drinking when it came to Big John. Usually if you could manage to do all of the above, Big John would have called that "one of the great days". He could hear that voice now, as the boat rocked listlessly on the calm lake waters. He knew how much Big John hated cell phones or anything resembling modern technology that forced people not to talk to each other face-to-face. Hearing her monotone voice made Roland think of Big John lecturing him about the dumbing down of the country, at the hand of technology.

"You only get a handful of the great ones. Only a handful of them, Roland. So, you gotta soak up every drop when they come around, my boy," Big John said, smiling ear-to-ear for the first time in a month since Agnes died.

Roland smiled back and cast his line out, enjoying the day just as much as his huge companion. They packed some ham and cheese sandwiches, homemade pickles, some deer jerky, and ice-cold beer in the cooler. The weather could not have been better. There was a slight breeze coming from the west, as if on cue, to make it a moment that Roland would put down as "one of the great ones".

Big John would continue, in between bites of the large sandwich, "You just never know Roland, you never know when it's your time. When it is – well, then it is. Only the big man upstairs knows when that is. So, you gotta enjoy everything – no matter how small."

"I hear you, John," I replied.

He let out a large belch, followed by a hearty laugh. "Hand me another beer or two, would you?"

Since Roland lost his father ten years before from a heart attack, Big John was like a surrogate dad. He was about the same age as Roland's real father, but the two couldn't have been any more different. While he was close to his father, Roland didn't talk to him about anything more than small talk. His father wasn't the kind of guy who liked to open up and was a loner most of the time. He was the postmaster for the post office in Pittsfield, Illinois. In his free time, William Wilson enjoyed keeping his lawn the best on the block and was an avid gardener. He did enjoy doing those things alone. Big John, on the other hand, was the opposite when it came to social situations, and he couldn't go anywhere without running into someone he knew. Everyone who met Big John loved him. Roland never heard anyone say a bad word about the man. Even former students were excited to see him, no matter how many years they were separated from the classroom. Former teachers looked up to him, and their adoration was unmistakable.

Big John taught at three different school districts in Illinois before becoming a principal in Franklin, and then five years later, he was promoted to superintendent. He was admired by all, and he genuinely loved them back. Agnes was a teacher at the school where he was the principal, and soon after they met, they began a

relationship, and they married the following year. She continued to

teach middle school English, and they had two children. Their son,

James, moved to Texas upon graduating college, and was a salesman

for a Dallas pharmaceutical company, while April stayed in town

and moved across the street, still unmarried in her 40's. She worked

at a local K-Mart. She did help Agnes and John as they got older,

and now that John was having some difficulty getting around, she

was doing much more. She knew how close Big John and Roland

had become and welcomed seeing her father happy again.

Just then, he realized the operator had asked him a question.

"1910 North Old Pine Road."

"OK, sir, an ambulance is on the way. Please stay on the line

until they arrive."

Roland continued to stare at Big John's chest as it rose and

fell. He could feel tears welling up in his eyes, worrying about what

would happen if John's breathing stopped. What would he do?

They had annual CPR and first aid training at the General Electric

plant that he managed in nearby Quincy. It was one thing to sit in a

classroom and practice on dummies, but it was another to be looking death in the face, as a man he idolized hung on to life by a thread. In the distance, he heard the first whine of the ambulance siren. Roland held his hand tighter. It looked like Big John's breathing was slowing down, but he couldn't be sure. He noted that it was 2:19 pm.

He remembered that soon after meeting him, Big John had invited him to a wild game feed that he put on for all his friends who loved to hunt, or who at least enjoyed eating all the food he prepared. Big John and Agnes put on one hell of a spread in the back yard, and it usually was held on the first Saturday in October. His friends made sure they put it down on the calendar each year, because no one wanted to miss it. John would cook a variety of game, typically venison, wild turkey, pheasant, rabbit and quail. Some years, he would surprise everyone with something different. The first feed Roland attended featured a whole hog that Big John roasted over an open pit all day. Between the fantastic food and the kegs of beer that Big John changed out like a member of a seasoned pit crew, everyone had a great time. When it got dark, Big John would start telling some of his classic stories that the little ones shouldn't be hearing. Even if you heard the stories countless times, his knack for telling them kept the laughs rolling well into the night. No matter what, Big John would always manage to tell one that Roland hadn't heard before. The first time hearing one of his stories was special.

Roland's favorite wild game feed was about ten years ago when Big John introduced him to one of his old high school friends as "his other son". Roland loved Big John like a father, but hearing him refer to him as a son made the relationship between them even more special. Just listening to John weave those great stories made Roland swell with pride. He felt like he knew the man all his life.

Now Roland could hear the ambulance getting closer. They lived out in the country, so he knew it was at least a ten-minute trip, and another ten minutes to the nearest hospital. Gripping Big John's meaty hand, Roland didn't know if his friend would make the trip. He felt John squeeze him back, but he wasn't sure if it was real or wishful thinking.

"Stay with me, John. Stay with me." Tears were falling.

Staring at him on the couch, Roland thought he saw a slight twitch in John's face. It looked like the slightest tear began to trickle down Big John's wrinkled countenance. Roland wiped it away, and did the same with his own tears, knowing the ambulance would be there any moment. April was still weeping and not offering any help. There really wasn't anything either could do. Big John was slowly slipping away.

The ambulance was in the driveway now. Roland heard two doors shut one after the other, as the EMTs made their way into the house with a stretcher and bags of gear. He knew that any moment they would ask him to move aside while they did what they could to save their patient. It was then that Roland thought about Big John, and how he had lived his life. While death scared Roland, he knew that Big John had a different outlook on things. He always talked about those "great ones" and how you only got a handful. Roland smiled when he realized that the great man he was kneeling before had bucketfuls of them; buckets upon buckets of "great ones". As a matter of fact, Big John himself was one of the great ones.

Roland thought about the St. Louis Cardinal games they went to, all the amazing fishing trips, deer hunting every fall, and shooting ducks from a blind, sharing a flask of Jack Daniels on a crisp fall morning. Through knowing Big John, Roland had several of his own bucketfuls of "great ones". He almost felt selfish now, holding

John's hand, and wanting him to stay behind with the living. Roland knew that Big John was probably ready to reunite with Agnes again, the woman he adored every day they were together. How could he be so selfish and want him to stay?

He let the big man's hand fall as he stood up, looking down at his unforgettable friend. His chest was no longer rising or falling. He could see another tear fall across John's weathered face, yet he was at peace, and all was OK with the world. Roland knew that he was witness to the passing of one of the great ones, and he knew he was a better person for having known him.

Blackened Spiral Down

1

I had been watching him for the past two weeks. I just knew the bastard was up to no good. There is just no good reason a man would be going into an old, abandoned church at all hours of the day and night. No good reason at all. After two days of it, I began to keep a diary of the visits. I took good, accurate notes, including times, what the weather was like, and other pertinent information. It took two weeks for me to get the courage to go over there to see what was going on. I only wish I had done so much sooner. I could

have stopped the horrible things that were happening in the basement

and maybe saved some lives. No one deserved what that sick

bastard was doing to them over there at the old church. I only

actually saw him going inside the church one time, but I could see

light from a flashlight or maybe a camping lantern coming from the

basement. I knew it was him, and I kept account of everything in my

diary. I knew the police would want to know the information I was

gathering at some point. In some strange way, it felt like I was doing

a good deed, a sort of civic duty.

Living in the small village of Armington, Illinois, doesn't

offer many distractions from the daily grind of a dying, small

Midwestern town. Not much ever happened in Armington, and

most of the business and younger residents left many years ago. It is

surrounded by several similar small towns and is 25 miles from

Bloomington to the northeast. With barely 300 residents, it seems

hard to believe that Armington was once a wealthy farming

community, three times the current population, with a busy

downtown, albeit only four square blocks. At one time, the Norfolk

& Western Railroad came through, providing steady business with the conductors and railroad employees. Mama Norma's Diner served the best biscuits and gravy around and did a great lunch business with her famous horseshoe sandwiches. There was also a hardware store, a few retail shops, a barber, a tavern, and of course a grain elevator which served the corn and soy farmers for miles. There was a Baptist church that has stayed open (somehow) and the Our Redeemer Christian Church that closed more than 10 years ago. It sits across the street from my house on Old Farm Road, on the far north edge of town.

It was fast becoming an eyesore from neglect, and now that the roof was starting to cave in, raccoons and other small animals were taking up residence in the attic. It was only a matter of time before they took over the entire church. The couple that owned the land and building retired to Florida, and while they paid the property taxes, both were unwilling to do anything else to keep the building and grounds presentable. Residents complained to the Village of Armington, with no response. Thankfully, one long-time resident had a nephew on the board at Tazewell County, and he was able to appropriate the funds to demolish the old church, and force the owners to either pay for it or give the land back to the Village. The nephew scored lots of political points in closing the deal, and the Village of Armington was pleased to have the demolition planned for the fall, when the crops would be in and the local contractor would have the time to raze the old church.

The town had been dying since the late 1960's. When the grade school and high school closed, the kids were forced to consolidate with the other small towns to form the Olympia School District. When the railroad stopped coming through and the schools went away, Armington began its slow death. Kids grew up and fled to the larger towns and cities, and the older citizens eventually died off and sold their rich farm ground to the big corporations, who gladly bought up the acres.

There isn't much of anything in Armington now. The tavern barely stays open, just like the Baptist church, and one tiny convenient store remains. The post office doesn't even deliver mail, and the townsfolk have to go pick up their mail each day. Armington is the classic story of a small town gone down the tubes. The other two houses near mine, on Old Farm Road, are vacant. The "for sale" signs in the yard are rusty and have weeds growing up around them. So no one else would have ever noticed the strange visitor going in and out of the old church. It was all up to me to find out what was going on and help the police catch the bastard.

2

It was two weeks after he started going over to the old church that I got the nerve to go over there myself. He had a key and went in the front door the one time I saw him. Since it was locked up tight, I decided to go around back and try getting in where no one would be able to see me. Despite Armington being a ghost town the last 10 years, there was still the occasional passerby, and in a small town – everyone knows everyone. There are few secrets.

I've lived in Armington all my 44 years. I was raised by my grandparents, who both lived in the house on Old Farm Road, where I still reside. Grandma had a massive stroke in the fall of 1985, and it left her nearly incapacitated. Grandpa and I did our best to take care of her, but it wasn't easy. Six months after the stroke, Grandma hadn't improved. I walked in one night to Grandpa shoving a pillow into her face. Tears were streaming down his face while he did it. I knew it was an act of love, even though it was murder. She barely put up a fight, as if she wanted to die and pass on to the other side.

Grandpa turned around to find me standing there in the bedroom

doorway, and told me to keep my mouth shut about it. He told me

that he hated to see her like that, and he couldn't bear it for another

day.

When the deputies showed up with the ambulance to pick up

Grandma, they took me outside and away from Grandpa so we could

talk. They knew what happened, but it was difficult to prove that he

smothered her with the pillow. They threatened me and said I could

go to jail as an accomplice to the murder if I didn't tell them what

happened. I told them all about it. I figured they wouldn't do much

of anything to Grandpa since he was old and was a grieving

widower, putting his wife out of her misery. I was wrong. They

charged him with second degree murder, and his lawyer said that the

jury would probably feel sorry for him and only give him ten years.

Two days before his trial was to begin, I found Grandpa in

the basement, hanging from a noose he made with a bedsheet. He

swayed beneath one of the galvanized water pipes, his eyes wide

open and staring at me. Even though he was dead, I knew his eyes

didn't lie. He hated me for telling the police what happened. He never asked me about it, but he knew. I could tell by the way he acted around me. As he was swinging in the dim light of the basement, I felt an overwhelming guilt for putting him in this situation.

Now it was me all by myself in the big, 90-year-old, two-story Cape Cod-style house surrounded by cornfields on the north edge of town. I was surprised that Grandpa had left me a sizeable inheritance, and since there were only distant relatives, it all came to me. The old house was paid for, and the property taxes were relatively small. I now owned forty acres of farm ground that surrounded the house, and many years ago, Grandpa had leased it out to a local farmer to plant corn and beans for a nice sum of money. There were also the six wind turbines on the property that earned me $10,000 each on an annual basis. Thanks to Grandpa, I didn't want for anything, as long as I was smart with what he left me.

As I made my way through the tall grass in the back of the church, I noticed a small window near the back door was broken. I could reach in to unlock the door and gain access inside. The pungent smell of mildew was striking as soon as I walked in, probably from the rain coming in the gaping holes on the roof. As I

walked, floor boards creaked, and I could hear animals scurrying in

the attic above my head. I knew enough to bring a good flashlight

with me, because even though it was daytime, the boarded-up

windows didn't offer much light inside. The first floor was empty,

aside from the few boxes left behind when the church closed down.

There was also some broken furniture and piles of clothes in one

corner, probably donations that never made it past the bin they kept

for that purpose.

I stopped every few steps to listen for any noises. I didn't

hear any. I did notice another strong odor as I approached the door

that apparently led to the basement. It was an odd smell, like rotting

fruit, but a stomach-churning cocktail that almost forced me to vomit

before my hand touched the door. I knew it was something bad

coming from the basement, and I figured the police would really

need an upstanding citizen like me to tell them all about it. I

grabbed one of the t-shirts in the pile of donated clothes and placed it

over my nose and mouth in a futile attempt to mask the horrible

stench. The moldy odor of the shirt did little to hide the miasma of death ascending the stairs, as I opened the door and began my descent into the blackness.

The basement stairs creaked and groaned as I made my way down. I clutched the wobbly handrail, hoping the old wood wouldn't give way and send me cascading into the unknown. I was also thinking about the stranger I had seen enter the church and hoped that I was not going to see him down here. The smell was overwhelming and became increasingly stronger with each step. The dampness of the basement was palpable, and the humidity amplified the pungent odor, making it feel as if I was walking through a dense fog. It was then that I heard what sounded like a female voice calling out.

"Help me!" she cried, and then I heard what sounded like fingernails on wood, followed by a soft pounding. I believed she was on the other side of the basement from where I was, frozen on the last stair.

"Who is there?" I called out, shocked to hear any signs of life in the pitch black. My heart was racing as I made it past the last stair and to the damp concrete floor. She didn't reply, but I could hear a soft cry and whimpering in the void.

As I gingerly made my way across the floor, my eyes slowly began to adjust to the darkness. My flashlight beam was strong, thanks to a fresh set of batteries, and I tried to figure out where the faint voice was coming from. It sounded very weak, from a woman in obvious distress. I could still hear the soft cries coming from across the basement. Then I tripped over something on the floor that sent me sprawling face-first into the concrete. My flashlight bounced and was sent sliding across the floor, several feet into the darkness. When it came to rest, the utter silence in the basement was maddening. I could see the beam of light pointing to my right as I struggled to get up. My face stung from the blow, and I could feel sharp pain in my right arm, where I attempted to cushion the fall. I felt something cold but sticky touch the side of my face, and I jumped back in terror!

I scrambled to get to my flashlight. I wish now I never found the light. I also wished I had never decided to go into the church or into the abyss of the basement. Undoing what I had already done was not possible, as I held the flashlight in my now quivering hands, shining its light upon the source of the cold and sticky thing that touched me. The sight of it was horrible and etched into my mind, no matter how hard I would try to make it go away. There was a large wooden table in the middle of the basement floor. On that table were various body parts strewn about, in pools of coagulated blood and other bodily fluids. These sickening, rotting human pieces were in various stages of decomposition. This display of carnage was obviously the source of the disgusting, rotten smell. There was a woman's arm hanging off the side of the table, with three of the five fingers missing, and that is what I believed touched the side of my face. Reaching up, I could still feel a nasty, wet slime that her mangled hand left behind. The mere thought of it forced me to hurl up whatever was in my stomach. The cacophony of odors was unreal.

I was reeling at the sight of what was before me on that large table. I could see hand saws of various sizes, and an old vice attached the edge of the table, with what appeared to be a woman's leg in its grasp. The foot was covered in a nylon stocking, and barely hanging on, as flies swarmed to feast on the exposed flesh. Then I shined my light around the room, giving me a reprieve from the horror show before me, only to find a neat row of severed heads on an old dusty shelf! There were eight or nine of them, also in various stages of decomposition. It looked like they were all young

women, or even younger girls. It was hard to tell their ages, as the

gray pallor of the skin in the dim light gave a mercifully limited

view. Their dead eyes were staring at me, as my beam of light

seemed to disappear in the emptiness. It was incredibly terrifying!

The stranger who I observed only two weeks ago had surely been

coming down here for months, or even years, making it his

workshop of horrors.

"Help me!"

The voice cut the tension like a chainsaw through a

dollhouse.

"I'm coming," I told her, making my way across the

basement, hoping that maybe I could at least save one victim from

this sadistic maniac.

As I approached the other side of the room, my flashlight

picked up a ring of keys hanging on a rusted metal spike, firmly in

one of the floor joists. I reached for the keys and began looking

furiously for a door they would unlock. I could hear the woman

crying only a few feet from where I was standing, behind one of

three locked doors. The rooms were small, like the size of broom closets. My hands shook as I put the first key into the locked door. It obviously didn't fit, and I tried the next one. My heart was racing, as I couldn't help but feel someone was watching me. I wondered if the stranger could be somewhere in the darkness behind me. It was unsettling to say the least.

Suddenly I had the right key and turned it while I pulled the door open. A sickening smell of urine and feces swept over me. I winced and gagged slightly as I shined my light into the small room. There was nothing in the room aside from the bucket with the human waste and two sturdy chains that were bolted to the brick wall. The floor was concrete like the rest of the basement, and at one side was a pile of threadbare, filthy rags that were probably being used as bedding. It was horrendous, and I knew that it most likely was a makeshift cell used to keep someone for a period of time. The thought of what horrors the victim endured in her captivity, especially with the soundtrack of evil on the other side of the heavy door, was terrible.

I then opened the second door. I saw the same things in that cell. I did observe some dried blood on the floor and on one wall. It spoke of extreme misery and pain at the cruel hands of the sadist butcher. I quickly backed out of the cell, knowing now that the source of the subdued cries was in the third and final room before me. I glanced over my shoulder into the endless darkness of the basement and put the key into the lock, then pulled on the heavy door to reveal a quivering mess of a young girl. She was cowering against the back wall, where her wrists were chained to the brick. She was almost completely naked, except for a filthy pair of panties and part of a t-shirt. She couldn't have been older than 11 or 12.

I reached my hand out, and she recoiled at the sight of me, her body shaking with fear.

"I'm here to help you. What is your name?"

She kept her head down while her brown hair stuck to her skin, soiled in sweat and grime from her occupation of the third cell. She was incredibly thin and looked like she was at the end of her time on this planet, likely from the severe neglect and hellish conditions. The dampness of the basement would escalate into a humid nightmare at the middle of the day, continuing on for hours, until the darkness outside helped cool it down. There was a dog bowl in the corner of her cell. It was empty.

I stood at the threshold of her cell, in shock at what I was witness to. I knew I had to do something. My first instinct was to run across the street to my house and call the police. I didn't have a cell phone, and in Armington, it wouldn't have been much use with spotty reception. I considered that, but had second thoughts. I thought about the stranger, and how once the police showed up to the scene, he would never return. I couldn't bear the thought of him not being captured. I thought about the young women and girls who perished here, and how this madman was displaying their heads like putrid trophies of his handiwork. I thought maybe I could help the police catch this killer by continuing my observation. I spent a few minutes weighing the options, and I decided the best option was to go for some food and water, and leaving her behind, in hopes the beast would return and be snared in the trap.

She didn't make a sound when I put two bologna and cheese sandwiches in her bowl and gave her some water. She just flinched when I got near, shaking horribly at the sight of me. He had her so riddled with fear, it really bothered me to shut the door, but I knew it was for the greater good. When I got home, I made a lengthy entry into my diary to account for what I had just seen. I filled at least a dozen pages with the details. In the back of my mind, and through a

fitful night of insomnia, I hoped the girl would survive the night.

3

The following week, I made it a point to go to the church

every morning to check on the girl. I still couldn't get her to talk,

and she still flinched when I opened the door each day, as if she was

scared to death at my presence. I considered that due to the lack of

light in the basement, and her horrendous living conditions, she

probably thought the deranged stranger and I were one in the same.

Despite the fact I was bringing her food each day and water to drink,

she still shook uncontrollably while I was in the cell. I wanted to

bring her fresh clothes and a blanket to lie on, but I knew the

stranger would figure out someone was interfering, and the last thing

I wanted to do was tip him off that the cops and I were on to his

game.

Each day for that week, I stood vigil at my living room

window, peering through the shades and recording every painstaking

detail. One day an Ameren utility truck stopped in front of the church, with workers doing something at the top of the power pole along Old Farm Road. I figured it must have been the police, maybe installing some sort of surveillance camera, since I knew there was no electricity at the old church. I did not see the stranger again that week in broad daylight, but on Friday night, I observed what looked like flashlight beams in the basement. There were only two small basement windows that faced my house, but it looked like he was down there. The thought of what he might be doing to that poor, frightened girl enraged me. I debated whether to get my Grandpa's shotgun from his bedroom closet and take the law into my own hands. I was afraid that if the stranger got himself a good lawyer, or if the Tazewell County Sheriff's department, being inexperienced with a crime of this scope, would botch the investigation, it might set him free on a technicality. I was worried that if I waited another day, the girl wouldn't make it. She looked terrible that morning when I brought food and water to her.

I paced around the house for a good hour, looking out my window every two or three minutes. I knew that my reluctance to call the police was likely causing her more pain, or worse, signing her death warrant. That's when I decided the best choice was to grab

Grandpa's shotgun and make my way across the street, under the

cover of darkness.

4

I made my way down the basement stairs once again. It was

11pm, and it was the first time I had been in the church at night. I

could hear the raccoons scurrying in the attic. The stairway was even

darker than my previous visits, which I had not thought possible.

The horrible stench of death was hanging in the air, yet I was

becoming used to the smell and didn't vomit. I had the shotgun

firmly in my grasp, not knowing if the killer was still in the

basement, lurking in the shadows. I paused at each step, listening

intently for any sound, but there was none. I hoped that I would hear

the girl crying, or making some sort of noise. There were no sounds

at all. I tried to control my own breathing and kept my light off, so

as not to give my own position away, in case the stranger was

waiting for me below. My finger was on the trigger, ready to blast

him into the unknown if necessary.

Having been in the basement now many times, I knew how to avoid the trip hazards and disgusting, festering body parts the killer kept out on the heavy wooden table. I reached for the keys, still hanging in their usual place, and then turned on my flashlight, to see if he was still there. I saw no one. The collection of severed heads was still arranged on the dusty shelf, staring at me as I made my way around, to avoid being surprised by someone lying in wait. I was surprised at how much cooler the basement was at night, as compared to what it was like during the heat of the day.

I made my way to the third cell, where the young girl would be huddled in fear. Not hearing any noise coming from the other side of the door worried me, but I thought it was possible she would be sleeping. I unlocked the door to check on her. I was shocked to see she was not inside! The heavy chains with manacles hung from the wall, with no one attached. The small cell was empty, except for the bucket, her food bowl, and a few dirty rags she was using to sleep on. Where could she be?

I quickly turned around, my light frantically looking around the basement for her. That's when I noticed something was different on the table. There was more added to the display of human carnage

I had seen many times now. The body of the frail, young girl was

naked and lying spread-eagle on the table, her rib cage filleted open,

exposing her organs. Her hands were bound with twine to nails on

the table, and her feet as well. I shined my light on her face, which

was contorted in a display of sheer agony, as if she was alive when

the maniac opened her up. My eyes welled up seeing her this way.

My grief was endless, wondering if I had called the police when I

first saw the lights in the basement, if she would have been saved.

Her short life was met with a diabolical end, at the hands of this dark

stranger, who invaded our small, simple town.

Just then I heard footsteps above me! There was someone on

the first floor, making their way toward the basement door. Did the

stranger come back to finish his work with the fresh corpse? Was it

someone else who maybe saw his flashlight in the basement

windows that faced Old Farm Road? I knew that I had the

advantage of surprise, as I shut off my light and crouched down,

steadying the barrel of my shotgun at the stairway. My eyes had

already started to adjust slightly, and I kept them fixed on the stairs.

I heard the basement door open. Whoever it was didn't call out, but

began to descend the stairs one at a time, the creaking of the old wood filling the stillness of the basement. I could feel the tension.

My heart was racing as I did my best to keep the barrel steady and

my finger on the trigger. One by one, the figure in darkness made its

way to the basement. I couldn't make out detail, but it did appear to

be a male. He didn't stop, slowly taking one stair at a time, until he

stood on the concrete floor.

 I knew this had to be the stranger. Who else would be here at

almost midnight? I decided the best thing to do was to turn on my

flashlight, in hopes of blinding him for a moment, and then sending a

deer slug into his chest. Once he was dead, I could go to my house

and call the police, knowing I would be considered a hero for

capturing the sadistic killer and avoiding a costly trial for the county.

I could see in my mind the Peoria Journal Star or the Bloomington

Pantagraph, complete with my picture on the front page – above the

fold of course. I would be standing outside the church with one or

more of the deputies, beaming with pride that I had done my duty. I

used my left hand to turn on the flashlight, so my right hand was

ready with the gun.

 The click of the flashlight caused him to flinch, yet as the

figure was awash in the bright light, I was taken aback and nearly fell over with shock at who was standing only ten feet from me! I knew it had to be a dream. There was no way he could be here in this basement right now. Yet he was, in the flesh, standing there and grinning at me.

"Hi, Ronnie. Seen a ghost?" he said, laughing at me. It was my grandfather, standing there in the same clothes I found him in that day in the basement, swinging from the water pipe. He had on an old pair of blue jeans, a flannel shirt, and a John Deere ball cap.

I stood up, unable to say a word. I blinked a few times, hoping that I would make the mirage go away. That didn't work. He was still standing there, now taking a step closer toward me. He didn't seem concerned about the gun pointing at him.

"Stop where you are!" I yelled out, pulling the trigger as my slug tore into his left shoulder. He only laughed as he jerked back, and then continued walking toward me.

I put another shell into the gun. I shot at him again, this time I hit him center mass in the chest. It only stopped him for a moment, while the gaping hole barely bled at all!

"I'm already dead, Ronnie. That's not going to do anything. You've been a bad boy here at the old church. Look at what you've done!" His voice was cold; his stare was colder.

"I didn't do any of this. I've been helping the police catch the bastard."

"You lying son-of-a-bitch! Just like you lied and told those cops that I killed your Grandma," he continued to walk toward me, "after I told you to shut your mouth!"

I moved back toward the three cells as he moved closer. I could see the bruises on his neck from where he hung himself years before. I was staring into the eyes of a dead man, but he looked very alive as he crept closer. He was now only a couple feet away, his rancid breath was cool yet foul.

"There's been no one over here but you, Ronnie. No one else. Just you and those poor girls. I've been watching. You were picking up prostitutes in Peoria or Bloomington and bringing them here. The ones you paid were the only girls that would have anything to do with you."

Images were rushing through my mind as he spoke. I could see a young girl in my car, driving down Old Farm Road toward my house. She was pretty, but dressed like a hooker, wearing too much make-up and trying to hide the track marks on her arms. Then I could see myself on a country road, stopping to talk with a girl walking home from her bus stop. She couldn't have been older than 11 or 12. She looked very much like the girl I found in the basement alive! She was the same one that was on the table now, ripped open and spread-eagle.

"You've been doing this for years. I've seen it all," he said, only a foot away from me now, "I let it happen, because I wanted to damn your soul to Hell. You turned me in, your own flesh and blood. You knew I did that to put your Grandma out of her misery. You . . . "

His hand reached out and knocked the shotgun from my grasp. More images were running through my mind. I could see myself sawing a woman's foot off, with a leg tightly in my vice. I could see me standing back to admire the collection of severed heads, as if they were trophies in a case at a local high school. To me, I guess that's just what they were.

Now my grandfather was holding open the door to the middle cell and pushing me inside. I was helpless to resist. I felt as if I were a rag doll in his firm hold, as he put the manacles on my own wrists. I tried to scream, but no sound came out. I tried to fight him, but there was no strength to do so. He slammed the door, and I could hear the lock engage. I was now trapped in one of the cells. His laughing echoed throughout the basement. It sounded more distant as he made his way back up the stairs. Faintly I could hear him walking on the floor above, and then silence.

5

Days pass, and I'm still in the middle cell. No one has come to give me any food or water, and I'm fading slowly. I'm left to my own thoughts, which, as I relive every encounter in this basement, are my own living hell. I can hear their screams and cries for help as I did those horrible things to them. I only wanted someone to love, but they wouldn't love me back. No matter what I did to make their stay in the basement better, they still cringed in my presence. They still recoiled at the mere sight of me. When I raped them, they kicked and punched at me, until all I could do was knock them out and finish my business. I just wanted someone to love. Instead, I continued my spiral down into madness. Now, in the darkness of the basement cell, I curse my grandfather for putting me in this situation, and hope that death comes to call.

As I stare into the blackness, I fear I will be here for all eternity, waiting for someone to love me back. All I hear is their screaming in the silence, and it's deafening.

Contraption Number 12

1

Freddy Frankfurt was worn down to the nub. He had a bad week at work, and all he could think about right now was picking up an extra-large Arctic Pop and a Charleston Chew before going home for the weekend. Freddy had enough! Since he didn't have a car, Freddy walked three miles to and from work - rain or shine. He lived in a Midwestern town with a population of approximately 20,000 and no public transportation. Today, it rained in torrents, and

Freddy was soaked to the skin. Every step he took, his feet sloshed

inside his sneakers, followed by an annoying squeak. Freddy's

blisters had blisters, and each step was painful. His diminished

height, chubby legs, and large protruding belly made him waddle

when he walked. Several cars drove by on his way home,

intentionally weaving into puddles, sending massive waves of dirty

rain water at him – honking their horns and screaming insults Freddy

did his best to ignore. Unfortunately, he was used to it. He had been

the favorite whipping boy to adults and children alike since he began

kindergarten at age five.

Freddy had been bagging groceries and herding shopping

carts at Ray's Food Mart for the last ten years and hated every

minute of it. The only reason he tolerated his job was to be able to

support himself – he had no family that he knew of. He had been

raised by elderly foster parents who had both died the year after he

graduated high school. The worst part of the job was when it rained

or snowed and Freddy had to round up the carts. The owner's son,

Ray Jr. (or "RJ" as they called him), was supposed to help. Yet he

was usually nowhere to be found, especially when the weather was

bad, or one of his girlfriends showed up to see him. He would go missing for hours, and no one could ask about it, for fear of Big Ray finding out. No matter what his father heard from others, RJ could do no wrong. Big Ray dismissed most of the criticism of his son as jealously and gave it no credence. Any employee who dared say anything negative about RJ would typically find themselves working the next holiday or a shift that would be difficult on them for a variety of reasons. Big Ray knew that one day, he would retire and move to Florida, and RJ would take over the family business. An insult of RJ was a reflection on Big Ray, and he wasn't having any part of that. As the owner of the largest grocery store in town, the big smiling rotund man was a celebrity.

Freddy had spent the day limping through heavy downpours, helping old ladies to their cars with groceries for quarter tips, and collecting shopping carts. He had only seen RJ once, when he was on the phone with his feet up on Big Ray's desk. Big Ray was at a funeral for a high school friend and had left RJ in charge. Freddy knew that RJ would take over when Big Ray retired, and he cringed at the thought of working for the spoiled brat. He was everything that Freddy wasn't. RJ was given unlimited access to money, drove a brand-new car, and had dozens of girls chasing after him. RJ was likely one of the drivers that had soaked Freddy as he limped home

in his sloshy shoes and battered body.

Now Freddy was in a long line at the gas station, picking up

his Arctic Pop and Charleston Chew. He was only two blocks from

home. While Freddy stood in the line, he noticed there were two

people staring into the screens of the video poker machines. Both

were middle-aged, a man and woman, in a trance. They didn't even

appear to blink! Occasionally they would push a button, but that

appeared to be the extent of their movements. Freddy was intrigued

by their intense interest in the machines and also marveled at their

sleek design and hundreds of moving parts. Yet it gave him the

creeps as he watched their robotic movements. He wondered how

much money they spent, sitting there, pushing buttons and watching

the vibrant colors. Freddy found himself jealous of the person who

invented the machines, and wondered how many millions of dollars

resided in their bank account. He knew it was more than he would

ever see in a lifetime.

"Well, well, well! If it's not ole Freddy Frankfurter!" a voice

cried out from the end of the line. "Sorry if I soaked you back there.

You're dripping all over the floor!" He laughed hysterically.

Freddy heard him. Everyone did. It was Johnny Kovacs. He knew that voice and laugh all too well. Freddy heard a few more giggles behind him, but he was used to it. In high school, it was the worst. Most of his classmates were terribly cruel. It didn't help that Freddy had a nasally voice and a slight New York City accent that stood out like a skyscraper amidst the surrounding blandness of the corn and bean fields. That was 11 years ago. Now he heard them laughing and calling him Frankfurter. The only thing he had for family was his last name. It was the one thing he knew of his father. So, when the kids called him Frankfurter, it burned him deep down inside. It stayed white-hot for a while. They picked on him at Ray's, and he often bagged groceries for the same jerks who had picked on him in school. Jerks like Johnny Kovacs. He was the worst, and whenever Freddy ran into him, Johnny made it a point to degrade him every way possible. Especially when he had an audience. One time, Johnny rumbled past him walking to work one morning and threw a large cup of urine out his truck window, showering Freddy in sour piss. He couldn't get the sickening smell off himself that day, and many customers complained. Big Ray yelled at Freddy in front of several other employees, telling him to "go home and take a damn shower."

"Don't ignore me, Frankfurter. You still stink like piss?"
Johnny howled with laugher again, as several others in the line
laughed with him.

Freddy set his drink and candy on the counter, then began to
dig for change from his pocket. The measly tips from the old ladies
paid for a week's worth of fountain sodas and candy. The cashier
was Angie Pugner. Her older brother Tom was in a few of Freddy's
classes, and was just like the others who picked on him. Angie was
usually very mean to him about using change to pay for things. She
rolled her eyes as Freddy dumped his change on the counter and
began count it out slowly.

"That will be $2.89." Angie smacked her gum. "Tell me
you're not doing this again, loser. Do you see the line I got?"
Freddy could hear people talking. He knew they were making fun of
him and complaining about him holding up the line.

"There. It's all there." Freddy pushed the change toward
Angie, not making eye contact.

"Hurry up, Frankfurter. Some of us have dates tonight,"
Johnny said, "and not with Rosie Palm and her five sisters!" He

laughed again. A woman in the line sighed. The others appeared to think it was funny.

Freddy grabbed his candy and drink and began to walk toward the door, noticing once again the trance-like state that the video poker machine players were in. There was a third one now, an elderly man in a Cubs baseball cap. Freddy could hear Johnny to his left, saying something to him, but he chose to ignore it. Suddenly, he tripped over something and landed flat on his face – his glasses sent sliding across the floor. His Arctic Pop went flying, spilling soda and ice, then crashing against the glass doors with a loud bang. His candy went in another direction. Freddy's face stung at the blunt impact. He could see Johnny move back into the line; it was obvious he must have tripped him. Freddy wanted to strangle him, but he knew that would make it worse and would get himself beat up in the process.

"You clumsy son-of-a-bitch!" screamed Angie from behind the counter. "Now I gotta mop the floor! God damn you!" It sounded like the entire line of people were all laughing. Even the video poker player in the Cubs hat snapped out of his trance long enough to laugh at the spectacle. He shook his head, then went back to pushing buttons, muttering under his breath.

To say Freddy was humiliated was an understatement. He struggled to get up from the floor, his face red with anger and from meeting the hard floor moments before. The laughing continued. He slipped a bit on the wet floor, drawing an encore of laughter from the crowd. Now customers were standing outside the doors – pointing and laughing too. Finally, he stood up.

"Get out of the store! Get out! Don't come back!" Angie cried out.

"Freddy Frankfurter. Thrown out of the Gas N' Go! Once a loser, always a loser!" Johnny yelled at him as he made his way out of the store and back into the rain, now coming down in sheets. Freddy put on his glasses, the frame bent from the fall, but thankfully the lenses weren't broken. That was probably the only thing that went right for him this day. Until he got home.

2

Freddy shook out his wet clothes in the mudroom of his small house on Walnut Street. Immediately, he was greeted by his three cats, who were the only things that showed him love at all. He

loved classic rock music and named them Jimmy (for Jimi Hendrix,

despite the fact Freddy spelled it wrong), Robert (for Robert Plant),

and Stevie (for his crush, Stevie Nicks). The three circled him,

which meant they likely wanted to be fed. Freddy didn't mind it at

all. It made him feel wanted. He didn't notice the strong stench of

cat piss, that, if you stood at the door for more than a moment, you

could smell from outside.

Inside the mud room were piles and piles of cardboard boxes

of various sizes. Freddy had them stacked in illogical ways with

some smaller boxes bulging beneath much heavier, larger ones. The

cats loved to get on top of the boxes, no matter how many times

Freddy shooed them away. Heading into the kitchen, it was much of

the same. A small path was available between the piles of more

boxes, so he could access the sink, his toaster and microwave, and

the refrigerator that rattled until you punched the right side of it. He

didn't do much in the kitchen beyond heating up canned goods in the

microwave and making waffles. Every now and then, Freddy would

treat himself by moving some boxes out of the way and making a

frozen pizza. Tonight, he felt like one, and dug the last pepperoni pizza out of the freezer, knocking chunks of ice to the floor in the process.

Following the path, while the oven pre-heated, Freddy made his way through the endless piles of cardboard boxes to his living room, where his desk and office chair were located, a few feet from his small 19-inch television. Freddy couldn't afford cable or satellite, so he made due with the few local channels he could pick up on the tall antenna attached to the house. As Freddy approached his desk, he noticed one of the medium-sized boxes had fallen, blocking his path.

"That's strange," he said, bending over to pick it up. It was upright and nothing seemed to have fallen out.

On top of the box was written in black sharpie, "Contraption Number 12". He picked it up and sat it on the desk. It felt heavy to him, but his long day in the rain may have impacted that assessment. He peered inside the box, not remembering exactly what Contraption Number 12 was. It had been a few years since he came up with it. Inside the hundreds of cardboard boxes that were slowly filling up Freddy's house, were his many inventions – which he called contraptions. Freddy had the grand notion that one day he would invent something that would make him rich beyond his wildest dreams. He loved to watch commercials on TV and dream about being the person who invented the products. Most of Freddy's contraptions were made of things he found in the dumpster, or setting on the curb on trash night, or sometimes the at junk yard on Race Street. In his mind, Freddy was one good idea away from millions of dollars. The last one he came up with was Contraption Number 274. So Number 12 was many, many ideas ago.

Robert jumped up on his chair, also curious about Contraption Number 12 and what it was doing on Freddy's desk. Freddy enjoyed the captive audience as Robert purred, and he took out the contents of the box, setting them on the desk. It was one solid piece that he had constructed from a small portable television, an old rotary-dial phone, and small keyboard with several letters and numbers missing. It made no logical sense, but to Freddy, every contraption had a purpose. He knew that one day he would be on the news for inventing the next great thing. Looking at Contraption Number 12, Freddy even marveled at his own genius. Immediately ideas began to clutter his mind, as he recalled now what he was trying to do when he came up with the idea. Despite his excitement, when Freddy plugged in the TV, it didn't come on. Freddy felt that

there was a reason that Contraption Number 12 was lying right-side

up next to his favorite chair. For all the bad things that happened to

Freddy on that rainy Friday, the fact his glasses didn't break and

finding Contraption Number 12 were two things he had going for

him.

3

It was just before 10 pm when Freddy made a breakthrough

with Contraption Number 12. With the back of the TV open, Freddy

had been busy checking every solder point and touching them up.

He used a large magnifying glass mounted to his desk that enabled

him to see the tiny connections. When he was inventing, Freddy was

in his favorite place. Having the tools to make his creations was

paramount, and when he found the old magnifying glass, he felt like

he had risen up in the world of inventing already.

This time when he plugged it in, something turned on inside

the TV. Freddy looked at the screen as it slowly came on, and he

was greeted with blessed snow and white noise. He got the TV to come on! Contraption Number 12 was already looking to show promise. Nervously, he picked up the receiver of the old 1960's rotary phone. Amazingly, he heard a faint static in his ear! The phone worked as well!

"Checking 1, 2, 3. Checking!" Freddy said into the mouthpiece.

Still only static, crackling from what sounded far, far away.

"Is anyone there? Can anyone hear me?"

Static again. This time, Freddy thought he heard someone reply. It was very quiet, and among the static, impossible to understand.

"Hello? This is Freddy Frankfurt, inventor," Freddy said, straining to hear a reply.

The static still droned on, but this time, Freddy thought he heard a man's voice. It sounded like he said, "I'm here."

"Hello, who am I talking to?"

Only static was heard. He wanted so badly to hear someone reply. Still static.

"If you can hear me. Give me a sign."

The snow on the screen began to pulsate a few times, then

went back to the way it was. The sound of the white noise was barely audible through the single small speaker on front of the TV. He began to doubt he had ever heard a voice now. Freddy felt dejected, and thought about his terrible experience at the Gas N' Go.

"If you can hear me, I want you to do something for me." He could see the laughing face of Johnny Kovacs in his mind. Endlessly laughing. Hurling insults like fastballs whispering at his chin.

Still only static, but the snow jumped again on the screen. Freddy thought whatever was out there was communicating with him.

"Kill Johnny Kovacs for me. Kill that bastard." His voice was strong, a built-up hatred shining through.

The static continued. Once again, Freddy thought he heard a voice on the other end. What it was saying, he couldn't understand.

"His address is 304 S. Poland. The ugly green house by Buzzard's Smoke Shop."

With that, Freddy got up from his chair and made his way through the maze of boxes to his bedroom. The only thing that was accessible was his 4-drawer dresser and the old twin bed with the stained mattress in the middle of the floor. It was midnight, and he was asleep fast after a long day, despite his promising breakthrough with Contraption Number 12.

4

Freddy was awakened at 7:30 am by the incessant whining of his neighbor, Dewey Carver, racing his radio-controlled (RC) car around the block. This sound was like a rite of spring on Walnut Street. It wouldn't be so bad if Dewey didn't run the car at early hours or late at night, but he did it all the time, fueled by a 12-pack of Natural Light beer. Everyone on the block was sick of it, even though it meant winter was officially over and spring had arrived. Dewey sat in his lawn chair, reclined back and enjoying the good weather, with a cold can of Natural Light and his car racing down the alley for another lap around.

Despite the musty smell that permeated the house, it was now filled with the rich aroma of coffee. While waiting for it to finish brewing, Freddy turned on the TV and plopped down at his desk. Contraption Number 12 was still there, stoic and silent. The screen was blank.

"Police are investigating a crime at 304 South Poland this morning. Family members of John Kovacs believe he was taken from his home earlier this morning. Police were called and found obvious signs of a violent struggle, with pools of blood on the kitchen floor that splattered the cabinets, appliances, and even the walls. Blood outside led police to agree the man was taken from the home. It is unknown if he is dead or alive, but the family remains hopeful."

Freddy sat frozen at his desk. He couldn't believe what he just heard. Again, the whining of Dewey's RC car sped past his window, bounding down the sidewalk.

"Holy shit!" he said aloud, looking around as if he were afraid someone heard his exclamation. Only Robert and Stevie were within ear shot. Jimmy was patrolling the neighborhood.

Freddy shut the TV off. He was astonished by what he heard. Could it mean that Contraption Number 12 really worked? Or was it a coincidence? After drinking two cups of coffee with several spoonfuls of sugar and some milk, Freddy decided to pick up the phone on his contraption. As soon as he did, the TV monitor blinked a couple times, then turned on. Snowy static and white noise again. In his ear, Freddy could hear the same static that he heard before.

"Hello? Is anyone there?" he said.

The static crackled slightly. It sounded like a voice replied, "Yes, I'm here."

Freddy's heart skipped a beat. "Did you do that to Johnny?"

The static remained, but no voice replied.

"If you did kill Johnny, give me some sort of sign."

The static continued in the receiver. The snow on the screen flickered three times, then continued!

Freddy stared at the screen. It was an obvious sign of acknowledgment! Once again, the screen flickered three times, then went back to constant snow, the white noise crackling away.

"If you can hear me, can you do something for me again?" Freddy said quietly, then looking out the window to check and see if Dewey was still in his lawn chair. He was.

"I want you to kill RJ. Ray Matthews, Jr. He lives with his parents on Main Street. The big brick house across the street from the main fire station. You know the one."

The screen flickered three times. Freddy was sure that whoever was on the other end heard what he said. He knew that whoever it was, had also killed Johnny Kovacs. What he did with the body, who knows? Freddy didn't really want to know. He was happy the jerk was dead.

The rest of his Saturday, Freddy sat at his desk, marveling at his own creation. Contraption Number 12 was now a source of pride. Finally, he had made something that was changing lives.

5

The rest of Freddy's weekend was uneventful. He checked the news periodically, but there was no mention of anything happening to RJ. As much as the town worshipped the Matthews family, Freddy was sure he would hear about it somehow. He knew that he couldn't appear too eager to avoid suspicion. Who would believe that Freddy Frankfurt was the inventor of a contraption that could kill people? For the first time in his life, Freddy enjoyed his anonymity and the fact that very few gave him credit for being good at anything. The tables had turned. Now it was Freddy with a huge secret and a thin smirk on his portly face, realizing that no one else knew about it but him and whoever was on the other end of the phone.

The sun was shining on Monday morning as Freddy walked to work. There was a bit of a skip in his step. When he arrived at the store, the day suddenly took a sharp turn for the worst. There were three police cars in the parking lot and two officers walking around RJ's car. It was parked where it always was, in a reserved spot for the Matthews family.

One of the cashiers, Brenda, came running up to him. "Oh, my God, Freddy! It's terrible!" Her face was red and puffy, tears still wet on her cheeks.

Freddy was surprised for a moment, then his thoughts went to Contraption Number 12.

"What's going on?" he asked, trying to hide his excitement.

"It's RJ! We found his car here this morning, but he's gone. There's blood all over his front seat, and the door was wide open! Oh God, Freddy!" she said, sobbing.

One of the police officers walked over to them. "You guys need to go inside, please. We're going to shut the parking lot down.

The whole front of the store is a crime scene."

Freddy walked with Brenda back to the store. He glanced over at RJ's car and saw a lot of blood on the driver's seat and inside door, as well as on the asphalt parking lot. He knew that this was too much of a coincidence to not be Contraption Number 12 doing his bidding. The hubris that swept over Freddy was overwhelming. For a man who never felt euphoria, even for a moment, it was amazing!

"Do you think it's that same creep who took Johnny Kovacs? Did you hear about that on the news, Freddy? Oh my God! What the hell is going on?" Brenda asked, standing next to him with two other cashiers and a stock boy. The others acknowledged her. Freddy was distracted, watching the police assess the scene. He wondered if they had any clues.

"Could be. Could be," Freddy replied distantly.

Standing inside the store and staring out the large windows, Freddy watched as Big Ray wept, being consoled by one of the police officers. Freddy felt alive!

6

Brenda gave Freddy a ride home. If it wasn't for the mess inside, he felt confident enough to ask her to come in. He knew that the condition of the house was not suitable for anyone, let alone one as-pretty-as Brenda. She had just graduated the year before and was going to cosmetology school. Her long brunette hair and hazel eyes had him in her spell. She reminded him of Stevie Nicks when she turned her head a certain way. Ever since she dropped him off, Freddy felt like he was soaring through the clouds. She had probably never said more than ten words to him before, but today she talked to him for an hour before they found out the store would be closed for the day. Then she asked him if he wanted a ride home. Freddy knew that she liked him. She must have felt the tremendous power he now wielded thanks to Contraption Number 12.

Freddy heated up a can of Spaghettios (with sliced franks) and grabbed a cream soda from the fridge. He sat down at his desk and turned the TV on. He knew the 5 pm news would be wall-to-wall with news of RJ. After a few commercials, Freddy saw images of RJ's car in front of the store with police putting up crime scene tape.

"A stunning situation at Ray's Food Mart earlier today, as Ray Junior was abducted in broad daylight. A truck driver making an early delivery saw the incident and after a review of the security tape, police believe they have made a positive identification on a suspect," the female news anchor said on screen.

"Yeah, this old beater of a truck pulled up next to that kid and this older guy got out. He stabbed the kid over and over before I could even get out of my truck. He had someone with him, too. They threw that kid in the back of the truck and took off. I got the plate though," the driver said, running his hand through his hair repeatedly.

Freddy watched the TV with undivided attention. Jimmy had jumped up on his lap, but he pushed him off. He watched the remainder of the news, but they had no other information about the crime. They showed fellow high school seniors on camera, talking about how great RJ was. They showed pictures of him playing football, baseball, and even wrestling. RJ had done it all. Freddy wouldn't be surprised if they changed the name of the school in tribute to his deity.

Suddenly, there was a breaking news report. Freddy was

glued to it. A still picture of an older man was shown. He was wearing a Cubs hat.

"Police have this man, Sam Tribbet, in custody at this time. After looking at the security video, they were able to positively identify him. The truck that was used to take the body away was found to be registered in his name, thanks to the witness who provided police with the license plate number."

Freddy couldn't believe it. It was the old man at the video poker machine on Friday night! He was definitely that guy. He was the one who was on the other end of the line? The one who killed two men more than half his age?

"Police are still looking for the second person on the video."

They flashed a blurry picture of another person who appeared to be a middle-aged male. Freddy couldn't tell who it was.

"If you have information, please call the police at 555-8998." The phone number flashed on the bottom of the screen.

Freddy turned the volume down on the TV. He ate some of his dinner, staring at the screen of Contraption Number 12. He was still in awe of what was happening, and despite two obvious signs that it was operational, it sounded unreal. Freddy couldn't imagine telling someone about the contraption. He would sound like a raving madman.

Freddy went to bed early and did not pick up the phone on Contraption Number 12 again. He would be lying to say he didn't like the outcome, but there were some strange and unanswered questions. Was it a coincidence that the old man in the Cubs hat that he first saw at the video poker machine was the same one police arrested for killing RJ? Was he the same one who killed Johnny? Despite the fact the bodies had not turned up, Freddy knew the two were dead. He didn't know how he knew, but he was sure of it.

He stared at the ceiling until midnight, unable to sleep. Frustrated, Freddy got up to use the bathroom and meandered through the piles of boxes to his chair and desk. He was exhausted, but there was too much going on inside his head to sleep. Staring at the screen of Contraption Number 12, he debated whether he should pick up the phone. Jimmy was sleeping on top of one of the boxes near his desk, but when Freddy put his hand on the phone, Jimmy woke up, arched his back – fur bristling up. He let out a loud meow and quickly darted away toward the kitchen. Freddy caught only a glimpse of the cat's orange body in his peripheral vision.

Freddy decided not to pick up the phone. He knew he had to get some sleep before getting up for work in the morning. He did look forward to seeing Brenda again and considered cleaning the house up so he could have her over soon. Where he would put the hundreds of contraptions was unknown. Freddy didn't know if he could bear to throw even one of them away. They meant so much to him. He knew that one day one of his contraptions would make him millions. At this point, Freddy didn't know how Contraption Number 12 was going to make him any money, unless he came up with a new approach on how to use it. He wondered if he picked up the phone and asked for money or other valuables, if they would arrive on command. He almost went back into the living room to try it, but wanted to give sleep another chance. This time he would fall asleep within ten minutes, waking to the shrill beeping of his alarm clock at 6 am.

7

Freddy stopped at the Busy Corner Convenient store on his way to work the following morning. He didn't want to go to the Gas

N' Go, fearing he would see Angie, who told him to never come back. The thought of seeing any of the customers there from Friday, after what had happened, was frightening. He was also afraid of seeing the video poker players, in their trance-like state, pushing buttons. He couldn't help but wonder if they were really listening to his commands and acting on them.

He stood in line with a cup of coffee, trying desperately to wake up. He only got a few short hours of fitful sleep, thinking about his contraption and the power it wielded. Freddy was the next person up to the counter, and as he set the dollar down, he noticed the Busy Corner Convenient also had video poker machines. There were four of them, with a person at each machine. As Freddy walked by, each of the four looked at him. There were two men and two women. The men were older, only slightly younger than the man in the Cubs hat. One of them had a strange milky left eye. One of the women was in her 30's and very obese. She winked at Freddy. The other woman was older, and used a cane to steady her on the stool in front of her machine. She smiled with dentures slightly too big for her mouth.

Freddy punched in on the time clock at the store and noticed that Brenda had not arrived. She was usually there before him and always remembered to punch in.

"Have you seen Brenda this morning?" he asked Sandra, the senior cashier acting as manager for Big Ray. He was a mess over the situation with RJ and had a lot of family at the house in support. They were organizing searches of the town, hoping against hope that RJ would be found alive.

"No, I haven't." Sandra looked at the large clock in the break room. "It is strange, she's never late."

Several hours passed, and still Brenda had not arrived at work. Freddy was worried about her. He was surprised none of the other employees mentioned it, but at noon, Sandra called a meeting with the cashiers and baggers. Freddy was nervous, noting that Sandra looked very concerned. Her face awash with worry.

"Brenda's mother just called me. Apparently, she went out last night with a few friends and never came home. Her mom found Brenda's car in the driveway with the keys still in it, blood everywhere. The police are there now," Sandra told the group, fighting back tears. "She's missing."

"Oh, my God," said one of the other cashiers. She started to cry.

Freddy was shocked to hear the news, as were the rest of the employees. Brenda had been working there since she turned 16 and was very well-liked. He couldn't believe it.

"I guess the police think this has something to do with the other abductions that have been happening," Sandra added.

Freddy thought about Contraption Number 12. He didn't ask it to do anything to Brenda, a girl he really liked. Despite his new-found confidence, Freddy felt empty inside thinking about what happened to Brenda. He could see those beautiful hazel eyes, and he felt like wanted to break down and cry with the rest of the employees.

Freddy's walk home was slow, and he spent the time thinking more about Brenda, hoping she was alive. Things didn't sound good. The police now had three people missing, each one leaving a violent and bloody crime scene behind. He walked past the Gas N' Go, considering the window and the mindless video poker players. Each of the six machines had someone sitting in front of it. Freddy thought about the old man in the Cubs hat and wondered if he was the one behind it all. Was it possible that Contraption Number 12 was a mode of communicating with the video gamblers?

He continued walking the remaining two blocks to his small house on Walnut Street and was greeted with Jimmy, Stevie, and Robert, all swirling at his feet and purring to be fed. In his distracted state, Freddy walked right by the cats, not stopping to feed them. Each of the felines stared at their master in disbelief and then in concert at their empty food and water bowls.

8

It was just after midnight, and Freddy found himself in a very deep sleep. Even the three cats were sleeping soundly. Suddenly, the quiet of the night was broken by a loud banging noise. Within moments Freddy jumped out of bed, hearing the banging once again. He quickly realized that someone was pounding on his front door. Looking at the small clock next to his bed, Freddy couldn't imagine who could possibly be beating at the door at this late hour.

Shuffling toward the front door in his slippers, Freddy rubbed his eyes, trying to wake up. He stood about ten feet from the front door as the banging continued, this time with a heightened urgency.

NOTE TO THE READER:

The decision on how to proceed is in your hands! If you would like

for Freddy to answer the front door, go on and proceed with ending

#1. If you think he should grab a baseball bat from the closet and

hide amongst the boxes, then proceed with ending #2. Of course, if

you like, you can read both endings and decide for yourself which

one you like the best! Choose wisely!

ENDING #1

"Hang on, hang on!" Freddy cried out, tying his bathrobe

together to hide his bare belly and the fact he slept in his boxers.

"This better be good, waking me up like this."

Upon opening the door, Freddy was surprised to see two

uniformed police officers on his porch.

"Sorry to wake you, Mr. Frankfurt. We need to talk with

you. May we come in?" asked Sergeant Tom Johnson. He was a

40-year-old barrel-chested man with a military "high and tight" haircut. "We have a warrant." He held it up for Freddy to see.

Freddy's heart was thumping. "Yeah, come on in. Sorry about the mess."

Sergeant Johnson and Officer Benton walked in, looking around in awe at the sea of cardboard boxes stacked in every direction. Robert Benton was a young officer only two months from graduating the police academy.

"I'd ask you to sit down, but . . . " Freddy began, "there isn't really a good place. I don't have company over much."

"That's fine. This isn't a social call. We have some questions to ask you, sir. Do you know Johnny Kovacs?"

"Yeah, I went to school with him."

"Yes, I heard that," Sergeant Johnson said, looking through a small spiral notebook he kept in his pocket. "Did you have a run in with him at the Gas N' Go on Friday?"

Freddy began to get nervous. He wondered if this is when he should not say anything and get a lawyer. He thought that would make him look guilty. Plus, how the hell could they link him to anything? No one would ever believe Contraption Number 12 was involved.

"Yeah. He's always bothering me."

"That's what the clerk said. What about RJ Matthews? You know him, right?"

"Well, yeah. I work at Ray's Food Mart. Everyone in town knows him."

Sergeant Johnson stared at Freddy, while Officer Benton looked around in disbelief at all the boxes in the house. Jimmy yawned, sprawled out on one of the boxes only a few feet from the police officers, and stared at them before nodding back off.

"What about Brenda Willis? She works at Ray's too?"

"Yes, she does."

"Someone there said they saw you two leave the store on Monday together in her car."

Freddy cleared his throat. He could feel his palms getting sweaty and took a deep breath.

"She gave me a ride home. That's all."

The sergeant wrote something down in his notebook. "I see."

Just then two more police officers entered the house through the open front door.

"Sarge, you better come into the back yard."

The sergeant asked, "Why, what did you find?" He put his notebook back in his pocket.

"Three shallow graves. Looks like a body in each one. Barely a foot under the ground. The smell back there is awful. I think we should call County and have them send some cadaver dogs out here."

"I agree. I'm calling homicide and requesting they send some crime scene investigators to process this scene. The entire house and property is the scene in my book," said Sergeant Johnson, pulling out his radio. "The warrant Judge Fulks signed is solid."

Freddy was shocked!

"Bobby, put the cuffs on him. Read him his rights."

Freddy felt like he was in a dream as the officer put the hand cuffs on him. He read the Miranda Rights from a small card he kept in his wallet. It was just like he saw all the time on "Cops" - his favorite TV show. Now he was living the nightmare. Everything began to swirl around him, as the police were drilling him with questions, and he could hear people talking back and forth on the radio about bodies and lots of evidence in the back yard.

They led Freddy to one of the squad cars, his hands cuffed

behind his back. He saw Dewey standing on his porch in a pair of ripped jean shorts and flip flops. He held up a can of Natural Light, toasting his small, chubby neighbor, as he was being taken in for murdering three people and burying their bodies in his back yard.

In two years, Freddy was found guilty of first degree murder. Sam Tribbet, the old man in the Cubs hat, testified against Freddy for a life sentence. Freddy was now residing on death row at one of the state penitentiaries. His case was mired in appeals, and it would be many years before he would get his date with the executioner. Freddy swore his innocence to anyone who would listen, and often talked about his many contraptions, and how he was destined to be a millionaire one day.

ENDING #2

Freddy quietly opened the closet near his front door and grabbed the wooden baseball bat he kept on hand for protection. The banging on his front door became louder. Then he heard banging on the back door. Listening intently from behind some of the cardboard boxes, Freddy thought he heard some noise outside the house, like the mumbling of a crowd. He didn't know what was going on, but there were people outside his house, and they wanted him for some reason. Did this have anything to do with Contraption Number 12? Were they coming to steal it from him?

The banging became more intense on both the front and back door as Freddy instinctively crept further into the nooks and crannies of the boxes. Then he heard glass break in what he believed was the kitchen. He didn't know what to do. Then more noise came as the front door began to creak and then finally split down the middle as Freddy could see arms reaching inside, pulling the remainder of the door apart.

"Shit!" he whispered, clutching the handle of the bat tightly until his knuckles were ash white.

In that moment, the front door gave way as several people began to shuffle inside, their gaze fixed and glassy. As they entered the house, Freddy could see them in the porch light outside. He saw the middle-aged man with the milky eye. Then there was the older woman with her cane and big dentures, the same one that he saw playing the video poker machines. Several others were there with them, looking around and sniffing their air for what they had come for. Freddy knew they wanted him. Why, he wasn't sure. Yet he knew deep down inside, they were coming for him because of Contraption Number 12.

Freddy began to move quietly amongst the boxes, making his way toward his desk in the living room. The people moved through the pathways, searching for him. Then he heard more glass breaking, this time it was closer, as he could see arms reaching into the broken window in the living room, then more climbing inside. In the distance, Freddy also heard the back door breaking and more people entering the house from the mud room and kitchen. How many were there? Could he fend them off with his baseball bat alone? Were they coming for his contraption?

Then the video poker players moved down the path toward his desk. Freddy saw there were at least a dozen of them. He grabbed Contraption Number 12 with his left hand and grabbed the phone receiver with his right.

"I command you to stop! I am the master! You will stop right now!" Freddy screamed out as the things were grabbing at him, trying to pull the contraption from his hands. "I'm your master! I tell you what to do! I am in charge!" Freddy's voice was frantic and ravaged with panic.

Freddy dropped Contraption Number 12 to the floor with a loud thud as they grabbed at him, pulling on his limbs, tearing at his eyes, and forcing him to the floor. The mob growled like starving animals as they tore him to pieces, all while he clung to Contraption Number 12 with his pudgy dead hands.

Killing Machine

(first chapter of the novel, *Six*)

1

Benito Martinez leaned back in his chair with one foot up on the small wood security desk. He held a stained Illini mug, filled with the blackest coffee he could stomach, and a cigarette dangled from his lips. He was barely awake pulling all-night Christmas Eve duty. He drew the short straw this year, not only for getting the Christmas shift, but for some commotion that occurred at the start of his shift with one of the patients. A tiny excuse for a television, with a rabbit-ear antenna, was sitting on a nearby shelf, playing a marathon of sappy Christmas movies. His eyes were glazing over when the shrill ring of the desk phone nearly knocked him backwards and caused him to spill his coffee all over the desk. It was 11pm.

"Security desk. Martinez speaking," he said, putting his cigarette out in a heaped-over ashtray. He cringed at the sting of heartburn from the strong coffee and vending machine junk food. He reached for a roll of paper towels to clean up the mess, with the phone cradled on his shoulder and left ear.

"Martinez, this is Gilbert Anderson. I just got off the phone with Dr. Henson. He said patient Six is in bad shape. I hear he's burning up with a 102-degree fever and his pulse is weak. He said he didn't think the patient would make it until morning."

"That's what I heard sir. The Doc left about an hour ago. What do you need me to do?" There was a pause. Martinez could hear Gilbert breathing heavily. He didn't want to do anything. It scared him to death to even walk by that last cell.

"I've called Father O'Donnell. He'll give the last rites. I'll be in sometime tomorrow to check on things. If he passes in the night, just cover him with a sheet, and I'll deal with it when I come in. He's not going anywhere. I don't want anyone in the Bunker after the chaplain leaves," Gilbert said, quietly drinking bourbon on ice and chain smoking. The stress of the night was wearing thin. So many things were going through his mind right now. He debated against last rites, but with all things considered – it was the least he could do for the poor bastard. "Are we good then, Benito?"

"Yes, sir. We're good to go. Merry Christmas. We'll see you tomorrow." Martinez did find it odd they weren't going to try and save the patient. He only had two years until retirement, and he wasn't going to question a thing. He just needed to show up and collect a check for two more years, so he and the wife could move to San Antonio, where they both had a lot of family.

"Merry Christmas to you as well." Gilbert hung up the phone and rubbed his eyes hard with the heels of each hand. He could feel one hell of a headache coming on.

2

Thirty minutes later there was a knock on the door leading to

the Bunker. The Bunker was originally designed as a bomb shelter

in the late 1940's, when the country was worried about the Soviet

Union and imminent nuclear attack. After William Anderson was

hired as the Peoria State Hospital administrator in 1946, he ordered

the construction, but never did anything with the space. His son,

Gilbert, oversaw the hospital's nursing school and was the head of

security on the grounds. He found a use for the subterranean rooms

that were kept very secret - even from his own father. Only a select

handful of security guards had keys to the Bunker, and that was the

way Gilbert liked to keep it.

Martinez jumped up to answer the door and turned the

television down a bit.

"I thought you'd never get here, Father," he said, opening the

door for the elderly priest, who had served as the hospital's chaplain

for 22 years. The door opened in from one of the steam tunnels that ran beneath the ground of the 200-acre campus. The tunnels were dark and humid from the many steam leaks in the old galvanized pipes that delivered heat and hot water to the 66 buildings that made up the hospital. It was almost like walking through a sauna.

Father O'Donnell was out of breath and sweating. He was a small man, barely 5'8" with thinning gray hair. A lower back injury caused him to stoop over, and a stroke forced him to walk with a slight limp. He was wearing a simple brown hassock and black walking shoes. His glasses were slightly fogging over from the steam. "I got here as quickly as I could. Is he still alive?"

"As far as I know he is, but the Doc says he's not looking too good."

Father O'Donnell didn't respond for a moment, then said, "Take me to him." He had not been down in the Bunker for years. He recalled coming down there once in 1960, when Gilbert first started using the rooms. At that time, all six cells were occupied. That was before his stroke. Some of the chaplain's memory was compromised after that, and his right side had lost most of the strength he once had. He struggled to get from building to building at the hospital. Some days he spent 10 hours on his feet, and at 68 years old, he wasn't holding up well. He longed for the days when he coached boys' basketball and was full of vigor.

Martinez led the way down the dark and narrow hallway, past five empty cells. Father O'Donnell shuffled along, trying to keep up. The lighting was poor, with bare light bulbs that hung from the ceiling. Some bulbs were out, and some flickered, giving the hallway an extremely creepy feel. The cells looked just like jail cells, with metal bars and gaudy old locks. The bars were corroded from many years of exposure to the humid environment of the Bunker. The cells were sparse; each one contained a small metal bunk attached to the wall and a bucket each patient used for a toilet. The accommodations were stark. The walls were brick and mortar that were beginning to crumble from age, as they approached 30 years since construction. The humid conditions had accelerated the process. The floors were concrete and damp to the touch, and a faint odor of mold permeated the subterranean landscape. As the two men stood outside the sixth and final cell, Martinez paused before he put his key into the lock. The number six was stenciled to the metal header above the door like an Army footlocker. Father O'Donnell peered into the dim light to find the patient they called Six lying on his back in a fitful sleep. A foul smell emanated from the darkness -

a combination of excrement and rank body odor, from showering

only once a month.

Martinez opened the cell doors and then stepped back into

the recesses of the hallway, his black uniform making him almost

invisible. His hands shook slightly as he lit up a cigarette. "He's

been moaning for the past two days, but today his skin got real red,

and it looked like he was burning alive with fever. That's when I

called the Doc." He exhaled a cloud of smoke.

Father O'Donnell knew that the young man was in his early

twenties. They had a past. He found it odd that Gilbert wanted him

to conduct last rites, since he never knew the man to be religious in

any way. He also wondered why they didn't take him to one of the

two hospital buildings on the campus. The chaplain knew better

than to question it out loud. Gilbert obviously had his reasons.

The priest noted that the man was sweating profusely through

his uniform and onto the threadbare sheet beneath him. On a white

cloth at the foot of the bunk, the priest laid down his bible, a small

container of holy oil, and a large metal crucifix that his mother got

him as a gift for his First Communion. In his 45 years as a Catholic priest, he administered last rites more than one hundred times in a variety of denominations. Since becoming the chaplain, he performed several last rites a week, with more than 2,000 patients in his spiritual care. While he knew the last rites prepared the dying person for the afterlife, it was still a somber ritual.

"In the name of the Father, and of the Son, and of the Holy Spirit – Amen," said Father O'Donnell, as he made the sign of the cross. The old priest put one feeble hand on the young man's shoulder, and the other grasped the crucifix.

"You want me to lock the cell doors, Father?" asked Martinez, his large frame standing several feet away from the cell, in the shadows of the hallway.

Father O'Donnell looked toward him in the shadows. "No. This young man is dying. There's no need to lock the doors."

The patient was mumbling something under his breath. Sweat was beading up on his gaunt face, as the priest mopped his brow with a handkerchief. Father O'Donnell could feel the heat of the fever that had driven the patient to his death bed. He wondered why Martinez appeared so apprehensive and was standing several steps away from the cell doors, as if he was afraid to come closer.

"Are you scared, Benito?"

Martinez lit another cigarette. "A little bit, Father. I don't like being around this little bastard, especially when he's not locked in his cage. When I first started working down here a few years ago, he almost killed one of the guards." He exhaled a cloud of smoke, shaking his head.

"Really? I don't recall that."

"Yeah. The kid had only been on duty for a month and was here helping a doctor make rounds. That bastard lulled the kid into thinking it was safe to get close to the bars of his cell. When he did, Six grabbed both his arms and pulled him face-first into the bars. Damn near knocked him out! He broke his jaw and busted several teeth." Martinez took a pull from his cigarette, staring at Six while he writhed on his bunk.

"My God!" said Father O'Donnell, keeping his eyes on Six the whole time.

Martinez continued, "It was brutal. He nearly ate all the meat off that kid's face, while he held him tight against the bars. He even broke both his arms before letting him fall to the concrete. The screaming was unreal. The Doctor nearly passed out himself. I'll never forget that. So yeah, he scares me." His eyes remained glued on Six. He didn't trust him.

The priest shook his head at the graphic details. "Why don't you go back to your office, and I'll let you know when I'm done. This shouldn't take long. He's not even conscious. I'll be fine."

"You sure, Father?"

"Yes, I'm sure. Thank you."

As the priest turned toward the young patient, he could hear the guard's shoes echo on the concrete floor of the hallway that led back to his security office. The young man had chiseled features and a military-style buzz haircut. Scars were evident all over his head through the stubble. He had led a tough life. His baggy patient uniform reeked of body odor and was stuck to his feverish body.

"Robert. Can you hear me?" Only the faint sound of Christmas music could be heard down the hallway from the security office. Six's lips were moving, but he still appeared to be unconscious. Father O'Donnell knew the man's real name, though not many at the hospital did. He knew him long before his stay in the Bunker. He also knew his mother.

"If you can hear me, Robert, do you wish to make a confession? A final act of contrition, my son?" The elderly priest looked intently at the young man for some sign of acknowledgement before he proceeded with the last rites. Six's eyes remained closed, his breathing labored. The fever was consuming him.

The priest turned to pick up his Bible and continued, "I believe in God, the Father Almighty, creator of Heaven and Earth."

As he turned around, Father O'Donnell was shocked to see Six no longer lying down next to him. The bunk was empty! His heart began to thump loudly in his chest beneath the brown hassock he wore. He looked under the bunk. He saw nothing in the gloom.

"You've got a lot of fucking nerve asking me to confess my sins, Father!" His voice was ice cold and steeping with vengeance. His face was contorted into a snarling fury.

Father O'Donnell turned around as a lump settled in his throat. He knew that voice. Before he could cry out, the young man was upon him, shoving him down to the damp concrete floor in the middle of the cell. He could smell the stench of human feces and urine in the wooden slop bucket as Six kicked him across the floor toward the back wall. The crucifix fell from his grasp and clanged on the concrete. In one fluid motion, Six picked it up and landed on

top of the priest, who was on his back and panicking at the situation.

"I trusted you! You took advantage of a scared kid!" Six

uttered through clenched teeth. His eyes were alive with anger.

With incredible power, Six forced the priest's mouth open

and grabbed for his tongue. The clergyman desperately tried to

resist and instinctively bit down on his attacker, but within seconds,

Six forced the metal crucifix into his mouth, and hacked off his

tongue with a crude cutting motion. The metallic taste of blood

filled Father O'Donnell's mouth as only muted grunts could be

heard. The priest felt intense pain and a burning sensation, while

blood poured down his hassock and onto the concrete floor of the

cell. He felt like he might choke on what was left of his tongue, as

frothing blood filled his mouth. His eyes were open wide in terror!

Six laughed, tossing the tongue to the floor. "Cat got your

tongue, Father?" He paced the cell like a wild animal, sizing up his

next meal.

The priest was on his knees, as the cell began to spin around

him. He tried to speak, but nothing came out – only a garbled mess of grunts and cries. The pain was unbearable! *My God, please help me! Please save me!*

"God isn't going to save you tonight, Father. God isn't anywhere near this fucking hell hole," said Six, while the priest was in disbelief that he had read his mind.

Six pulled the hassock from the old man, leaving him cowering on the floor in a white t-shirt and boxer shorts. Then he reached down and grabbed the priest's left hand and slammed it with tremendous force to the floor, shattering his wrist in several places. It was the hand he wore his prized 1950 Illinois State high school basketball championship ring on. He coached a boys' team from Peoria to the March Madness games in Quincy and won it all, beating a tough Catholic high school in the final game. He was known throughout the hospital for always wearing that ring. It was a large gold ring with a bright red stone. Despite his vow of poverty, the Peoria Diocese allowed him to wear it.

Now Father O'Donnell was fighting for his life with everything he had, as searing pain radiated from his broken wrist and up his arm. Years of captivity in his cell gave Robert lots of time to do push-ups, sit-ups and other strength exercises – in hopes that one day he would be given the chance to escape. It seemed almost too easy to convince the guard and doctor he was dying. He had learned how to slow his body down and control even his temperature in the countless days and nights he was captive. Six knew his mind was an incredible weapon and had a genius-level IQ. With the malnutrition he endured, he was often sickly and had a fever. So it wasn't hard to pull it off at all. Now he had the old man face down, his left arm stretched out on the floor and twitching under his force. He used the same metal crucifix to hack into the flesh of the priest's forearm, just below the elbow. He screamed out, but it was barely audible without his tongue and with a mouthful of blood. A mist of blood spattered on the brick walls and across the cell to his bunk, as Six held the priest down and continued to cut into muscle, bone, and cartilage - tugging with ferocity at the forearm of Father O'Donnell. Bone crunched and splintered while blood poured, as he tore the remnants of flesh holding the two pieces of his arm together. The priest was mercifully slipping into shock.

Six was clearly in a frenzy of blood lust as he stood up, and the priest was on the verge of passing out. The bloody stump of his left arm was quivering in unimaginable agony.

"You're a miserable piece of shit! How many others did you rape?" Six's eyes were intense, staring down at the priest as he rolled on the floor, silently begging for his life. He was a blubbering mess – tears streaming down his face and blood still pouring from his mouth. "Now I'm in control! I hope you rot in hell, you bastard!"

Six unleashed the pain that had been bottled up inside him for eight years. All the misery and hatred that boiled for what felt like an eternity now erupted in a display of incredible and sadistic violence.

"Robert died in 1959. No one calls me that any more. There's a headstone at the cemetery with that name on it. You motherfuckers killed the old me and created a monster. A fucking monster! You bastards did this to me!" He glistened with sweat, and his chest heaved. He felt alive for the first time since his captivity. "You're supposed to help people, not allow what they did to me!"

Six proceeded to kick and stab Father O'Donnell with the crucifix, as the chaplain barely held on to life. By the time he was done, the dead priest was naked in the corner of his cell, the metal crucifix sticking out of the middle of his chest. Father O'Donnell's lifeless body was covered in deep gashes and stab wounds. Steam

rose from a dark red pool of blood on the concrete floor, and Six was

gone. Only his name remained on the back wall of the cell, written

in the blood of the priest that he claimed as his first victim the night

his rampage began. The killing machine was unleashed.

Thirteen Nuns

(part 1, first chapter of the novel, *The Dreadful Lives of Enoch*

Strange)

March 1927

1

Sister Mary Concordia was running as fast as she could. The
March night was cool, and a blood moon was high, providing an
eerie red filter over the path that led deeper into the woods

surrounding St. Michael's Academy. The young sister knew she wasn't supposed to be outside the convent at this hour as a novitiate in only her second year. The punishment for such a violation would have resulted in hours of punitive chores, 24 hours of fasting, and at least 30 days of confinement to her room, other than to attend daily mass and use the bathroom. A second offense would mean expulsion from the order and going back to her prior life as Emily Randuski in Palatine, Illinois. Still she ran, her chest barely rising more than at rest.

Her mind wandered as she ran, thinking about how Mother Mistress would be furious to know the convent's cat, Boris, had run away again. After a year being well-cloistered from society, Sister Mary Concordia was finally enjoying socializing with others in the church. The older nuns at the convent had begun to accept her, teaching her their secrets, and Mother Mistress let her take care of Boris, which she enjoyed a great deal. Mother Mistress made it known how much she and the other nuns loved the orange and white tomcat and the inherited responsibility that came with caring for him. Her eyes darted back and forth, hoping to find Boris and get him back inside before anyone noticed his jail break. She slowed down to a stop for moment, listening.

"Boris, Boris!" she whispered, fearing discovery. "Where are you? Boris!"

Only the night sounds in the enveloping darkness replied. There was no sign of Boris. The usual choir of crickets, nocturnal creatures that stirred in the brush, and the call of a distant owl were the only noises the young woman heard. Her mind was focused on the idea that Mother Mistress was likely to come check to see if she was in her room. She felt a chill from a stiff breeze coming from the west, and the leaves flapped above her while she shuddered at the thought.

"Boris!" she called out again. There was no reply from the feisty tomcat.

She decided to go a little further into the woods before turning back. Approaching the crest of a small hill, Sister Mary Concordia heard something she couldn't make out. It sounded like a low rumble. Holding her breath, she strained to hear what now sounded like voices. It seemed like a gathering of people, very low and distant – deeper in the blackness of the forest. Staring up at the blood moon, Sister Mary Concordia questioned whether she should continue. She heard the nuns talking this week about the rare blood moon that would appear on this night, but they acted like they didn't want her to hear what they were saying about it. There were many times when she felt like some of the sisters were guarded about what she was able to hear, so Sister Mary Concordia didn't give it much thought. She had never seen a blood moon before. Staring up at a crimson full moon, it almost seemed unreal.

She feared being discovered, knowing the punishment would be severe. With one more year of study as a novitiate, Sister Mary Concordia would begin five years of work in the convent before taking her final vows. She didn't know if an offense such as this would cause her to be removed from St. Michael's, but the curiosity of the source of the voices in the darkness drew her in. She stopped thinking about Boris and stepped quickly, yet gingerly, down the path toward the unknown. The young novitiate knew if she thought about it for a moment more, she would run back to St. Michael's.

The voices got progressively louder as she moved closer. The timber became almost opaque, and the brush was like a wall of impenetrable thorn and thicket. There was now a glow in the distance from what appeared to be a campfire. The voices were clearer to her, yet still low in tone and measured in timbre. One voice was more prominent than the rest, and as Sister Mary Concordia continued ahead, she could make out the other voices in unison answering the apparent leader. To her, it sounded like a religious ceremony, such as a Catholic mass. She still was not able to make out the words, but as she got closer, she decided to take cover off the main path to avoid discovery. Although she had no idea what was going on one hundred yards in the valley below, her gut reaction was dread. Still, she continued forward, the runaway cat still removed from her thoughts. The blood moon was casting an ominous red blanket across the valley in every direction, like paint poured from a giant bucket.

A few minutes later, Sister Mary Concordia found herself quivering with fear behind a dense cluster of bushes, only twenty feet from the gathering. There was a fire pit and an altar of dark stone, with a man standing behind it. He was dressed in little more than an animal skin that obscured his head and upper body, and he spoke with the command of a seasoned preacher at the pulpit. There was a small congregation of men and women kneeling before him, and they were naked in the crisp evening air. She didn't know what to make of this strange perversion. On the altar was a crucifix, yet it was upside down, and the man in the animal skin was drinking from what looked like a human skull. Then he continued to speak to them in Latin.

"In nomine magni dei nostril Satanas! Introibo ad altare Domini Inferi!" he cried out as the congregation before him repeated the infernal words. She didn't know exactly what he was saying, but she had sat through enough Catholic mass to pick out some words.

Suddenly, a woman in a black robe stepped from the shadows and walked to the altar, carrying something in her arms wrapped in a blanket. Sister Mary Concordia was mesmerized at what she was seeing. The naked men and women then began to fornicate as a group, intertwining themselves in carnal lust, of the likes she had never witnessed before. At only 22 years old, the young novitiate had never seen the naked body of a man, let alone the mass of indecency now only a breath away. Being found out by these evil people was a terrifying thought. She was afraid to run back to the path, knowing they would hear her. The noise of breaking twigs and branches underfoot would surely give her away. All she could do was hide behind the bushes.

Now the woman in the black robe was at the altar and laid down whatever was in the blanket upon it. The man in the animal skin dipped his hand into the skull he was drinking from, his fingers stained with a dark red substance. Sister Mary Concordia assumed it to be blood, as the woman opened up the blanket to reveal a naked infant boy squirming in the cool midnight air! The baby was crying, his arms and legs flailing, as the man rubbed the blood on his forehead, saying something she couldn't make out. He reached down behind the altar, then abruptly stood up, his congregation in the midst of their orgy before him, and held up a 10-inch knife. The blade gleamed in the moonlight. Sister Mary Concordia gasped as the man brought the knife down upon the infant's chest, the woman in the robe holding him down as his little voice screamed out in pain. His tiny body convulsed in agony! His screams shrill.

Things began to play out in slow motion to Sister Mary Concordia. The bright-red blood that flowed from the infant was dripping from the stone altar as the man held him up to the sky, speaking once again in Latin. Blood poured down his arms and dripped from his heaving chest. His breath was a frosty mist in the chilled night air. The woman let her black robe fall and pulled the animal skin from his body, and the two locked in a bloody embrace of horrific evil, sharing a deep kiss, rubbing the warm blood onto each other's skin. The young nun-to-be was in utter disbelief at what she had witnessed, the cries of the congregation escalating, and the two at the altar now joining in the fornication. They appeared older than the rest. He bent her over the dark stone, knocking the inverted crucifix over; her writhing body cried out, rubbing the sacrificial blood on herself as the disturbing act continued.

Sister Mary Concordia was speechless, the actions in slow motion before her, and the cries were distant and muffled, as though coming through a cup and string. She could hear the screams of the baby over and over again as she crouched in the darkness praying she would not be found out. Yet as the older man and woman continued their desecration of life, joined in an unholy union, she made eye contact with both of them. To her utter horror, they were both faces she recognized! In that moment, all she had been working toward since entering the sisterhood, and everything she held dear with her God, came crashing down like a high-rise building being demolished.   The man was none other than the

Abbott of St. Michael's Academy – Father Reilly! She would know

that face anywhere, even in the light of the blood moon, in mid-

fornication at the altar of evil. It was terrible enough he was

participating in this abomination, but the woman's identity shook her

to the very core of her being. Sister Mary Concordia questioned her

faith for the first time in her life as she gazed at the gasping

countenance of the Mother Mistress! She had been the young girl's

inspiration and rock through her training, and seeing her through this

perverse lens was too much to bear. Sister Mary Concordia's

bedrock was crumbling.

Without hesitation, she ran away. She fled from the

disgusting ritual toward St. Michael's. It felt surreal, like she was

running in a nightmare, as if she was moving in place – unable to

escape. Sister Mary Concordia didn't know if the Abbott or Mother

Mistress had seen her, but she did make eye contact and couldn't be

sure. As she ran faster, the visions she had just seen were already

haunting her, and she could only hope her presence was undetected.

When she finally got back into her room and to bed, she

closed her eyes tightly in a futile attempt to wish away what she had just seen, but the images of the blood orgy were engraved into her mind, and the cries of that innocent baby reverberated in the stillness of the night.

2

In a private dining room on the third floor of the monastery at St. Michael's Academy was a feast fit for kings. The four priests that sat at the table were not royalty, but the monks waiting on them would have a much different opinion on the matter. The way the four conducted themselves, looking down at the monks who served them, was appalling. A simple, yet magnificent oak table with six ornately carved chairs sat in the middle of the Abbot's private dining room. Before being seated at the table, the four had enjoyed drinks and Cuban cigars in the Abbot's office and spent the past hour talking about the events of the night before. To listen to the four of them, one would have assumed they were fraternity brothers from collegiate days gone by, instead of men of the cloth, who met each other years before in seminary school. These men were not the usual clergy – far from it.

Father Patrick Reilly sat at the head of the table, as he was the Abbot of the institution and had been for the past ten years. He was a fit man in his early 60's with a military-style buzz haircut, chiseled jaw and piercing blue eyes. The Abbot was pleasant enough to those who barely knew him, but to those who worked at St. Michael's, he was despised for his brash demeanor and elitist attitude. It didn't take long to pick up on that quality in him. He was hardly what most would have assumed a priest to be like. He spent his early years growing up in Albany, New York before his calling to enter the priesthood. It was years later, as an instructor at a seminary outside of Richmond, Virginia, where he met the other three priests that he chose to dine with on this Saturday afternoon in March of 1927.

To the Abbot's right was Father Cordero Rosa, who made the trip to McHenry, Illinois by train two days before, from his congregation at Holy Trinity Catholic Church in Cottonwood, Arizona. It was a four-day trip by rail, yet he didn't question the Abbot when he was asked to come to St. Michael's. To the Abbot's left was Father Roger Wilkes, who also had a long train ride to northern Illinois from St. Luke's Catholic Church in Hartford,

Connecticut. He was looking forward to catching up with the Abbot, as well as the other priests he kept in touch with since they were young priests-to-be at the seminary. Lastly, at the opposite end of the table from the Abbot, was Father Frank Bartolini. He arrived to St. Michael's by car the day before, since he had the shortest trip of the priests, from his Epiphany Catholic Church in Des Moines, Iowa. All three of the priests were roughly 20 years younger than the Abbot, and they looked up to him as a father figure. In some ways, they even regarded him more dearly than that.

There was a knock at the door.

"Come in," said the Abbot sharply, straightening up in his chair, and adjusting his red habit. He wore it for special occasions such as this.

"Lunch is ready, Abbot," said Brother Francis, the head chef at St. Michael's. His job entailed keeping a sensible menu designed for the high school students who attended the prestigious academy and the staff as well. Yet for the Abbot and his inner circle, the monk was tasked to provide some of the most extravagant meals he could conjure. In the ten years the Abbot had been in charge, Brother Francis showed off the culinary skills he learned as an apprentice for a French chef while living in Europe. He didn't like

the Abbot much, but in his subservient role in life, the monk never

said a word. He could recall a few rare times when the Abbot

disliked a dish he prepared, and he would be punished for it. One

time in particular, the monk had diarrhea for two weeks after the

Abbot had the monk's food poisoned. The Abbot was known for

exacting harsh punishment and for extremely narcissistic behavior.

Very few of the staff knew about the culinary decadence that went

on in the Abbot's private dining room.

"OK, Brother Francis, then bring it in," the Abbot replied.

The other priests could smell the incredible aromas entering the

room as two monks assisted the chef in bringing in the delectable

spread. The monks worked silently and quickly, wanting to leave

the room as soon as possible. They were afraid to be in the same

room as the Abbot.

The Abbot insisted his guests try some of the monastery's

homemade elderberry wine with their lunch, as well as a very

expensive sherry that he kept in a private stash. Despite the rest of

the country having to abide by Prohibition, the Abbot acted as if it

didn't exist. As the four men sipped their wine and sherry, the table was soon filled with an incredible array of fine foods the other three rarely saw. Since the monks and priests often hunted on the grounds, there was plenty of game to eat. They enjoyed a venison consommé Celestine soup, followed by succulent roast duck over baked rice Milanese, and haricots verts in a rich garlic and butter sauce. There was also fresh-baked french bread and homemade butter and honey. Freshly made pecan pie and apple cobbler, the Abbot's favorite, were kept warm on a small nearby serving table with two large carafes of black coffee. It took the monks nearly fifteen minutes to get everything situated.

"That will be all, Brother Francis. Let the Prior know we do not wish to be disturbed for the remainder of the afternoon. Now go!"

The chef nodded to the Abbot and said something quietly to the monks assisting him before quietly closing the door behind them. The Abbot rose and walked to the door, locking it securely before returning to his seat to begin eating his lunch.

3

The Abbot enjoyed his apple cobbler and black coffee, then looked around the table at his guests.

"I want to thank you all for coming on relatively short notice, but this is important."

Father Bartolini also sipped at his coffee, but he had passed on dessert after eating such a large lunch. "Of course, Abbot. None of us would have missed this. The blood moon is such a rare occurrence, and we hold it in such high regard."

"Yes, that's true. Last night was one of the most wonderful masses I've ever attended since our days in Richmond," Father Rosa added. "I have read that many Christians believe the blood moon has a foreboding quality, a prelude of bad things to follow. You know, the superstitious types." He laughed.

"I thought you would all enjoy that. The sisters from the convent haven't seen much male companionship lately," the Abbot said, smirking from behind his coffee mug, "but from the sound of it, you all gave them something to remember for a long time."

The four priests laughed out loud at his reference to the black mass they all attended the night before. Father Wilkes was correct in the power of the blood moon when it came to occultists like the four men seated around the table. The Abbot had picked the date years ago, long before any of them had any idea of what his plan was.

Father Wilkes said, "If I may say so, Abbot, you looked like you also gave the Mother Mistress a good time across the altar."

"Yes, indeed I did," the Abbot replied, his smirk widening. "She gets horny when the moon is full, and so do I." He laughed aloud, gazing out the window, as if imagining them engaged in the act the night before, savoring every bloody kiss and decadent stroke.

"The ritual last night and the infant sacrifice was necessary for what we are about to embark on," the Abbot continued, "and the true reason I asked you all to come here to St. Michael's will now reveal itself."

Father Bartolini had wondered where the infant came from, but was too afraid to ask the Abbot.

As if on cue, the Abbot said, "The sisters brought that infant from the church. It was found two weeks ago in the vestibule of the convent. No one knows who left the boy, but he was wrapped in blankets and left for the sisters to find. It was like an omen from Lord Satan himself." He smirked at Father Bartolini with a sort of infernal amusement. The priest felt a pit in the bottom of his stomach that nearly forced him to vomit at his seat. As quickly as the feeling came over him, it fled in fear.

The three priests sat in uncomfortable silence as the Abbot explained his true motive for the visit. The only noise that could be heard in the third-floor private dining room, aside from the Abbot's voice, was the wind and rain against the large picture window that faced the east.

"I need each of you to find three nuns from your region of the country, who we can use to participate in a special tour of hospitals, infirmaries, and asylums, to cheer up those less fortunate for Christmas," the Abbot said as they squirmed amidst the tension. He knew they would be confused. He also knew that staring at them like he was would ratchet up the fear. Despite their many years removed from the seminary, the teacher-student roles were difficult to absolve. Though their continued friendship over the years, the younger three respected and revered the dark and mysterious Abbot.

"Surely you didn't ask us to come all the way here for this, Abbot. I'm sure you could do such a thing with the fine nuns here at St. Michael's," said Father Rosa, "or certainly with the large pool of sisters from the many churches in Chicago." He forced a smile, wondering if he was going to be reprimanded for speaking out of line.

The wind continued to howl outside as the sun hid behind the clouds and made the grounds outside darker than before. The temperature in the dining room dropped several degrees as well. Father Rosa noticed, as did the Abbot.

"The nuns I need for this mission are not just any nuns. I need nuns who have experienced pure evil in the world. I need nuns who have come face-to-face with the worst of the worst." He leaned back slightly in his chair, noting the curiosity in each of their faces. The Abbot could see their wheels spinning voraciously before him. It was for their incredible intellect and devotion to the cause that the three priests were picked many years before to assist him with this most precious mission.

The Abbot continued, "I've been working on this project almost my entire life, gentlemen. I have spent countless hours studying and translating texts from various languages around the world, but in secret, for fear that someone would know what I was working on. I have been reading in the shadows and compiling an incredible amount of data. I even kept it from all of you. I hope you know I did it because it was just too important to trust anyone. Even all of you, my closest friends."

Father Wilkes finished the last of his sherry and poured himself another. His hand shook slightly. The Abbot noticed. It was his nature to notice such things. In the warehouse section of his memory, the Abbot kept every morsel of data collected, knowing it would likely become of use to him at some point down the road. He was almost always right.

"I believe that I have discovered a dark secret from the very manuscript of one of the earliest Satanists of the modern age. I bet none of you have even heard of Wilfred Weeks from England. He was a prominent doctor in London in the early 1600's. He was able to cure people of illnesses that no other doctor could. Many said he had made a pact with the Devil in order to marvel London with his medical capabilities. They weren't too far off, actually. Dr. Weeks was a Satanist and held some of the earliest black masses ever documented," said the Abbot, looking around the table at the other priests. They were amazed at what they were hearing. "Even Aleister Crowley was said to have been enamored with Weeks, but he was never able to read what I have read."

The Abbot went on, "He was working on something that no one else knew about. He believed that through a very precise satanic ritual, with lots of moving parts that involved magic he was still discovering, he could cause Satan himself to manifest in human form. Much like God claims to have done in the body of Jesus."

Father Bartolini continued to sip at his coffee. He was staring at the Abbot, focusing on every word he was saying, "Please continue, Abbot." He was still in shock from the odd mannerisms surrounding the Abbot reading his mind. There was no telling what dark secrets and magic the elder priest had mastered during his endless hours of study. His mastery of four languages, including Latin, and his encyclopedic knowledge of nearly any subject of conversation, put everyone else in the room several notches below his abilities. The Abbot knew this and was always the alpha male of the pack.

"A young woman stumbled on Dr. Wilfred Weeks' papers one morning, after he was found in bed ill. She was part of his cleaning staff and removed some documents that detailed his denouncement of God and celebration of Satan. She turned him in to a very politically influential Catholic priest in London, Father Portis Larimer, who had the good doctor arrested by police. Most of the papers were burned to ash, and he was hung by the neck in a public execution, for crimes against the church, only five days later. Only the documents I came across survived, and he hid them well. Dozens of searches of his house were conducted, but the secret documents remained safe. The rest I had to piece together myself, which was incredibly difficult."

"Amazing that you found them," said Father Rosa. "How did you secure such rare documents?"

"Don't ask questions you're not prepared to hear the answer to, Father Rosa." The Abbot was cold in his reply, yet his eyes burned holes right through the priest. Father Rosa's mind was immediately filled with dread as those icy blue eyes dug into the depths of his soul.

Father Rosa shifted uncomfortably in his chair. The other two priests looked down to avoid eye contact.

The Abbot continued, "This ritual would be a way to bring Satan himself into human form to walk the Earth and wreak havoc upon God's children. Only those of us who have accepted his infernal majesty would be immune from his wrath. We would live on Earth for eternity at his side, while the human race would be at our mercy. We would experience pleasures beyond our own imaginations – forever."

The three priests stared into the Abbot's piercing blue eyes, unable to speak or move.

"Each of us must come up with three nuns who have experienced true evil. Each of them will make up this procession of twelve, in a direct perversion of Christ's twelve apostles. It will be the residual evil that each of these nuns possesses which will combine to summon Satan himself into human form. They will be sacrificed as Wilfred Weeks' manuscript explains, in every painstaking detail, and we will have our own dark salvation, my brothers!" the Abbot said in a low whisper, as if to avoid anyone outside the private dining room from hearing what he was saying.

The Abbot was nearly short of breath at the excitement of being able to finally explain his life's work. Just hearing his own voice recount the happenings at hand was enough to get his blood to boil with anticipation.

"The sacrificial blood that was spilled last night will give each of us the drive to find these nuns. With the incredible magic of the blood moon, coupled with that spilling of sacred blood, our bodies will soar, and our search will be swift. Search every church in your region of the country. Find three nuns who have had traumatic experiences with the sinners of the world, and together we will have our twelve. We will send them on this pilgrimage, and they will end their tour at a location I have chosen, where the sacrifice will be done." The Abbot stared into every fiber of their collective being as he looked around the table. He knew these men had strong convictions from their time at the seminary, where he introduced them to Satanism. He knew even back then, this day would come, and he would need their help. Now was that time, and he could see each of them, in their own way, preparing themselves to fulfill his grand plan. The Abbot seemed pleased that his hard work had paid off.

"You each have nine months to get me three nuns. On the first Saturday in October, we will meet here again. You will bring those three nuns here with you. We will keep them in the convent, under lock and key, until their tour starts in Chicago. They will make their way down the state to an asylum outside of Peoria, in Bartonville," he continued, "where the last stop will take place. It is there they will die. It is there that Satan will walk the Earth."

Silence came over the room once again. Oddly, the wind and rain no longer made any sound outside against the window. It was as if a giant fishbowl had been placed over the four men who sat at the large oak table, plotting to bring Hell itself upon the Earth.

4

The Abbot sat in his office after the other priests had gone to bed in the guest quarters he provided them for the duration of their stay. They would all be leaving St. Michael's in the morning, to go back to their parishes, and to begin searching for the nuns. He had no doubt they would be successful. The Abbot had already done his own exhaustive search prior to the meeting and found three nuns who would be perfect for the job at hand.

There was one other person he needed to make the tour successful. The Abbot knew that most of the nuns were elderly and would need assistance. He needed someone who could handle the luggage, tend to the train tickets, and keep them together. The Abbot also knew this person would be killed along with the twelve nuns as part of the ancient rite from the secret manuscript of Wilfred Weeks. It was a sacrifice he had to be willing to make in order to see this plan come to fruition before he became too old. He was in his 60's now, and his fear was that if he waited much longer, he might die himself before seeing his life's work through to the end. The Abbot knew now was the time to strike, and nothing would get in his way.

Suddenly, there was a knock at the door.

"Yes, come in," he said from behind his large desk. He was still in the red habit from earlier in the day. It was dark outside now. He had the beloved Boris on his lap, purring loudly as he stroked his dense, orange fur.

Sister Mary Concordia opened the door gingerly. She was obviously afraid, as most were when summoned to the Abbot's office, especially late at night. Many heard stories of improper advances on the younger women. She didn't want to believe such things, but after what she had seen the night before, Sister Mary Concordia was repulsed to be in his presence. She could only see him in the strange costume, arms soaked in blood, driving the long knife into the trembling infant. She asked one of the other sisters to go along with her, but Mother Mistress insisted she go alone to see the Abbot. The Mother Mistress did not let on that she knew what the meeting was about, nor did she give Sister Mary Concordia any indication that she had seen her the night before under the blood moon, while she was being taken upon the stone altar.

The Abbot smiled at the attractive novitiate. "Please sit, Sister."

She immediately noticed Boris purring on his lap. Her heart was rising into her throat as she did her best to control emotions. She had thought Boris was gone for good. She hadn't seen him since he had run outside the night before, when she was throwing garbage away. Now he was purring on the Abbot's lap and she felt sure the priest was doing it for a reason. He had to know she had been there last night.

She felt a chill in his gaze. It was impossible for her not to think about him naked, thrusting himself into the Mother Mistress, their bodies entwined in the sacrificial blood. She was horrified to think that he had seen her in the woods, shaking from behind the bush on the other side of the congregation.

The Abbot set Boris down and stood up, then walked in front of the desk, leaning against it. He put his hand on her shoulder and felt her recoil at his touch.

"Are you afraid, Sister?" His jaw was clenched tight, the grinding of teeth was audible. The Abbot slowed his breath purposefully.

Sister Mary Concordia didn't reply. She was petrified. The Abbot moved off the desk and stood directly next to her, his hand still resting upon her frail shoulder. She felt nauseas, like she could throw up at any moment. Boris was sleeping with his back against one of the many bookcases in the Abbot's office. He was content here, yet she wanted to scream out at the top of her lungs.

The Abbot moved even closer to the young novitiate, his habit brushing up against her left arm. She was disgusted that she could feel that he was obviously erect underneath his red habit and was rubbing himself up against her! She abruptly stood up and moved toward the door, crying.

"Please don't hurt me, Abbot." She was sobbing.

"I suggest you sit down, Sister Mary Concordia. I suggest you sit down right now!" the Abbot said forcefully. He was enraged that she had rejected his subtle advances. None of the novitiates he had ever summoned to his office late at night had done so, and even at his advancing age, the Abbot's libido was alive and well. His hubris was bottomless.

He went back to his chair and sat down, and the sister did too. She was still crying, but she was doing her best to keep it under control. Boris climbed back up in the Abbot's lap. He used his left hand to cradle the tomcat's head as he rubbed his neck. It made Sister Mary Concordia very uncomfortable to see him hold Boris that way. It looked uncomfortable for the cat, and she couldn't take her eyes off the Abbot's hands.

"I called you here to tell you about a special calling I have for you. There will be a Christmas tour of nuns going to hospitals and nursing homes later this year. I'd like you to go with them, Sister. They are elderly and will need assistance. You would be perfect, and what a grand experience for you!" The Abbot smiled, barely.

Sister Mary Concordia continued to watch his hands. His right hand was still stroking the cat's neck, yet she wondered why he was waiting to discuss what happened last night. When Mother Mistress said the Abbot wanted to see her, the sister was sure she had been discovered out after curfew. In addition, there was her presence at the Satanic mass. She figured someone had seen her and turned her in to Mother Mistress.

The Abbot did his best not to raise his voice again, but the fact that she kept her head down began to upset him once again. His left hand began to apply pressure to the top of the cat's head, and Boris squirmed under the strain. The Abbot also tightened his hold on Boris' neck, and together, his hands formed a vice.

"So, what do you think? Mother Mistress raves about you, and the two of us think this will be a wonderful experience, Sister," he said. She was staring at his hands in horror, as she could see his grip tightening on Boris. His eyes were bulging with fear, but somehow the Abbot kept the cat still as he continued to squeeze even tighter. She thought she heard the bending of bone to the point of breaking.

She looked up at the Abbot, tears welling up in her eyes. She knew he was killing dear Boris, but she realized there was nothing she could do. Still, the flexing of bone was breaking the silence.

"Yes, Abbot. Thank you for the opportunity." His eyes stared deeply into hers. She could hear the strain on the cat's skull as the grip tightened – now bone was breaking.

The Abbot remained seated, despite his desire to reach out to the pretty, yet plain young novitiate. She looked down as blood began to stream from the cat's eyes, nose, and mouth. It quivered slightly and died in the Abbot's grasp. He let Boris fall to the floor like a swatted fly. She began to sob again. The lifeless body of Boris was bleeding on the original hardwood floor of the office.

He continued to stare at the young woman, then stood. "Very good. Mother Mistress will fill you in on the details as we get closer. That is all."

"Thank you, Abbot," she said, standing up and making eye contact briefly as she wept.

The Abbot stared at the door. He had seen the young woman in the woods the night before. He knew she saw the entire thing, and he was not about to take any chances with her talking to others. Starting immediately, she would be cloistered away in her room for private study. He couldn't have her talking with the rest of the staff, and especially any visitors. Sister Mary Concordia would be the thirteenth nun and accompany the rest on their death march to Bartonville in December. He laughed and poured himself one last glass of bourbon with an ice cube, before turning in himself. The Abbot wanted to get a good night sleep so he could deliver Sunday mass for his congregation the following day.

Chainsaw House Party

(part 2, chapter 1 of the novel, The Dreadful Lives of Enoch Strange)

Summer 1985 - Wichita, Kansas

1

Philip Edwards was trying to keep his composure. It seemed lately his temper would flare up at the most inopportune times. This was one of those days. It was Friday night, and he had a long week at the office. It was simply miserable dealing with incompetent coworkers to get the major sales report done for his boss, Andrew.

Philip spent several late nights working in his glorified jail cell, also

known as a cubicle. Death by cubicle was more like it. While other

employees seemed to ingratiate and accept the padded room without

a ceiling - Philip did not. The rest of his department adorned their

cubicles with pictures of their kids and grandkids, banners from their

favorite sports teams, or pictures of vacations in warm places so they

had some solace on those dreary winter days. Philip did none of

that. The only thing he had hanging up was one family picture with

his wife and two kids and a simple sign he bought one day at a yard

sale that read "TGIF". Philip loved Friday because it meant he

would have two days away from Andrew and his cubicle and time to

spend with his family. He loved them beyond compare. So Friday

was a day filled with anticipation of good things to come.

No one else in the department worked past 5:00 pm, but

Philip did, and he hoped that Andrew would realize how hard he was

working and give him the promotion. The report was very important

to a large corporate meeting where Andrew had to address the board

of directors to help explain why sales were lagging. Low sales

numbers put everyone on edge, especially Andrew who was

constantly catching heat from above. Praise was dealt infrequently and seemed to wane quickly, while the negative kind came up often, and when it did, it lingered. Philip knew he had been overlooked for far too long, and he refused to let this promotion slip by. He would simply will it to happen, or so he thought. Philip knew the promotion would come with headaches, but he was willing to deal with that for a lot more money and a ticket out of the cubicle into a real office. In his own office, Philip could shut the door and keep everyone else's germs to themselves. The cubicle offered none of that, and every cough and sneeze seemed to be amplified. Philip often reached for his hand sanitizer and vitamin C drops to combat the sickness all around him. He did his best to hide his fixation with germs, but you didn't have to work around Philip long to know, that he was bat shit crazy about being clean, orderly, and following procedures at all times.

He was trying not to lose his temper now in the line at the pharmacy, picking up some medicated cream that Tammy needed for a rash on her leg. His wife, Janice, thought it was just prickly heat, but Philip didn't agree and insisted she be taken to the doctor. When she was prescribed the cream, he volunteered to pick it up on his way home from the office. He would likely gloat when he got home about how he was smarter than the average guy for knowing it was something that needed medication. Janice didn't argue with him, because she knew that Philip had a low self-esteem issue. If it made him feel better for a while, then so be it. She had lived with his germ phobia and odd ways for nine years now. Their daughter, Tammy, was 8 years old now and well aware of her father's obsession with cleanliness, germs, and meticulous order. The youngest, Todd, was barely three and didn't know much more than what cartoons he liked and what time food was served. Both kids were his pride and joy, and he enjoyed spending time doing things together. He and Janice liked their Friday movie night the best, and the kids were still young enough to look forward to it with vigor.

Directly in front of Philip in line was a young Hispanic woman with a baby in a stroller and a toddler running around her yelling something repeatedly in Spanish. The toddler was sniffling and sneezing, and with each mucous membrane explosion, Philip felt like he needed to run away to a bathroom and thoroughly wash his hands and face. If he had his choice, he would have bathed in hand sanitizer. Speaking of sanitizer, Philip knew that he left a small bottle in the console of his car. He kept a larger container of it in his trunk so he could keep the smaller bottle full at all times. Right now, he was facing a sea of germs with nothing at all to stop it. In the distance, he heard a terrible instrumental version of "The Safety Dance" on the pharmacy intercom. *We can dance if we want to, we can leave your friends behind.* He always hated that song. He wished he was somewhere else. The storm around him swirled with ominous clouds and impending rain.

Finally, Philip was second from the counter, in a line that was winding into the vitamin aisle by now, as people stopped by on their way home from work. He noted there was an elderly couple behind him, talking about someone they knew who had the flu in July, and despite having had their shot, had to be hospitalized over it. Behind them was a man in his 30's on a cell phone, and as everyone within earshot knew, he was talking his mother about what lice shampoo to buy for his daughter. Philip felt his skin crawl at the notion. The man on the phone was telling his mother that she had gotten them at camp and that he had to wash all the bedding and upholstery. His mother was yelling back at him, but all anyone could hear was an inaudible static-filled rant. His mother sounded hostile, adding yet another layer of chaos that seemed to engulf Philip on this Friday after work. He was overwhelmed but keeping things under control. Barely.

He hummed along with the chorus of "The Safety Dance" and hated himself for it. *We can dance, we can dance, everybody's takin' the chance.*

"Thanks for your patience. How can I help you today?" said the young cashier, a round band aid covering her bottom lip piercing. Philip couldn't help but wonder how many germs would get into that small hole in her lip.

"Picking up a prescription for Edwards. First name is Tammy." He noticed a bottle of hand sanitizer on the counter and helped himself to a glob to clean his hands while the cashier worked on taking care of his request.

2

Philip was smiling now in the confines of his Honda Accord. It was meticulously clean at all times. He went to the car wash at least twice a week but vacuumed the inside top to bottom every other day. A lint roller was in the glove compartment just in case he needed a quick clean up.

Now he could resume his love for Friday as he took the usual route home, complete with Tammy's prescription, two rental DVDs for them to watch tonight and tomorrow, some assorted snacks, and a bottle of wine for him and Janice to enjoy when the kids went to bed. It was her birthday tomorrow, and he had made reservations at a favorite Italian restaurant of theirs. Then they were going to a new jazz club to watch a local band. Tonight was sort of a pre-game to all that, and Philip hoped that he would get lucky tonight after the movie, the bottle of wine, and the quiet of the kids fast asleep. Even something like sex was a thought-out activity that required a lot of preparation and planning. He always showered after.

Janice was ordering pizza for tonight, but Philip never indulged. He read a story once in a magazine about what young kids do to food in restaurants, and it featured a vile tale about a pizza place that urinated on pizzas if they didn't like the customer. Philip vowed to never eat a pizza again unless he was making it himself. Janice had some frozen pizza for Philip to make for himself and then eat with the family.

He tapped his finger to Cab Calloway's "Everyone Eats in My House" as he pulled on to Lake View Drive, only a few blocks from their house. It was 1212 Lake View Drive, and within a few moments he was pulling into the driveway. He could feel the stress of the week slowly leave his body as he hit the button to raise the garage door. It was a large 18-foot door for the two-car garage, and it took a larger opener to raise it. They had the door company add custom cedar woodwork in a herringbone pattern, which increased the weight of the door a great deal, but they both loved the way it looked. Slowly the door raised up. For some reason, someone had left the overhead lights on. Philip hated to waste electricity, so this was something he didn't want to see coming home on a Friday – or any day for that matter.

Suddenly he saw something that didn't look right in the garage. Philip shut off the engine and stared ahead in disbelief. He even took off his glasses and wiped them with the cloth he kept for that purpose in his glove compartment. The wall where he kept all his wrenches and assorted other tools was in shambles. There were several fist-sized holes in the pegboard over the drywall. Not even half of the tools he kept hung, in meticulous order by size, were where they were supposed to be. The metal hangers that he used were bent, and the rest were missing. His workbench below where the tools were hung was a mess. There were muddy footprints going into the garage from outside, to the work bench, and then into the house. Philip was furious! Then he heard the screaming.

3

Philip's head was swimming with thoughts and all of them were very bad. It felt like he was in a dream as he ran from his car into the garage, ducking his head under the door that was stuck part of the way up. Hanging from the overhead door track was the lifeless and bloody body of their neighbor, Brian Hagarty. Brian would come by and cut the grass, trim hedges and trees, clean the gutters, and do various things for Philip. He was more than happy to pay Brian, a senior in high school, to do those chores, and he enjoyed contributing to his college fund at the same time. The Edwards' home was on a large 4-acre lot with a sprawling yard, two dozen maple and pine trees, and large hedges to help keep the privacy Philip always wanted. The closest neighbor was two football fields away.

Now Brian was hanging from the metal track, handcuffs joining him at the wrists. His half-naked body was full of gashes and deep cuts in what had to have been a slow and miserable death. His face was frozen in terror. His eyes were open wide, telling a story so horrible it would freeze blood to ice. The mouth was agape in a mid-scream posture, while his lips were cracked and swollen. A pool of blood, still warm, was growing in size toward one of the floor drains. His body swung slowly in the summer night breeze.

Sickened at the site, Philip covered his eyes as he brushed by the bloodied corpse and made his way to the house. Outside the doorway, by the light switch, was a bloody handprint on the door frame. It was fresh, and Philip had no idea whose it was, yet the hand seemed large, like a full-grown man's. He heard the screaming again, and more agonizing thoughts raged through his skull as he staggered into the kitchen. A strong scent of body odor was prevalent.

"Where the fuck is the chainsaw?" a large, booming man said in the dining room, to the left and out of view.

A chilling scream pierced the air. "Please, no! No! My God, no!" It was a female voice, hoarse and ragged with fear. The terror was real.

Philip was panicking now. He realized the voice belonged to Janice, and it settled in his stomach like a rusty metal anchor.

"How should I know? Watch your mouth around these children!" another man sounded out. This voice sounded proper and more educated than the other much gruffer and gravelly tone. He sounded older as well.

Then a third person chimed in. This voice sounded like it had a Southern accent. He was loud and came across like he was in charge.

"Here it is. Now let's get this done!" Janice was screaming incoherently.

The motor of the chainsaw suddenly cut the warm, humid air. Whoever was holding the saw was pulling the trigger to make it whine louder, adding to the terror. Philip's anxiety and fear went to places he'd never imagined as he crept slowly through the kitchen and closer to the dining room. He was petrified of what he was going to see, but his family was inside. He knew there were three men to deal with, and he had no weapon. Slowly he rose up from his crouched position behind the butcher block table in the middle of the room to see if he could grab one of the kitchen knives Janice kept near the toaster. He didn't see them. They were gone! His fear ratcheted up at the thought of unknown people inside his house armed with six sharpened cooking knives.

"Daddy!" sounded from across the kitchen, as Todd came running toward him. There was fear in his little voice. He held up his hands to signal the toddler to stop, but Todd kept running across the ceramic tile floor. His little bare feet made a pitter-patter sound as he sped along toward Philip. He looked petrified!

Suddenly someone stepped out of the dining room and into the kitchen. He was large and clumsy in the dim light. Philip ducked down below an open lower cabinet door. The man turned on the overhead light above the butcher block. Todd stopped mid-step as the bright light forced him to cover his eyes. He was shaking with terror, and instinctively he began to urinate in his pants. Todd held his head down and cried as his urine pooled up at his own tiny bare feet.

"So that's where you went, you little bastard," said the man whose voice he heard asking about the chainsaw. He was a large-framed young man in his early 20's, with several tattoos on his muscular arms and a bald head that gleamed in the bright light. He grabbed Todd before he could get to Philip. The boy squirmed in the man's grasp, crying out and reaching for Philip.

"You're a nasty little bastard. You got piss all over me!"

Philip started running toward the garage when he felt something hit him hard on the back of his head, sending him sprawling across the floor. Then everything went black.

4

Philip awakened to cold liquid splashed across his face. He sputtered and shook his head back and forth quickly. Immediately he realized that his glasses were missing. Everything was blurry at a distance. He could feel a sharp throbbing pain in the back of his head, where something had hit him before he blacked out. He felt a wave of nausea sweep over him, and, realizing he was tied to one of their dining room chairs, Philip leaned his head to the left and vomited up whatever was left in his stomach. It stung his throat and left an awful taste in his mouth. Throwing up made his head hurt even worse. The throbbing was intense.

"It's about time you woke up, sleeping beauty!" said the same bald man Philip had seen in the kitchen moments before. The man backhanded Philip hard across the face, punctuating the intense pain he now realized was all over his face and upper body.

Philip was out of the daze he was in. He could hear Janice whimpering in the dim light. He couldn't make out anything but shapes at a distance without his glasses. His body was awash in terror at all the unknowns going on around him. Philip was a person who needed to be in control. His well-structured life, filled with schedules and procedures, was now in utter turmoil, and the stress that he was enduring was palpable. His heart was racing wildly, and he found it difficult to control his breathing. Things were slipping quickly out of his control. Thinking about the situation made Philip throw up again. The sting was even worse to his throat.

"Janice? Are you OK?" he said in a quiet voice, realizing they were not alone.

Janice only cried. She was trying to say something, but her words were unintelligible. She cried out as someone slapped her face. Philip pulled hard at his restraints at the sounds coming from his loving wife. Despite his sometimes-cold demeanor, Philip did love Janice and the kids more than anything. Hearing her cry and babble hurt him deeply, and he felt the ropes cut into his own flesh as he continued to pull at the restraints.

"Oh, she's just fucking dandy, my boy!" said another man in the room that Philip couldn't make out. Then the chainsaw sounded again, and Janice let out a scream. "Just fucking dandy!" A hideous laugh followed, still drowned out by Janice's hoarse screams and the whine of that 35-cubic centimeter chainsaw engine. The smell of gasoline and the exhaust was thick in the stagnant air of the dining room.

Suddenly Philip felt someone extremely strong grab him and the chair he was tied to and move him across the wood floor toward the family room. He could hear Janice whimpering and doing her best to communicate with him in a state of delirium. Her voice was raspy and drenched in misery. Philip wanted to reach out to her, but he was unable to move his arms even an inch the way he was tied down to the chair. He could not make out much in the shadows of the dining room as he was dragged past her. A tear fell down his cheek.

"It will be OK, honey," he said quietly. "I love you." Desperation had his voice in a choke hold.

"Well, wasn't that fucking sweet!" The man laughed again.

Abruptly, Philip was thrown down to the living room floor, his face hitting the polished hardwood with a crunch as his nose was broken to pieces. Blood was streaming from his nose and into his mouth, running down his chin. He spat out two broken front teeth. The pain was intense, but the terror that swept over him was all-consuming and maddening. *Where is Todd? Where is Tammy? Is Janice OK?* The questions ripped into his brain in rapid succession. Panic had fully taken hold. *Who are these guys, and why are they doing this? Was it a robbery?*

"Pick his ass up. He needs to see this shit," said a completely different man than he heard before.

In his jumbled mind, Philip was trying to assess how many people he was dealing with here in his house. Was it six? Maybe seven? He couldn't keep track. Before he could give it another thought, someone roughly picked him up from the floor with the chair and sat him upright. Philip felt someone put his glasses on, the right lens was severely scratched, and the frame was bent, but things slowly came into focus. He took one look and shut his eyes hard to protect himself from such a deplorable vision.

"Open your fucking eyes, fuck boy!" cried out one of the voices he had heard before.

"Daddy!" he heard Todd's tiny voice cry out. He was crying.

The large, bald man was now grabbing Philip by the hair and yelling into his face. Spit was flying as the burly man continued to scream at him.

"You better open those eyes, or I'll rip them out one at a time with a rusty spoon," he said in the Southern voice he heard before.

Philip looked up and saw a nightmarish sight. Both of his children were nailed to the living room wall across from the fireplace, with what appeared to be the tent stakes that Philip kept in the garage with his camping stuff. The stuff he had never used, but wanted on hand just in case. Todd was squirming in pain and crying out, held at a strange angle with one single metal stake sticking out of his collar bone. The toddler was going into shock from the pain.

He was losing blood and fading from consciousness. Philip was driven mad at the sight.

"It hurts, Daddy. It hurts really, really bad!" said Todd, barely coherent.

The bald man started laughing again. It was a cavernous, deep, yet dark laugh.

"It hurts, Daddy!" the large man squeaked, mocking Todd's cry for help.

"You son-of-a-bitch!" yelled Philip, tugging at his binds — both arms and legs. The ropes tore at his flesh in the effort.

Now the bald man turned toward him and got into his face yet again. His eyes were open wide and alive with madness. He was clearly off the rails of sanity.

"You better shut the fuck up, Daddy. You hear me?" his Southern drawl seemed stronger as his rage began to tick up a few notches. "You ain't seen nothing yet." He started laughing again. He reached down and picked something up that was out of Philip's sight. Then he held the lifeless body of Tammy in front of Philip. Her face was horribly swollen and black and blue. She looked like she'd been dead a while, as her skin was a light blue color. Her eyes were open, yet vacant and absent of any sign of life. He tore at the ropes once again, as the bindings ripped painfully at his flesh, causing his wrists to bleed profusely.

"You son-of-a-bitch!" cried Philip, tears streaming down his face at the site of his lifeless daughter. The man threw her down like a sack of laundry. Philip had an awful feeling at the heavy thud on the floor.

"I told you to shut up. You don't wanna listen, then?"

"No, please. Don't hurt anyone else. We can work something out. You want money? You want any of the stuff in the house? Take it. Take all of it. Just please let us go." Philip was hysterical, his voice ragged and strangled. His breathing was rapid and out of control, and his heartbeat continued to thunder on.

The bald man looked Philip directly in the eyes and laughed again. This time real slow at first, then building to a maniacal cacophony.

"I'm your nightmare maker!" his voice boomed into the vaulted ceilings of the living room and reverberated back and forth. In one fluid motion, the man grabbed a wood-handled axe that was propped up against the wall and swung it with precision, chopping off Todd's head with a dull crunch and sharp cry.

Philip tried to scream out, but there was no sound. He felt his entire world collapse on all sides. He was thrashing in his chair, desperately pulling at his restraints, but to no avail. The ropes were very tight and expertly tied. They continued to tear at Philip's wrists. He arched his back as much as he could, and again let out a silent scream. Veins were protruding from his neck, his entire face and neck bright red in fierce resistance to what he just witnessed. It was like a nightmare. A nightmare he couldn't wake from. Again, the maniac, still wielding the axe, laughed out loud.

This time the laugh was different. The bald man walked toward a dimly lit area of the living room, out of the view of Philip. He heard glass breaking, and then shouting – like two or three adult males arguing.

"Why do you have to do that stuff? I mean, really!" said the man with the proper, educated voice from earlier.

"Why don't you mind your own god damn business?" asked the large bald man in his Southern drawl.

"You two need to cut this out. We need to wrap this up, and then I'm burning this house to the ground. Too much evidence around here to hang us ten times," said a totally different voice Philip had not heard before.

The man with the proper speech replied, "You will do no such thing! Put that thought from your mind. You are not lighting this house on fire and bringing every cop and fireman in the area down the main road we need to take to get away from here."

Philip was breathing heavily, trying to do what he could to keep it together despite the fact he had seen his dead daughter thrown around like a rag doll, and then his little son decapitated by a blood-thirsty killer. *What is going on with Janice? Is she still alive? Thank God she didn't have to see that. My God! How can I go on without the kids?* He began to weep uncontrollably.

"OK, Philip. It's show time, my man! Pull it together!" said another man from the dark area of the room. He slowly came walking toward Philip, and it was the same bald man from moments ago! Yet his voice was completely different, and his demeanor was not nearly as aggressive.

He pulled out a hunting knife and cut the binds that held Philip to the chair. It was a welcome feeling as the ropes fell to the floor and blood began to flow into his hands and feet again. His wrists were gouged by the rope, but it was still a good feeling to be out of the bindings. Philip tried to stand, but the man put a firm hand on his shoulder.

"Now, don't go getting cute on me. You don't do a damn thing without me telling you what to do. I'll slit your throat if you even think about trying to run. Plus, your legs will be tingly for a good 30 minutes," he leaned into Philip's face, "so you aren't going anywhere." His eyes were pure evil. Like bottomless pools, all Philip could see was a cold darkness inside.

Philip merely shook his head in the affirmative and stared at the large bald man in disbelief that he was so different from before. Yet this new persona was extremely firm and deliberate. Now the man grabbed Philip by his shirt collar and belt and lead him toward the dining room where he last saw Janice alive. His legs were asleep, and it felt like he wasn't even walking at all. The bald man was so strong and powerful that Philip felt like a marionette in his firm grasp.

"You ready for this shit, Phil?" the man said, laughing in a more high-pitched tone than before, as they crossed the threshold into the dining room. He tightened his grip on Philip's shirt collar, twisting it to almost choking him.

Suddenly the dining room was filled with light, and the true horror of what was waiting for him was in the middle of the room. His wife, Janice, was spread-eagle on their formal dining room table. It was a gift from his grandparents when they got married. Now his beautiful wife was barely dressed, bloodied, battered, and holding on to life by fraying threads.

"Oh my God!" cried Philip, falling to his knees. Tears were streaming down his face. His entire body shook with anger, rage, and helplessness. His nerves were like stretched piano wires, frayed and snapping one at a time.

Janice turned her head slightly and acknowledged her tormented husband. She had been beaten up by the large bald man, savagely raped for hours, and now the metal tent stakes were through each of her hands, keeping them down to the beautiful oak table. Her bare feet were also staked down to the table, but in a spread-eagle position, so she was available to the bald man if he chose to take her again. Janice continued to pray for death to come. Her

entire body was sore, and she was in and out of consciousness.

Janice was so hoarse from screaming that no sound would come out.

Like her husband, she would let out the most primal silent screams

until her eyes bulged out with a vengeance. Death could not come to

claim her soon enough.

5

As Janice lay on the table, knowing that the end was about to

come, she remembered earlier in the day and how everything turned

upside down. She was getting the kids ready for day camp. She was

cooking breakfast and making lunches, and they were buzzing about

what was going on that day in summer camp. Life was good. Then

the doorbell rang. She went to answer it, and a well-dressed young

man was standing outside with a briefcase. He was bald and broad-

shouldered, and obviously strong, yet there was something very

charismatic about him. The man told her he was a salesman and

sparked her interest talking about a new laundry detergent that was

the best to get stains out of clothing. He was a natural, and he won her confidence to invite him inside. Once he gained access and realized there were no other adults in the home, the man erupted into a raving maniac, and the day became an eternity of sheer terror. Tears escaped her bloodied and crusted-over eyes, knowing that it was her bad judgement which had lead to all this. If she had listened to Philip and never allowed the man inside the house, this all would not have happened. The guilt was unbearable. It was a dagger in her dying heart. Still, death would not come to call.

Suddenly the quiet moment was shattered with the roar of the chainsaw. The bald man walked into the room laughing in an unnerving way, waving the chainsaw around, while revving the motor to add to the mayhem. Philip was cowering on the floor as the man walked past him, lowering the saw as he approached the table and Janice. She looked so pitiful, completely defenseless as the maniac had the chainsaw only a few inches away from her crotch. Janice closed her eyes as tightly as she could and began to whisper prayers, as she did her best to blot out her reality. She braced for unimaginable pain and hoped it would be over quickly.

"I'm your nightmare maker, baby!" the bald man screamed out, his Southern twang now back, and his volatile persona back in full gear. His eyes darted about the pathetic victim before him, and he became aroused at the idea of what he was about to do.

He lowered the chainsaw down and blood flew in every direction possible. The bald man let out a booming laugh, and continued to push the saw into Janice's flesh and bone. The saw jumped up and down as it met with resistance, and the blood continued to spew, painting the dining room walls and ceiling. Janice's back arched awkwardly, and her mouth was open wide in a final silent scream. Then the pain was over. Still the bald man pushed on until he literally cut the woman in half. The saw idled now, and the man backed up from the table, covered from head to toe in blood, brain, and bone fragments. Philip was still on his knees, completely catatonic from what he had witnessed. He also was covered in her blood – only the whites of his eyes could be seen as he knelt down in defeat. He had nothing left to give after what he had seen on this night.

"I hope you liked the show," the bald man said, turning to Philip. He laughed, in a low guttural way. The man raised one of his powerful arms and wiped the blood from his face. It didn't do much good.

He shut off the chainsaw and tossed it to the floor. He pulled the hunting knife from its sheath and moved with stealth toward the dazed Philip. He didn't say a word as the bald man swiped the large blade across his throat, severing his jugular vein and spouting his own blood now like a fountain. Phillip imagined the picture of his family that he kept in his cubicle at work. He almost laughed at the irony that he was thinking about that cursed cubicle he hated so much, in the fleeting swan song of his life. The last thing he saw before collapsing to the floor was the bald man wiping the blood off on his pants before putting the knife back into its sheath.

6

An hour had passed when the bald man walked away from 1212 Lakeview Drive. It was early morning, and the sun was casting a fresh light upon the landscape. Freshly showered, fed, and a clean set of clothes was just what he needed to move on. A red and white 1973 Ford pick- up truck was parked in the woods off one of the country roads nearby. He had parked it there earlier.

"Let's go," he said in a bland Midwestern tone.

Turning on the engine, the cassette player came on, picking up where he had left off. He smiled when he heard "Back in Black" and turned it up a little. He also pulled out an old spiral notebook from under the seat. He spent a few minutes writing in it and enjoying the music. He felt alive.

Glancing in the rearview mirror, something caught his attention. Looking into his own eyes, he felt like himself now. He felt like the Nolan Weeks that he had been his whole life. Over the past two months, Nolan would start to feel weird right before one of the people inside of him would take over. There would be nothing he could do to stop them, and even worse, he would be a bystander watching from the sidelines while they acted out their horrible fantasies upon the innocent. Nolan lost count at how many there were. The sights he had seen since they invaded his body were dreadful. Just when he thought he knew them all, another would step out of the shadows and take over for a while. Yet now, as he looked at himself, he knew that for the time being, it was only Nolan. Despite that fact, his eyes were still cold. No matter who was taking charge, his eyes couldn't lie. His eyes told the tale. His eyes would present him to anyone who wanted to look, as someone who was the embodiment of pure evil.

He began to question if he was any better than the others. As they moved seamlessly in and out of the control seat, there was almost no way to know who was who. It was those eyes, though, that he saw in the rearview mirror, and he knew they would show his enemy that he meant business. Deadly business.

Then he thought about something his Uncle Donny told him about his time in Vietnam. He remembered him talking about setting up claymore mines around the camp perimeter, so if the enemy attacked, the good guys could set them off. He told Nolan that the side that you pointed toward the enemy said right on the mine, *this side toward enemy.* He could still hear Uncle Donny sitting at the kitchen table, chain smoking and drinking black coffee, talking about how the mines were filled with hundreds of small BB's. He seemed to enjoy telling Nolan how the mines could tear a man in half if he got close enough. Nolan thought of that now and how his own hate-filled stare would be like his own claymore mine: ready to explode and eliminate anyone who tried to stop him.

I'm back! Yes, I'm back! Back in black – I'm back in black!

Nolan turned up the stereo before pulling away in search of some hot, black coffee. Thinking about Uncle Donny and his old man made him want some even more, and maybe even a pack of cigarettes. Camels – just like the old man. It sickened Nolan to think of himself acting like his Dad. He knew what his Dad was. He had seen what his Dad did. Some things can't be unseen.

For now, Nolan sang along to the music and knew he had a lot of ground to cover and plenty of hunting to get done. It was only a matter of time before he would be a spectator again and one of the entities inside of him would erupt and need to feed. This side toward enemy.

Sifting Through the Ashes:
Afterward and Acknowledgements

I started writing short stories when I discovered the craft at a very young age. I've always enjoyed writing and reading short stories, appreciating the artform for its unique niche in the world of literature. I recall my Uncle George making cassette tapes of Vincent Price reading Edgar Allan Poe's classics like *The Telltale Heart*, *The Pit and the Pendulum* and *The Black Cat*. I also loved the classic Alfred Hitchcock short story anthologies, where he recruited writers from the horror, suspense, and thriller genres. One of my all-time favorites of those stories was one by Ray Bradbury, entitled *The Wind*. I loved the way it kept the reader hanging at the end, almost inviting him to pull up a chair and discuss with the author some possible endings to the story. There were many other short story writers that influenced me a great deal, such as Stephen King and HP Lovecraft.

The beauty of the short story is that it's a brief glimpse into another world, often only a tease served alongside an unsettling feeling that the story hasn't ended. That may be why some of my stories end in unpredictable ways, while others wrap things up in a bit neater package. A good short story sucks you in quickly, but then leaves you wanting much more at the end.

Now, as I write novels, too, I see short stories additionally as palette cleanses, a way to try a different perspective, such as first person, or stories that really broaden the scope of my usual subject matter. I have enjoyed emailing them to friends and family who asked about what I am working on and who want a little taste. I have been very pleased with the feedback. I enjoyed writing every one of the stories for a variety of reasons. I thought you might like learning a little more about each one and hearing the back story which inspired me to write them.

Long, Dark Hallway was created by several visits I have made to an older hospital for my day job as a building inspector. The office I had to go to was in the same hallway as the morgue. While it wasn't a long, dark hallway, it was eerie and creepy enough to cause my imagination to run wild with possibilities. Also, my son Joe (intentionally the same first name as the main character), is a school custodian, and has shared with me some of the odd feelings he's experienced when working late at night, often by himself.

Carnival of Atonement was conceived while sitting in an auditorium at a local grade school, waiting for my granddaughter to perform in a Christmas program. Sitting there, looking around at the large gathering of family and friends, my mind couldn't help but wander. I thought it would be odd if we were there for something dark and disturbing, instead of something pure and innocent like a children's Christmas program. From there, the ideas came at me quickly. The fiery preacher bears some resemblance to a character (Dr. Wilfred Weeks) from my novel, *The Dreadful Lives of Enoch Strange.* The town is completely made up, so don't waste your time trying to find it on the map. I did use some real geographic references, but the unincorporated town of Atonement is pure fiction. That's a good thing! I went for a real shocker of an ending with this one, only because the ending I had in mind just seemed too predictable for my liking. Up until the end, I wasn't sure how I was going to end it, and the ending that I used popped into view just in time. I think the story is better because of it.

Man With Spots is a long-standing story in my family and has exalted itself to folklore. As a young boy in the Bronx, I experienced some very terrible nightmares about him. I was too young to remember it, but my parents told me about how I would wake them up, frantically recalling dreams of the "man with spots". At the time, we were living in an apartment on Fish Avenue. I went to nearby PS 78 – which for you non-New Yorkers, the PS stands for public school. In my short story, I made him a "good guy", but in my nightmares, I was afraid of him. I have searched online for a scary villain in the cartoons I used to watch back then to see if I could find one that matched my description, but I have had no luck. To this day, I don't know if I saw him on TV or if he's a complete figment of a very active young imagination.

I must admit that with *Elvis and the Two Dead Hookers*, I went for a sensational title first. I thought it would make readers want to find out what the heck the story would be about. I set the story in the town that I lived in for about 12 years, Bloomington, Illinois. Many of the local readers that follow me enjoyed the street names and other real things I used to color the story. Thanks to my good friend, Les Aldridge, for the excellent information on hot rods that was a pivotal part of the story. The 1950 Mercury was his suggestion - right down to the glowing skull eyes on the shifter. During my research, I came up with the Pontiac Chieftan, but Les informed me that it wasn't "hot rod enough". I did work the Chieftan into the story, but not for Elvis' ride. This story was a bit of a departure from the horror stuff to more of a "Twilight Zone" type of tale. Based on the reactions of my readers, I think it was a hit. It's hard not to like and feel a bit sorry for Elvis Lee Lewis.

The Jesus Tree was a tip of the hat to my friends from Danbury, Connecticut, who know all too well about the tree. It's probably my favorite of this batch. The Jesus Tree was a local legend when I attended Bethel High School in nearby Bethel, Connecticut. The story was that you could see Jesus on the cross if you stared hard enough at the tree, and if you defaced the tree in any way, you would be cursed. That's the sort of thing that makes most kids want to go out there and party, which they did every weekend.

The tree was actually in Brewster, New York, which borders

Danbury to the west, and it was chopped down several years ago. I

thought it would be fun to write about the legendary tree, but instead

of making it a cheesy story about kids terrorized by a cursed tree, I

thought it would be more challenging to provide my own back story.

None of the back story is true – including the Mansville family

living there or the monks of St. Bede coming to the rescue. There

really is a St. Bede Academy in Peru, Illinois, but it has nothing to

do with the real tree or this story at all. I also experimented with

writing this story in the first person, which is something I haven't

done recently. I think it worked well and gave the story a sort of

Edgar Allen Poe or HP Lovecraft feel. Poe, especially, was a huge

influence on me in my formative years of wanting to read and write

stories from the dark side. I admire Lovecraft, too, but I didn't

discover him until a bit later in life.

They Came to Darkness was inspired after hearing a dark

local legend story on TV. I thought it would be interesting to come

up with my own, and so that's how this one came to be. I came up

with Darkness as the name of the town only because I thought it would make a reader want to know more about such a mysterious name. Some of the geographical references are real, but there is no such place (that I know of) named Darkness. I intentionally used some stereotypes and common themes of horror stories in the beginning, so the reader would let his/her guard down, and when the shapeshifting monster comes down from the mountains, the nape of their collective necks would be more vulnerable and dangerously exposed.

The story *Unfit For Human Occupancy* was inspired by some real experiences I have had in my day job. I have inspected hundreds of abandoned buildings and houses, prior to demolition, which were very similar to the creepy one in the story. The mind begins to wander and play tricks on you when you're in a dark place and hear things crawling around, coupled with a dripping noise from somewhere in the distance. I've come close several times to falling through a floor in a dilapidated building, and that's where all of that stuff in the basement comes from. I've worried about what would happen if an accident like would occur. It was unsettling to say the least! I always thought writing about one of those inspections would make for a good story. The sign on front door, with the words "unfit for human occupancy" is real and is put on the front door once a city official condemns properties. It does make you wonder what might possibly be on the other side.

The story *Cross to Bear* was inspired by my paternal grandmother, Theresa, who suffered for years with dementia. In addition, my late wife, Sheilie, suffered from COPD and was on oxygen at home. At the time I wrote this story, my wife was alive and was a bit unnerved about my idea to write such a tale. Of course, she knew me all too well, and just shook her head as I pitched the idea at her. Most of my close family members and friends have heard these "pitches" of new ideas that my crazy mind has concocted. Combining experiences is something that I enjoy doing, the challenge to make it work in a story without it coming off as forced. I think it worked well here, and this story impacted readers in a variety of ways. My beta reader, Chris Kovacs, was especially affected by this one, since he lost his father to cancer and could relate to my descriptions. Ironically, both Chris and I are cancer survivors, so it's a subject that hits close to home on many levels.

The story *Bodies In My Pocket* is another one that follows a concept I wrote about while I was in Low Twelve. This is another story with a very sensational title. The song was about a sniper who struggled coming home from Iraq with PTSD. I spent some time researching this topic and interviewed two former soldiers that I served with in the Army. Huge thanks to Sam Delle Donne for his help. The other soldier asked to be anonymous, and I respect that. Their experiences in Iraq were vital in putting this one together. It was difficult to discover the many problems they have both endured after returning from multiple deployments. I was fortunate to have never deployed due to an injury I sustained on active duty in 1992. The therapy technique of the "bodies in my pocket" is completely invented by me. I have unwavering admiration for all branches of service and what they do to protect this county. It's too bad that politicians often foul things up by making war political. Then again, politicians foul up everything they touch.

Hand of the Dying was inspired by a close friend of mine who experienced death firsthand. When he told me the story, it reminded me of the subject matter of a Low Twelve song I wrote bearing the same title. The song was a true story about a Marine,

Jason Dunham, who died jumping on a grenade to save his brothers-in-arms. I was moved by a book on the subject, *Rule Number Two* by Dr. Heidi Squier, about her experiences in Iraq at a M.A.S.H. The true story, and the one I created, share a similar concept of the struggle between the living and the dying. I imagined what each party would be thinking about at that moment just before death. My friend who shared his experience with me liked the way the story turned out, so I believe I was successful here.

Blackened Spiral Down was a story that I started without much direction, only that I wanted the main character to discover something evil in the abandoned church across the street from his house. Stephen King's book, *On Writing,* explains that good characters will tell you what they want to do. He could not have been more correct, and this story is a great example of that. I let Ronnie tell me what he was up to in the darkness of the church basement. As you now know, he was a very, very bad boy! This was one of the darker stories of the bunch.

Contraption Number 12 came to mind after I completed the rough draft of *The Dreadful Lives of Enoch Strange*. There are some real-life people who inspired a few of the characters here, namely the main character, Freddy Frankfurt. Freddy's love for inventions was completely made up, but I thought it would make for an interesting story to have a person who lived his entire life being bullied, and how he would handle having the ability to strike back. Like with all my stories, the tale went very dark, very fast. This was the first time I tried writing two endings and gave the reader the chance to choose which way he/she wanted the story to go. This was a hit with my readers, and so I'll likely try this again in future short stories. Just about everyone said they liked the ending that involved the undead coming to Freddy's house to pay him a visit. Truth be told, so did I.

Killing Machine is the first chapter of my novel, *Six*. I came up with this title to include it in this collection. I felt it would be a good way to tease you, the reader, and to let you experience the exploits of the escaped madman, Six. The story is set at the Peoria State Hospital in Bartonville, Illinois. I worked at the former hospital back in 1995 for a project involving my day job. I spent some time in the steam tunnels below the hospital, and it inspired me to want to write about it. It was eerie, to say the least, and 20 years later, I finally wrote the novel. This story is only the first chapter, but it gives you a taste.

Thirteen Nuns is the first chapter of *The Dreadful Lives of Enoch Strange.* Years ago, I wrote a novella, *This Side Toward Enemy*, that I was thinking about releasing as a graphic novel. The artist who was set to do the illustrations was not able to make it happen at the last minute, so the book sat idle. I always loved the concept, so when I thought about a follow-up to my novel, *Six*, I thought I could work this one into a full-length novel. *Thirteen Nuns* provides some of the back story to the original, *This Side Toward Enemy*.

I couldn't resist including *Chainsaw House Party* in this collection. It's also part of my novel, *The Dreadful Lives of Enoch Strange.* It is the first chapter of part two. Sixty years pass between parts one and two, so I thought bringing in the modern part of the story with a bang was appropriate. Keep in mind, there is not much at all appropriate with *Chainsaw House Party.* It's meant to be a sick and twisted ride. This story is merely the opening salvo to the change in time periods and meant to shock and pummel the reader down to the floor. If you're picking yourself up to read this afterward, then you must agree that I was successful.

Some of the stories in this collection were originally released in my book, *Blackened Spiral Down*, that was sold only as an e-book on Amazon. I took those original stories, wrote some new ones and decided to create a brand for my short stories with the *Creation of Chaos* series. This is of course volume I, and subsequent releases will continue after that. I do still enjoy writing short stories, and I plan on releasing them periodically as I find the time between other projects.

Once again, I'd like to thank everyone who has helped in various ways to make these stories come to life. My beta reader, Chris Kovacs, is probably the biggest force in my corner, because he gives me instant feedback, and we bounce ideas back and forth often. We talk nearly every week about different things, but the writing has been at the top of our list for the past few years. Also, my proofreader, JBS (who wishes to be semi-anonymous), is a major help in tightening up the grammar and making things flow better. Thanks to Ron Curry and Derek Stephenson for assistance with my firearm questions, and Kristina Conder, RN for her help with all things medical. Thanks also go out to my friends, family, and of course you – the reader! Without you, writing wouldn't be as much

fun!

Pete Altieri
Heyworth, Illinois
September 2017

Made in the USA
Lexington, KY
01 October 2017